THE BIG EMPTY

D0096399

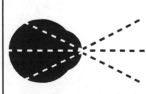

This Large Print Book carries the
Seal of Approval of N.A.V.H.

THE BIG EMPTY

JIM JONES

WHEELER PUBLISHING
A part of Gale, Cengage Learning

GALE
CENGAGE Learning·

Farmington Hills, Mich • San Francisco • New York • Waterville, Maine
Meriden, Conn • Mason, Ohio • Chicago

GALE
CENGAGE Learning·

LIBRARY OF CONGRESS CATALOGING-IN-PUBLICATION DATA

Names: Jones, Jim, 1950– author.
Title: The big empty / Jim Jones.
Description: Large print edition. | Waterville, Maine : Wheeler Publishing Large
    Print, 2017. | Series: Wheeler Publishing Large Print western
Identifiers: LCCN 2016049883| ISBN 9781410483638 (paperback) | ISBN 1410483630
    (softcover)
Subjects: LCSH: Large type books. | BISAC: FICTION / Historical. | FICTION /
    Westerns. | GSAFD: Western stories.
Classification: LCC PS3610.O62572 B54 2017 | DDC 813/.6—dc23
LC record available at https://lccn.loc.gov/2016049883

Published in 2017 by arrangement with Cherry Weiner Literary Agency

THE BIG EMPTY

CHAPTER 1

They call it the Big Empty. Works for me. The land stretches out and seems to go on forever out here. The wind blows like a banshee all the time and you can go for days without seeing another human being. A few antelope now and then, that's about it. It's not that it's quiet, exactly, what with the wind and all. It's just that it's . . . well, it's empty. It can feel lonely right down in your soul, like you're the only person left alive in the world. That tends to make some folks nervous. Me, I kinda like it.

My name is Tom Stallings but most folks call me Tommy. I turned twenty-one on my last birthday, which makes me a full-grown man. It bothers me when people use that childish nickname. I try to correct them as often as I can. It doesn't seem to make much difference. It's 1886 and I'm the deputy sheriff of Colfax County here in the New Mexico Territory. Folks say we'll become a full-fledged state one of these days. I'll believe it when I see it. Those thieving polecat politicians have been making a killing for years grabbing property from the land-grant families and small ranchers. They got a good thing going for themselves. I don't reckon they want the United States government looking over their shoulders too close.

That's not my problem right now, though. My boss, Sheriff Tomás Marés, has me chasing after a gang of bank robbers out here in the Big Empty. That's not even my problem. Best guess, it's Jake Flynt's gang. Pierce Keaton, Dave Atkins and his brother, Charlie, Patricio Baca, maybe some others. They pulled a bank job in Taos just a few days before this one and the law chased after them hot and heavy. At least they did until they crossed the county line, then they seemed happy enough to let them be somebody else's problem. They're all pretty bad hombrés, killers every one. Still, it's my job to go after men like that, although what I'm supposed to do with them when I catch them is a bit of a mystery to me. I think I'm pretty tough but I'd probably need a bit of help to bring them in.

When the gang robbed the bank in Cimarrón, two witnesses said they saw Garrett

O'Donnell riding with the gang. The thing is, somebody blew the vault. John Burr, the bank's president, had bragged that nobody could crack that safe but danged if this bunch didn't make a liar out of him. They blew the door off without either damaging the money or killing themselves, which are two little problems bank robbers who use dynamite run into from time to time. The witnesses heard an explosion. Not long after that, one of the outlaws set a bag down by the front door of the bank. They couldn't identify him because a bandanna covered most of his face. A few minutes later, a different fella came along and when he bent over to pick up the bag, his bandanna slipped. Both witnesses swear it was Garrett.

That part's probably true. Garrett O'Donnell used to rob banks in his native country of Ireland. He was the dynamite man for a pack of Irish rebels who were fighting against the big landowners in something called the "land war." I don't understand all that Irish Rebellion stuff but I know they been fighting the English for a long while. Garrett told me himself one night on a cattle drive we went on together. We'd gone into town and gotten ourselves about three sheets to the wind and that's when he told me about his past.

9

After Garrett picked up the bag, the witnesses say he rode away headed south like his horse's tail was on fire, still carrying that bag.

So here's my problem. I don't believe Garrett O'Donnell is an outlaw. He told me the reason he and his family came to America was to get away from that life and make a new start. After he told me about being a bank robber in Ireland, I told him when we got back to town, he'd better hotfoot it over to Sheriff Averill's office and fill him in. Old Nathan kept an eye on Garrett for a long while and came away convinced that the man had indeed chosen a different path. All he wanted was a piece of land for him and his family where he could raise a few head of cattle and scratch out a living.

If he was riding with Jake Flynt, I believe somebody must have forced him into it. Maybe they threatened his wife and children or something, I don't know. It's a mystery is what it is.

I spend a lot of time worrying about justice. That drives Sheriff Marés to distraction. He thinks I should just worry about enforcing the law. I figure that's more his problem than mine.

Right now, my other problem is figuring out what's over the next rise. When you get on the high ground and look out toward the horizon, it can appear like this country is flat as a flapjack. Turns out that's not the case. When you're riding in it, you find out that it's all rolling hills, low spots, coulees, and short grass. Places where a man could hide if he was of a mind to ambush someone. That can sure make a fella nervous, particularly when he's on the trail of dangerous men.

We've had some good spring rains so things are already pretty green out here. It's June now and once July comes, we'll be into the rainy season. It'll green up for sure then and the grass will be taller, which makes the ranchers happy. I'm glad the ranchers will be happy. As for me, I'm mostly concerned about who lies waiting over the next hill. Like I said, these are some pretty bad hombrés I'm chasing out here in the Big Empty.

CHAPTER 2

Jake Flynt's eyes flashed fire as he and the rest of his gang dismounted. He stormed over to where the terrified man stood quaking in front of the door to his dwelling. With a howl of rage, he drew his pistol and slammed it into the side of the man's head, bringing him to his knees. He kicked him hard in the ribs. With a groan, the man slid down into a fetal position.

"Take that sheepherdin' trash over there by that tree. Bring me my whip." As the dazed man continued to moan, Flynt shouted back over his shoulder, "Now, Pierce. By God, I said bring me my whip."

Pierce Keaton scurried over to where Jake's striking white-legged sorrel stood and untied the ten-foot bullwhip from the saddle. "I got it, Jake, I got it." He scuttled like a cockroach back to where his boss stood waiting impatiently and held out the whip. Without a word, Flynt took it and stalked over to the tree. Keaton shivered with revulsion as he watched his boss walk away. Although he rode with the man, they were not friends. He was terrified of him. Pierce Keaton was afraid that Flynt was crazy . . . and sliding steadily down the well of insanity by the day.

Dave Atkins and Patricio Baca grabbed the semiconscious sheepherder by his arms and drug him around behind the sod house. Hank Andrews followed along behind them. The man's wife stood by helplessly wringing her hands. She cried and begged them not to hurt her husband. She might as well have been talking to the wind for all the good it did. Her two young children cowered behind her skirts. Moments later, the woman sobbed uncontrollably as her husband's agonizing screams reverberated across the rolling hills.

Dave Atkins's younger brother, Charlie, turned to Pierce Keaton, who had chosen not to accompany the others and witness the gruesome torture. In a frightened whisper, he asked, "Why does he do that, Pierce? That fella didn't do nothin' to him. Hell, he ain't even got anything here worth stealin'."

In an equally hushed tone, Keaton replied, "If I's you, I wouldn't never ask him that." He shuddered. "What I heard tell was that when he was no more than sixteen years old, some Union soldiers came to his parents' farm in Missouri. They'd got'em a tip from some Jayhawk sodbusters that Jake and his family was Confederate sympathizers. They went at Jake and his daddy with a bullwhip. Near 'bout whipped all the hide off his daddy's back." Keaton turned his head and spit a stream of tobacco. "He died. Jake's still got scars all over his back." He leaned over and whispered. "I seen 'em once myself. Walked in when Jake was with a whore. I guarantee, I walked out quick as a cat on a hot stove so's he didn't see me."

Charlie Atkins's eyes had gotten bigger and rounder as the story unfolded. "You seen them scars?"

Keaton nodded. "Reckon I did." He paused to consider the inflammatory nature of the information he had just shared with the young man. Apparently, he had second thoughts about the wisdom of having done so. He reached over and grabbed Charlie's arm in a vice-like grip. "Don't you go tellin' Jake I seen him. Don't you breathe a word of it, you understand me? I don't even want to think about what he'd do to me if he knew." He gave Charlie a rough shake. "I tell you this. If I found out you told him, I'd take that bullwhip to you myself."

"Duh . . . duh . . . don't you worry," Charlie stammered. "I ain't gonna say nothin' to nobody." He squinted a bit as he mulled over the state of affairs. It appeared as if he was taxing his brain. "Still, I don't get it. This fella couldn't have been the one who told them soldiers about Jake and his family. Why's he whippin' him, Pierce?"

"Not rightly sure," Keaton shrugged. "Reckon he just don't like sodbusters."

"Oh," Charlie said, as if that explained the situation. Clearly, in-depth thinking was not something he engaged in often. He took a breath and changed the topic.

"Well, how come that Mick, O'Donnell, didn't come with us on this raid?" he asked indignantly. "Does he think he's too good to ride with the likes of us now?"

"That's another thing I wouldn't bring up with Jake if I's you," Pierce warned. "I tell you one damn thing, if he sees that Irishman, he's gonna do more than horsewhip him, I promise you that."

"What'd the Irishman do?"

"He up and disappeared is what he done," Keaton replied. "After we done that bank job in Cimarrón, nobody's seen him." Pierce Keaton paused as if he were afraid of what might happen if he said the next words out loud. In a hushed voice, he whispered,

"He took the money with him."

"Well, if you ask me," Charlie said haughtily, somehow missing the most important part of Keaton's statement, "he wasn't worth havin' around anyway. After he blew the safe, he didn't do much. Usually not much call for blowing up safes when you can get the bank manager to open it for you. Wonder why we didn't do that in Cimarrón? We ain't never had to blow up a safe before, why'd we do it this time?"

"Well, Charlie, it ain't exactly the case that he didn't do anything." He shook his head at his simple-minded comrade. "Did you not understand what I said? That crazy Irishman took all the money." Pierce looked around quickly. "Shush now, here comes Ben."

About that time, Flynt, Baca, Ben Ralston, and the older Atkins brother walked around from the back of the house. Jake stalked over to the front of the sod dwelling and surveyed it intently. The front door and two small windows were supported by wooden planks and were embedded in a wall of adobe bricks. After a moment, he reared back and with the heel of his boot, gave the door a powerful kick, knocking it off its rusty hinges. The rest of the gang looked at each other with unease. They knew what came next. Flynt looked around the interior of the house, and then he backed out.

"Damn thing won't burn," he said with disgust. "Not enough wood." He turned and surveyed the property. His eyes settled on a dilapidated wooden barn about twenty yards from the house.

"That'll do," he said with a satisfied tone, as if he had just located a suitable campsite for the gang. He turned and said, "Patricio, Charlie. Go get that sodbuster and drag his sorry tail over here. Put him and the others in the barn. Barricade the door."

The two men looked at each other with disquieted expressions, then headed over to where the unfortunate man was lying bleeding and semiconscious.

"Pierce," Flynt barked viciously. "Get a fire started. We're gonna burn that barn to the ground." He turned to Dave Atkins and the other members of the outfit, Ben Ralston and Hank Andrews. With an unnatural and malevolent smile, he said, "You boys get that woman and those pups of hers. Put 'em in the barn."

Atkins glanced at the terrified woman, who pulled her children behind her in a feeble attempt to protect them. In her eyes, he saw the shock as the meaning of Jake's words sunk into her consciousness. She looked as if she were about to faint. The miniscule portion of his being that passed for a conscience protested weakly. Sure, they had burned sodbusters before. Atkins didn't have a big problem with that. Including the wife and children was a different matter, though. Turning back to Flynt, he said cautiously, "I thought we was tryin' to lay low. We're not really gonna burn the woman and them young'uns, are we Jake?"

"The hell we're not," boomed Flynt. "Get moving or I'll use this whip on you." Jake brandished the bloody bullwhip in Atkins's direction.

Cowed by Flynt's ferocity, Atkins's meager conscience ceased its protest. "Well, sure, Jake, whatever you say. I was just askin'."

"Well, don't ask," Flynt snapped. "Just do what I tell you. You understand?"

"All right, Jake, I understand." Atkins nodded briskly.

Atkins turned and started in the direction of the woman, who shrank away. Ben Ralston followed a step behind him. Before they reached the woman, a rifle shot boomed and Ralston dropped in his tracks, shot in the chest. A strident voice echoed off the barn ordering men to spread out and surround the outlaws. From the sound of the commands being barked in rapid-fire fashion, there had to be at least five men circling the band. Jake Flynt sprinted to his sorrel stallion and leapt into the saddle. The rest of the men milled around in confusion for a moment as several more shots rang out.

"Mount up," Jake roared. "Let's get out of here."

Jake's order brought the men to their senses. They ran to their horses and struggled into the saddles. Pierce Keaton let loose with a high-pitched scream as a bullet tore the heel off his right boot. He let loose with a string of profanity as he awkwardly found the stirrup with his left foot. Jake Flynt spurred his horse and galloped off to the north toward the next rise. More shots chased the bandits as they fled, though none found their mark.

The shooting stopped when the last of the outlaw band cleared the distant hilltop. The silence was deafening. The woman huddled in front of the fallen door to her house, her two children clutched tightly in her arms. She remained that way, frozen, for several moments, sobbing quietly. Then she heard the sound of hooves as a horse trotted down the slope toward her from the west. She was blinded by the afternoon sun until the lone rider was within twenty yards of the house. "Howdy, ma'am, are you and the young'uns hurt?" Tommy Stallings pulled up a few feet away from the woman and dismounted.

In an unsteady voice, she answered, "I reckon we're all right. My husband's hurt bad, though." She looked around. "Where's the rest of the posse?"

Tommy said, "There ain't no posse, ma'am."

CHAPTER 3

It was a chore getting that sodbuster patched up enough to load him and his family in their wagon. I was going to toss the dead outlaw in the back as well but the sodbuster's wife would have none of it. She said she didn't want him lying there next to her husband after what he'd done to him. I wasn't pleased about it but I took the time to dig a shallow grave and dump him in it.

It was chaos for a while with everyone crying and screaming. I have to say, I'm not real good at handling those kinds of things. I tell you for sure, it's not easy digging a grave while you try to calm down a woman so she can calm down her children, while her husband is moaning loudly. It near about broke my heart seeing those little ones with their eyes wide with fear. They hadn't done anything to deserve that kind of misery. The memory of this day will haunt those poor children for the rest of their lives. You can't let things like that get in the way of getting the job done.

I did get it done, though the wagon trip took at least an hour more than it would have under normal circumstances. I figured the children might need some comforting from their mother so I tied Rusty to the back of the wagon and took the lines. Around mealtime, we pulled into Cimarrón and I went to see if Doc Adams could do anything to help that unfortunate man, Bill Malone. I swear, if I've ever seen anything as bloody as that poor fella's back, I sure can't remember when. That bullwhip must have had a piece of metal, like a barb from fencing wire, on the end of it. I can't believe that leather by itself would do that much damage. He almost looked like a grizzly had been at him. I don't know if Malone is going to make it or not. There's not much I can do for him other than get him to the doctor, though.

At Doc Adams's place, the Malone children got more upset at the sight of their father's bloody injuries. Doc called me aside and asked if I could remove the family as they were interfering with his ability to treat the man. I took the hint and asked Mrs. Malone if it would be all right if I found them some lodging where they would be more comfortable. She hated to leave her husband's side but it was clear that the children were suffering and there was nothing she could do to help the doctor.

I took them over to the St. James, Cimarrón's fancy hotel. I told the clerk to give them a room on the town's ticket. He tried to tell me the town didn't have a ticket. I had to threaten him a little to get his attention. It's kind of like when you're working with a horse . . . sometimes you got to give them a good swift kick so they know you mean business. I told him we had some questions about how he was using some of his hotel rooms. In my most official voice, I said we'd had reports of young ladies drifting in and out on a frequent basis and we . . . we, of course, being me and the sheriff . . . wondered if he might not be running a house of ill repute on the side. Of course, there's nothing to that, I made it up. I managed to buffalo the clerk for the moment although once he thinks about it, he'll probably tell his boss, Roger Smith, about it and he'll complain to my boss, Sheriff Marés. The sheriff doesn't like it when I do things like that. He says hoodwinking citizens is not part of the job, a point on which we often disagree. Still, it did serve to get the man's attention and his cooperation. I'm mainly interested in getting results.

After I report in to Sheriff Marés, I'll see if I can get my wife, Mollie, and her boss, Miss Christy, to look in on the woman and her children. Those poor folks will be in a tough situation if Malone doesn't make it. Mrs. Malone told me they have no kin in the area. I figure there's going to be a lot more crying and such, and like I said, I'm no help with anything like that. If you need me to shoot somebody, I can do that. Providing comfort to a crying lady is not my cup of tea. Heck, I don't even like tea.

I walked into the sheriff's office and found Sheriff Marés sitting at his old rolltop desk looking over some wanted posters and reports from the sheriff over in Taos. The reward for Jake Flynt is up to five hundred dollars now. That's a nice pile of money if you ask me. I can think of a lot of things I could do with it. Of course, that's the reward for any brave citizen who helps capture that lowlife cur. Me, it's just part of my job. I'd get nothing if I bring him to justice. Nothing, that is, except for the satisfaction of seeing a no-good sidewinder like him locked up and then strung up. After a fair trial, of course.

I walked over and sat down in the chair in

front of his desk. "Howdy, Tomás . . . I mean Sheriff Marés." I've known Tomás Marés for five years. He's only been the sheriff for the last two of those years so I have trouble not calling him by his first name. I don't mean any disrespect, I just got used to calling him Tomás and I can't seem to quit. Of course, I don't try that hard because it gets on his nerves a little bit. A fella's gotta take his fun where he can find it. "I got a bit of a mess to tell you about." I smirked a tad. "That is, if you've got a moment you can spare from all your important paperwork."

I did mean the tiniest bit of disrespect with that last remark. In my opinion, Tomás spends too much time on paperwork and not nearly enough time out looking for outlaws. Of course, he didn't ask me for my opinion so my smart-aleck comment didn't go over too well with him.

"For your information, Deputy . . ." He kind of drew out that last word like it had a bit of a disagreeable taste that he was trying to spit out of his mouth. "I am trying to keep myself fully informed about the dangerous criminals that lurk in Colfax County. This paperwork *is* important." I notice that they list the names of Jake Flynt's gang on the poster along with a drawing of Jake's face. I see Garrett O'Donnell's name on the list, which bothers me quite a bit. I figure this might not be the best time to question this since I've already got him a little stirred up with my smart-aleck comment about his important paperwork.

"Sorry, Sheriff," I said, a bit sheepishly.

I was sorry, too. Even though I like to get his hackles up every so often, I have to say that Tomás really is a pretty fine fella. He's a good man to ride the river with and we have done just that in the past . . . and his heart is in the right place for sure. It's just that he's so serious and buttoned down. He never wants to bend the rules if that's what it would take to solve a crime. He says we got to follow the law. That's another one of his problems. It's sure not one of mine. I decided when I took this job that I was gonna get things done and I wasn't gonna let the law get in the way of seeking justice. Kind of a funny point of view for a lawman, I realize. Still, there it is.

Tomás waved his hand dismissively. He gets over these things pretty fast. Lots of practice. "Tell me what happened. I have a bad feeling that you are going to tell me something about Jake Flynt."

Like I said, he's a pretty sharp fella. "Yep, that's what it's about. Looks like we were

26

prob'ly right that Jake and his gang pulled the job here. He found him another sod-buster and was goin' about doin' that vicious, hateful thing he does." Jake Flynt was infamous for his irrational hatred of sod-busters. "I was able to stop it before he burned the place down." I had to stop for a moment so I could push down the sick feeling in my stomach. The image of that sod-buster's back looking like raw beef was gonna be hard to forget. When my insides quit rolling, I continued. "Afraid I didn't get there in time to stop the whippin', though."

Tomás shook his head in what appeared to be a combination of revulsion and resignation. "I do not understand how a man becomes so twisted and evil. I have seen it before and yet I still do not understand." He struck his desk with his fist, causing me to jump like a spooked deer. "We must catch this outlaw before he commits any more of these horrible crimes."

I was a bit taken aback by this show of emotions from my usually buttoned-down boss. He's generally pretty calm. The fact that he could work up a good mad about it made me respect him even more. "You're right about that, Sheriff. Course it's a lot easier to say than it is to do."

I took off my nice silver-belly Stetson hat and placed it carefully on his desk, crown down. I hoped he didn't get mad again and wind up smashing my hat. A good Stetson can set you back a few dollars. "You know, it would help if we had a couple more deputies to ride along with me out there. That Big Empty is a whole lot of territory for one man to cover. There's a whole bunch of places for a man to hide out."

"We have talked about this before, Tommy," he said patiently. He was buttoned down again. "Even after everything that has happened here in Colfax County, we cannot get more money from the county coffers for another deputy. For some reason, the mayor does everything he can to prevent the council from voting on it. It does not matter what we wish for, we must deal with what we have."

"You're right, I know," I said with disgust. He was right, too. He's tried as hard as a person could to convince that silly bunch of gutless wonders that control our village council to put up or shut up. They raise a big fuss when we don't catch these outlaws yet they don't do what it takes to help us out. Turns out they won't put up *or* shut up. Can you tell I'm a little frustrated?

"Do you have any ideas where they are

28

hiding out? If we could figure out where they hole up, we might be able to sneak up on them." I appreciated that he said "we." This is not a job I want to try all by myself.

"You know there's lots of peaks and buttes in that country north of Springer. Any one of 'em would make a dandy hideout that'd be tricky to sneak up on." I leaned forward in my chair. "Near as I can figure, they're either holed up at Black Mesa or Buckhorn Mesa. I've tracked 'em in that general direction, but I can't really get too close 'cause they got the high ground."

"I understand," Tomás said. "Still, if we could follow them from a safe distance and determine where their hideout is, we might be able to put together a small posse."

I think this time when he said "we," he meant me. If I could track them to their hideout without getting shot, we'd know where to look. All I have to do is find them. Sounds easy enough unless you're the one doing the finding.

"Who you plannin' to have ride with us when the time comes to go after 'em?"

"My father and brother. Jared Delaney. Maybe Tom Figgs, too," Tomás said. His mouth turned up in a hint of a smile. "It would not be the first time we have fought outlaws together, *qué no*?"

As a matter of fact, we'd had a lot more experience handling bad men than I ever would have expected in the course of my young life. Miguel and Estévan Marés along with Jared Delaney had given more to the town of Cimarrón than could ever be repaid, though, as far as I could see, nobody was scrambling to line up and start the repayment process.

"Kinda funny, ain't it? Estévan workin' for Delaney now," I chuckled. A few years back, Estévan blamed Jared for the death of his friend and mentor, Juan Suazo. They'd managed to get through that rough stretch, though, and now they were amigos. "Estévan has sure nuff calmed down from his wild ways."

Tomás shook his head and smiled. "I suppose you could say that. He is still impetuous; there is no doubt about it. He stays away from the mescál though. That helps."

In case you couldn't tell, Estévan is a bit of a hothead. Mescál never helps with that. "Well, I'd ride with Estévan any time," I said.

"I have always loved my brother," Tomás said. "It is only in the last few years that I have been proud of him as well."

"Your ma and pa did right by you boys, no question about that," I said. I meant it, too. I had a whole bunch of respect for Miguel and Anita Marés. They were good, solid folks, the kind you were proud to call friend.

"*Es verdad,*" Tomás said, reverting to his native tongue. He leaned toward me. "Here is what I need you to do. Pick up the trail of these *cabrónes* and find out where they hide out. Once we know this, we will go after them." Tomás smiled but there was no warmth in the smile.

I sighed. My wife was not going to be pleased. She already complained vigorously about my long absences. Of course, she complained in that lovely, lilting Irish accent of hers so I didn't really mind the nagging all that much. I could listen to my wife talk for hours . . . which she often did. That reminded me.

"I'll get right on that, Sheriff." I can't say that I said this with a great deal of enthusiasm. I wasn't looking forward to this job. Still, it was what I'd signed on to do. "First, I got to talk to Mollie and Miss Christy about that sodbuster's wife and young'uns. The woman is gonna need some help over there at the St. James while she waits to see if her husband survives that whippin' Jake gave him."

"You say they are at the St. James?" Tomás

cocked his head and looked at me suspiciously.

"Yep," I replied with some degree of satisfaction. "I told the clerk to put it on our ticket."

"We don't have a ticket," Tomás snapped.

"That's funny; the clerk there at the St. James said that same thing. After I reasoned with him, though, he saw his way clear to put 'em up for a couple of nights, no charge."

Tomás looked at me for a long moment. Apparently, he decided it might be best if he didn't know any more details about my interaction with the clerk at the St. James. He sighed. "All right. Talk with the ladies. After that, I would appreciate it if you would saddle up and go do your job."

He had that look he gets and I could tell he was aggravated. I didn't much care. I figured if I got to go risk my life chasing those egg-suckin' dogs that ride with Jake Flynt, the least I could do was aggravate my boss a little bit.

"Mollie, darlin', you got to understand," I said as calmly as I could. I'm not really known for my patience but since I married my lovely Irish colleen, I've had the chance to develop a great deal of it. "It's my job. If

Tomás says I got to go ridin' around the Big Empty lookin' for outlaws, then that's what I'll do." I reached out to pat her on the arm and she slapped my hand away. She does that when she's upset. It's not her most charming feature. *Patience,* I told myself.

"Don't you be tryin' to sweet-talk me, Mr. Tommy Stallings. You just got home from ridin' around out in that desolate land, now you're tellin' me you're goin' back?" I could see she was getting ready to cry. Damn. I'd take her being angry anytime. I hate it when she cries. I've also asked her to call me Tom. Sometimes she does, just not when she's mad. I think I'll let it pass right now.

"Mollie, we both knew what I'd be doin' when I signed on. You know I hate bein' away from you. Like I said, though, I got a job to do."

I reached out my hand to her again and this time, mercifully, she didn't slap it away. Instead, she melted into my arms and burst into tears. As much as I wanted to find the pump handle for those waterworks so I could shut them off, I've picked up a trick or two over the past couple of years. I just hugged her and kept my mouth shut. That's also not something I'm generally known for. Finally she stopped crying and pulled away from me. Although her eyes were a little

33

puffy, she was smiling.

"Sure and you got a way about you, Mr. Stallings." We were in the schoolhouse where she assisted Christy Johnson in teaching the children of Cimarrón. Christy had already walked over to the St. James Hotel to meet the wife of that poor sodbuster, Malone. Mollie had assured her she would come right along after we had talked. When I heard that, I knew it was going to be a rough stretch for me. I don't generally like it when we "talk." It was looking like it might not be too bad after all.

"Honey, you know I love you more than life itself. If I could, I'd be right by your side every minute of every day. It's just that there's work to be done and somebody's got to do it."

"I know that. I just don't know why it's always got to be you." She made a sour face. "Why doesn't Mister Tomás Marés get off his fancy arse and ride out into that wilderness instead of you?"

I love it when she cusses in Irish. "Mollie, Tomás has a lot of official business to take care of as the sheriff. And besides, you know as well as I do that when trouble comes to a head, Tomás will be right there with me. He's proved that and you know it."

"You're right," she said with a sigh, "he

34

has. I'm just upset." Some of the wind seemed to have gone out of her sails. Slowly, an impish grin appeared on her face. "And Mr. Stallings, if the time ever comes when you can be right by me side every minute of the day, please don't do it. Sure and you'd drive me plumb insane. I might have to shoot you."

When she starts giving me a hard time like that, I can tell the worst is over. She likes to tease me. It means she loves me. "I'll keep that in mind."

"Enough of this fiddle-faddle, I need to get meself over to the St. James and help Miss Christy look after that poor woman and her wee bairns."

Being married to an Irish lass has been educational. I've learned words like "fiddle-faddle" and "wee bairns." As best I can tell, they mean "nonsense" and "children." It never ceases to amaze me that Mollie can switch so fast from tears to all business. The storm seemed to have passed, though. She seemed like she was ready to leave so I wasn't going to do anything to stop her.

"I know Miss Christy will appreciate the help. I'm gonna stop back in Tomás's office and let him know I'm ridin' out. I'll pick up some supplies from the house and hit the trail."

For a brief moment, Mollie looked like she might cloud up again. She took a deep breath and then grabbed me in a fierce embrace. "I love you, Tommy Stallings."

I didn't bother to correct the "Tommy" this time, either. The ride seemed to have smoothed out, no sense in rocking the wagon. "I love you, too, Mollie Stallings."

She'd been Mollie O'Brien before I made her my wife. I was getting better at saying things like "I love you, too." It's not something cowboys say a lot. I've found that since I met Mollie, I've gotten a lot of practice with it. It's starting to feel natural.

She pulled away, kissed me on the cheek, and walked out of the schoolhouse. I took a deep breath of my own and walked out to go track down some bad men.

CHAPTER 4

I decided that before I took off back out into the Big Empty to chase outlaws, I was going to ride out and have a chat with Garrett O'Donnell's wife, Ashleen. I'm still trying to figure out why Garrett is caught up in this mess. I hope maybe she can shed a little light on that subject. On top of that, I've got a sneaking suspicion that the president of the bank, Mr. John Burr, is not as much of an innocent victim in all this as he tries to pretend he is. This whole thing is like a big puzzle and I'm trying to understand how all the pieces fit together.

I have to say, that the things I've seen over the past few years have made me a bit cynical. I like that word. I learned it from my schoolteacher wife. Now that I'm cynical, it seems to me that quite a few of these men who are in powerful positions in the territory abuse their power. They tend to take advantage of your average citizen by grabbing more than their fair share of the money and land. Speaking of fair shares, we've sure had more than our share of trouble with that dirty bunch of corrupt politicians that call themselves the Santa Fe Ring. Can you tell they're not my favorite group of people?

For more than ten years that I know about, those no-good scoundrels in Santa Fe have been taking advantage of the small landholders, using the law to steal their land. They say that poltroon by the name of Thomas Catron owns more land than anybody in the whole United States of America. All those fellas, they're lawyers. They trick folks by telling them they'll defend them against the people who are trying to steal their land. Right. Then they turn around and demand most of the land as payment when they "win" the case for the poor folks they're supposed to be helping. They even justify it by saying it's legal. It may be legal but it sure ain't right. It's just dirty dealing in my book.

When they can't hoodwink folks in the courts, they hire outlaws and bullies to force the small landowners off their land. They use the banks to foreclose, never giving a rancher an honest chance to sell his cattle and make his payment. That's where I think old Mr. John Burr fits in with this bank robbery scheme. It's a little too convenient that right after his bank gets robbed, he goes right out and forecloses on three small outfits that were behind in their payments. I heard that each one of those folks had money in the bank and lost most everything they had in the robbery. I wonder if Garrett O'Donnell was one of those folks. Maybe I'll ask his wife when I talk with her.

"It's been more than a week since I last saw him." Ashleen O'Donnell said this in a subdued voice, defeat written all over her young face. "Sure and I don't know if he's ever coming back to us."

When she said "us," she was referring to herself and her two young children . . . a girl, probably around the age of four or five, who had freckles and her mother's long auburn locks, and a baby boy who hadn't yet begun to walk. My first impression was that Mrs. O'Donnell seemed awful young to have two children. I snuck a closer look and reevaluated my assessment. Although she was pretty, I could see that the wind, weather, and worry were already beginning to take their toll. There was a roughness to her hands that comes with hard work and there were fine lines around her eyes. Of course, you can get them when you have trouble on your mind, too.

"Mrs. O'Donnell, I knew your husband." I stopped myself and started over. "What I mean to say is that I *know* your husband. We've got witnesses in town that saw him during the bank holdup. I don't know what to make of that. I don't think he's an outlaw." I took a polite sip of the tea she'd made. Nasty stuff. "I'm just tryin' to make sense out of why he would be ridin' with those men."

"I don't know how to explain it to you, Deputy," she said warily. "I don't really know if I understand it myself."

I took a deep breath. "Mrs. O'Donnell, your husband told me about his past in Ireland." She started to protest but I raised my hand to silence her. "He also told me he'd given that up and came here for a fresh start. I believed him." I spread my arms, trying to convey to Ashleen O'Donnell that I was wide open to hearing any explanation she might have to offer. "It seems likely to me that somebody forced his hand." I waited.

Ashleen O'Donnell pressed her lips together so tight, I thought her face might explode. She glared at me for a moment before saying, "I don't know anything about any of that. I just want my husband to come

40

home." I looked around the place, trying to get a picture in my mind about what their life might have been like before all this trouble. They lived in a two-room weathered wooden house. Although it wasn't much, I could tell Mrs. O'Donnell tried to keep it clean and neat, fighting a losing battle with the dust that blew through the chinks in the wall. I admired her spirit. I believe there's a certain nobility in fighting a battle you can't win. There was a barn and stable west of the house. I could see one broken-down old nag in the small corral. Appaloosa. That figures.

"Can you tell me about anything Garrett might have said before he left? Was he havin' some kind of trouble, maybe somethin' weighin' on his mind?"

Mrs. O'Donnell looked at me like I was a first-class idiot. "He had worries troubling him all the time, Deputy. Sure and we didn't have much else, as you can see for yourself if you got eyes, we had more than our share of worries. I planted a vegetable garden, he ran a few cows." She shook her head. "Someone stole our cows, Deputy. We had a buyer for them . . ."

Then she burst into tears. I don't understand why this keeps happening to me. As usual, I didn't know what to do. I took

41

another sip of tea, tried not to gag, and waited until she calmed down.

"Somebody stole your cattle?" I prompted her.

She sort of hiccupped and caught her breath. I was relieved. This crying business was unnerving.

"That's what I said, Deputy." She was a little testy. I reckon I can understand that under the circumstances. "We had part of the money saved to make the payment on this place. We were counting on that money for the rest of the note."

"You kept the money you had saved in John Burr's bank?" Ashleen O'Donnell had Tommy's full attention.

"Certainly not," she scoffed. "Garrett said banks were too risky. There's always someone looking to rob them."

Apparently, the irony of her statement went right over Ashleen O'Donnell's head. "You have a good point, Mrs. O'Donnell," I said sympathetically.

"Somebody took our livelihood." Her eyes flashed. "That bank was going to take our place if we didn't make the payment. They wouldn't give us any time to try to make it up." I could see the muscles in her jaw tightening in anger. "I can't tell you why my Garrett was riding with those men, Deputy, because I don't know. If you're asking me to feel pity for the bank, though, I feel no sympathy at all. That Mr. Burr, the man that owns the bank, is a monster."

I knew John Burr, the president of the bank in Cimarrón. It might be a little harsh to say he was a monster. I'd probably describe him as a rattlesnake. He had no compassion for the small-time ranchers who tried to scratch a living from the land. He wouldn't hesitate a second to foreclose if they fell behind on their payments. I'd heard that he was in pretty tight with that Ring bunch. As a matter of fact, since the bank was robbed, I knew he had foreclosed on three small ranches. Although I wasn't sure who was set up to get the land once he kicked the poor folks off their places, it seemed mighty suspicious. The whole thing had the unmistakable odor of another one of those Santa Fe Ring deals. All right, I reckon he is a monster.

"So you're tellin' me Garrett was in a desperate spot," I said. She nodded. "You'd lost your cattle and were afraid you were gonna lose your place?" She nodded again and looked away. "Was that about the time that Jake Flynt and his boys showed up?" She nodded once more. I asked her, "Has Mr. Burr sent you a notice that he's foreclosin' on your land, Mrs. O'Donnell?"

She shook her head. "No, he has not. Not yet anyway. Sure and it's only a matter of time."

A tear trickled down her cheek. I was afraid the waterworks would start gushing again and I'd sure enough had my fill of that. I'd had enough of her tea, too.

I figured I had a pretty good picture of what had led up to Garrett's riding with that band of villains. They needed a dynamite man, Burr had the leverage. I didn't think Ashleen O'Donnell was going to admit that to me. That's okay. I could always come back and talk to her again.

"Mrs. O'Donnell, I've taken enough of your time," I said. "I'll be on the lookout for your husband. If I find him, I'll do my best to bring him in without any trouble." I felt bad for the woman. "In the meantime, you're plannin' on stayin' around here, are you not?"

She avoided looking at me and her face held that wary expression again. "I can't say for sure about that, Deputy. We had been talking about selling this place, maybe going somewhere else to start over. If we did sell, we could pay the bank and maybe have some money left over. If they seize our land, we'll have nothing. The children and I may have to go back east until Garrett can find work. My brother, Terrence O'Reilly, lives in Boston. He might take us in."

There wasn't much I could say to that. She had next to nothing, two children to take care of, and the bank was putting pressure on her. The notion that someone might be interested in this hardscrabble piece of land seemed a bit far-fetched to me. Still, who was I to stomp all over her dreams?

"Well, do what you got to do, Mrs. O'Donnell. If you talk to your husband, please tell him that I'm sympathetic to his plight. I don't want to hurt him, I just want to bring him in so we can sort this mess out."

She nodded one final time. She continued to avoid looking me in the eyes. I had a feeling she wouldn't do what I'd asked. I had a distinct feeling that there was more going on here than I could see right now. I'd felt pretty certain that John Burr was up to no good. Now I'm beginning to think Garrett O'Donnell might be doing some conniving of his own as well. I don't know why things have to be so complicated. I thanked her for the tea. As I rode away, I decided against heading out into the Big Empty. Instead, I figured I'd better ride back to town and have a little parley with my boss. Trying to think my way out of this mess on my own was making my head hurt.

CHAPTER 5

"They did what?" I asked in disbelief.

"They robbed the bank at Springer," Sheriff Marés said. I don't know how in the heck he stays so calm. "I just received the telegram. They must have gone straight from that sodbuster's place when you ran them off. I think you had better head over there and try to pick up their trail."

"Those lowdown thievin' curs," I said vehemently. It took me a moment to calm down. "Anybody get hurt?"

From the solemn look Tomás had on his face, I knew what the answer would be before he said it. "They killed a teller. A couple of citizens were wounded, also. I think they are going to live."

"Thank goodness for that at least. Sounds like I'd better get a move on if I want to track down those gutless wonders." I walked over to the cabinet where we keep the guns.

I grabbed a Winchester and two boxes of shells.

Tomás turned toward his desk and reached for a stack of papers, then turned back around. His face was clouded with worry.

"You know they will use this robbery as support for moving the sheriff's office to Springer. They will say that if the sheriff had been there, this would not have happened."

I shook my head, disgusted. "That's just plain silly, Tomás. The sheriff's office is in Cimarrón and they managed to rob the bank here."

"I did not say it made sense; I just said they would try to use it." He shook his head. "Politicians." He looked like he might spit on the floor. Being Tomás, he didn't. I probably would have. That's just one of the many differences between the two of us. I tell you one thing, I didn't envy him this part of his job.

"Reckon I'd better get busy and catch these egg-suckin' dogs then. That might shut 'em up for a while at least."

"Sí, Tommy, that is an excellent idea, catching the outlaws." He smiled. "If I had known it was that simple, I would have suggested it myself. *Vaya con Diós, amigo.* Be careful."

I think he was having fun at my expense. I decided to let it go this time and headed for the door. As I reached for the handle, I stopped. "Anybody in Springer say they saw that Irishman, Garrett O'Donnell?"

Tomás gave me a quizzical look and shook his head. "No, no one said anything about that. Why do you ask?"

"Well, I don't think he's really a part of the gang, Sheriff," I said cautiously. Then I figured I'd just say what was on my mind. "I sure wish he wasn't on that wanted poster you been lookin' at. He ain't an outlaw, leastways not like Jake Flynt and those other no-good sidewinders."

"He was seen during the robbery, Tommy. The vault was blown and we know he is an explosives expert. We have several witnesses who identified him. He was with the gang."

There he goes with the Tommy thing again. I didn't call him on it but it got me riled up. "But he wasn't really 'with them,' if you can take a minute and look at the difference. Those other fellas in the gang are stone-cold killers and bad men. That's not who Garrett O'Donnell is." I inhaled. "He must've had some other reason for doin' what he did. I reckon they forced him into it somehow."

I could see the muscles in Tomás's jaw tighten as I made my speech. "That is not for us to decide, Deputy." The way he said "deputy" sounded a little better than "Tommy" but not much. "The courts will decide that when we bring these men to justice."

I exploded. "Dang it, Tomás, that's what I'm talkin' about . . . justice. You know that these territorial courts and judges ain't much interested in justice. They'll say he did the same thing as those other lowlife curs and treat him like a criminal. That ain't right."

"I have tried to explain to you before, Deputy, that we pursue those who break the law. We do not decide who is right and who is not. That is not our concern. We have to leave that to the courts."

"Well, maybe we ought to spend a little more time worryin' about who's right and who's wrong, Sheriff."

I was really mad. If I stuck around much longer, I might say some things I couldn't take back. Even though I didn't agree with Tomás on this, I did respect him. Also, he's my boss. I turned around, walked through the door, and headed out for the Big Empty again. I wondered if justice was waiting out there somewhere . . . or if it was just empty.

■ ■ ■ ■

I have to tell you I was mighty nervous as I rode the trail east to Springer. Although I was pretty sure Flynt and his gang had all ridden north to their hideout on one of the mesas, I was on the lookout for an ambush. They know who I am and they know I'm after them. I even know Dave Atkins. I'd ridden with him on one of Jared Delaney's cattle drives up to Trinidad and Pueblo and I didn't enjoy the experience much. Although he knew his cowboy work, he was a bully and a braggart. We had some young pups making their first drive with us and he sure did give them a hard time. I'm not talking about the typical hoohrahing we all do, I'm talking about cruelty. I didn't much like him.

The trip from Cimarrón to Springer takes the better part of a day because a lot of it is through the foothills. The trail is pretty good but there's a lot of spots where a fella could set up an ambush if he was a mind to. Did I mention I was nervous? Probably a good thing, too, since I reckon it saved my life.

Up ahead, the trail took a sharp turn to the left. There was a big old granite rock right there at the turn and an even bigger one a little bit past it and up the hill. I was just thinking to myself that if I was going to set up an ambush, this would be a good spot for it when I heard the sound of small rocks clattering down the slope. I reined in my roan gelding, Rusty, dismounted, and led him over to a pine tree where I tied him loosely to a low branch. I considered taking the Winchester, then decided against it. Too many rocks to climb over, too big a chance of knocking it against one of them and making a noise. I'd go with my Peacemaker.

Not to brag but something I'm pretty good at is sneaking up on people. When I was young, before I lost my family, my sister and I used to play games of hide and seek. She could never hear me coming until I was right on her. It used to make her so mad all she could do was stand there and sputter at me. I reckon it's a natural gift. Since I been a lawman, I've worked at getting even better at it. You never know when you're going to have to sneak up on a fella. I was sure hoping my skill didn't fail me now.

I set off carefully on the left side of the first rock, heading uphill with the intention of sneaking up behind whoever was on the other side. It occurred to me that it might just be a deer. That would be all right with me. Deer ain't likely to hurt you none. I'd shoo it on its way and get myself back on the trail. Of course, it also occurred to me that it might be a mountain lion. I sincerely hope not. They're not as easy to shoo away as a deer. They're also more inclined to do you bodily harm. I'd probably have need of the Winchester if that was what was waiting around the bend. Given a choice, I think I'd prefer one of Jake Flynt's gang over a lion.

There was a game trail up around the side of the hill where I was headed, which was fortunate. The footing was good so I was able to move without a sound up and around the first rock. I stopped there and listened. There's a trick to listening when you're alone in the wild. People think it's quiet but that's not really the case. You got all the noises of the birds and little four-footed critters plus the whispering sound the wind makes as it caresses the leaves of the aspens. You have to listen for something that doesn't fit with those natural sounds.

I thought I could hear something fidgeting about on the far side of the second rock. I figured the good news was that this whole thing wasn't my imagination playing tricks on me. The bad news was that some kind of living thing was waiting on the other side of the rock. Reckon it was time to find out what it was. I turned uphill and made my way up the steeper incline. Sweat tickled the middle of my back and a little bit got in my eye. I had to stop and use my sleeve to wipe it away. I have to admit I get a little bit jumpy when I'm tracking something, especially when I don't know what it is. By and large, I like surprises as well as the next fella, but not in situations like this.

It being early afternoon, the sun was just west of straight up. Since I was coming from the west and the high ground, this gave me an edge if whatever was waiting down the hill heard me and looked up in my direction. You take whatever advantage you can get. When I got to the top of the rock, I sat still as a tree stump for a couple of minutes. I was pretty sure I hadn't made any noise to alert whatever kind of critter might be on the other side. Still, you can never be too careful. I was getting ready to look over the top of the rock when I heard the sound of metal striking rock, followed by a low curse. I was relieved. I'd never seen a mountain lion carry a rifle and I don't believe they're inclined to cursing. Looks like I had me a human critter.

Slow as the rising sun, I raised my head up over the rock enough that I could get a glimpse of what was below. The first thought that crossed my mind was that it was Dave Atkins. It took me a second look before I realized that the man lying prone on the rock pointing his rifle down to where the trail came out below was a little smaller than Dave. I figured it must be his younger brother, Charlie. Looked like it might be my lucky day. If I could take him alive, Tomás and I might be able to find out some information from him . . . things like where their hideout was located. It occurred to me that I could interrogate him myself before I took him back to Cimarrón. Tomás tends to be a bit more patient and civilized than I am when it comes to extracting information from prisoners. It's like I said earlier about the horse . . . sometimes you got to give them a swift kick to get their full attention and cooperation. All I had to do was take him alive. At a snail's pace, I drew my pistol.

"Hello, Charlie," I said. "What are you up to on this fine summer's afternoon?"

That's what I meant to say. Before I got the word "Charlie" out of my mouth, the kid had jumped up like a bee had stung him on the backside. Instead, what I said next was, "Hold it right there, kid, I got you covered."

Charlie Atkins stared hard at me, squinting up through the glare. He held his rifle in his right hand out to his side at arm's length. Although he couldn't do any damage with it where he was holding it, I watched him like a red-tailed hawk eying a field mouse. If he made the slightest movement across his body with it, I would know he was making a play. That gave me an advantage, although not much of one.

"Who's there?" His voice started out high and squeaky, then came down a notch.

I said, "Why, it's Deputy Stallings, Charlie. Ain't I the one you're waitin' for?"

"I don't know what you're talkin' about," he said with as much bravado as he could muster under the circumstances. "I was out here huntin' deer." He didn't sound all that convincing to me.

"I believe you were huntin', Charlie," I said politely. "I don't believe you were huntin' deer. I believe you were huntin' me."

"That's a no-good, rotten lie," he shouted, working up an almost believable batch of indignation. "I ain't doin' nothin' wrong."

"Reckon we'll see about that," I said as calmly as I could.

No matter what anyone tells you, it's no easy task staying cool when you and some desperado are both holding on to deadly weapons. While I didn't want to shoot him, I doubt he had any qualms about shooting me. I tried to keep the tension out of my voice. I didn't want him to know I was scared, too.

"I'm takin' you as my prisoner, Charlie. We'll head back to Cimarrón, have us a little talk. I'm right curious about what your brother, Dave, has been up to these days. I heard he was ridin' with Jake Flynt. Didn't know you were ridin' with him, too."

From my vantage point, I could see the expression on Charlie Atkins's face begin to change just as soon as I mentioned Jake Flynt's name. Where he had looked scared before, he started looking mad now. I didn't think this was a good sign.

"You need to calm down, boy," I said. I was getting the feeling that this situation was going south mighty fast. "You also need to put that rifle down . . . slow."

He continued to squint uphill at me. He made no move to put the rifle down and it seemed to me that he was gradually moving his right hand, the one with the rifle in it, back toward the center of his body. Not good.

Trying hard to keep the edge out of my voice, I said, "Don't you get any ideas about throwin' down on me with that rifle, Charlie. I got the drop on you. You make a move, I'll shoot you."

"Maybe so," he said heatedly. "You take me in, though, Jake'll skin me alive when he finally gets at me. He'll think I turned on him. He don't tolerate that."

I had a sinking feeling in my stomach. The kid was more afraid of Jake Flynt than he was of me shooting him. I gave it one more try. "Charlie, once I take you into custody, Jake would have to break into the jail to get at you. He ain't gonna break *into* the jail."

"You don't know Jake." A grim smile spread slowly over his face. "He's loco."

Quicker than I thought he would be capable of, Charlie Atkins swung his right hand the rest of the way around, grabbed the stock of the rifle with his left hand, and started to pull it down into position to fire at me. I had no choice. I shot him.

"I hope that dim-witted brother of yours can get the job done, Dave," Jake Flynt said with equal parts misgiving and malice in his voice. "I'd feel a whole lot more secure if I knew that useless deputy wasn't dogging our tracks every minute of the day and night."

"Well, I sure believe he can," Dave Atkins said with an enthusiasm that he likely didn't feel. "That boy's got some sand, I'll say that for him."

"It's not his sand I'm concerned about," Flynt said scathingly, "it's his brains and his aim. I don't know why I let you talk me into this."

"Now that ain't quite fair, Jake," Atkins said cautiously. "You said you thought it was a good idea when I brought it up yesterday." Mustering his artificial enthusiasm again, he blustered, "Hell, even if he misses, he'll scare him all the way back to Cimarrón, maybe give us a little breathin' room. That'd be worth somethin' right there."

"Right," said Jake in a cold voice. "And if Stallings captures him, he can find out where our hideout is. I suppose you didn't think of that, did you, Dave?"

Atkins looked around at his compadres for support. Pierce Keaton and Hank Andrews avoided his gaze. Patricio Baca shook his head and sneered in disgust. Dave looked back at Jake Flynt and said, "Well, hell." He couldn't seem to think of anything else to say for a moment. After awhile, he said lamely, "Jake, I sure hope that don't happen."

Flynt glared at him. "You'd better hope it doesn't." He turned to the rest of the outlaws. "Looks like we may need a change of scenery, boys."

CHAPTER 6

I rode into Cimarrón leading Charlie
Atkins's little paint horse. Charlie was
draped over the saddle. I hate when I have
to do something like this. The sheriff's office is right there on the main street and
there's no way to sneak in quietly. Everyone
comes over and asks what happened, making a big deal out of something that is really
pretty sad when it comes down to it. I'd
wager not a single one of those folks who'll
want to celebrate me killing this misguided
young man has ever pulled a trigger and
taken another human life. There's nothing
to glorify about it. I believe the word my
schoolteacher wife would use is tragic. I
mentioned before that I try not to let the
law get in the way of justice being served.
That doesn't mean I enjoy killing.

Tomás looked up when I walked in the office. "Tommy, I am surprised to see you. I
thought you were riding over to Springer."

Tomás didn't really look surprised. Of course, he's not one to display his emotions so it's a little hard to tell sometimes. I'll bet he'd be a good poker player if he was inclined toward the game. Due to the serious nature of the situation, I let him slide on not calling me Tom. I even called him by his official title. "I didn't make it all the way there, Sheriff. I got ambushed about ten miles into the trip." I motioned over my shoulder. "Charlie Atkins, Dave's little brother."

Tomás perked up at that bit of news. "Well, bring him in. Did you already question him?" He stood up quickly, excited at the possibility of getting information that could lead to the capture of Jake Flynt and his gang. Well, as excited as he ever gets.

"Sorry, Sheriff," I said with genuine remorse. I really did feel bad about shooting Charlie. He was just a kid and not the sharpest tool in the shed to boot. It was probably his destiny to come to a bad end. Still, I'd rather it had come at the hand of somebody else. "He drew down on me even though I had the drop on him. I had to shoot him."

Tomás nodded slowly. "You had no other choice?"

If someone else had asked me that, I

might have taken offense. I'm no cold-blooded killer. I knew Tomás had to ask the question. He can't have his deputy going around shooting folks whenever it strikes his fancy.

"No, sir, I did not. He was dead set on killin' me. I tried to talk him out of it. There weren't no reasonin' with him." I shook my head. "I don't believe thinkin' was Charlie's biggest talent."

Tomás didn't respond right away. He looked like he was contemplating the situation. That's one of the things I like a lot about him. Unlike me and his brother, Estévan, Tomás takes the time to think things through before he does something. Me and Estévan, we tend to barrel on in. I suppose there's some use for either approach, depending on the circumstances. I'm trying to learn to stop and think. I believe it's fair to say that my progress in this area is uneven.

"These outlaws are becoming bold," he said in a clipped tone. "They have no respect for the law. We must show them that if they ignore us, there will be a price to pay, Deputy Stallings." His eyes narrowed. "I want you to get the body over to the undertaker. As soon as that is done, I want you back out on their trail. They need to know we are not cowering in fear here in

Cimarrón while they are on their rampage." I could see his jaw muscles clinch for a moment. "They need to know we are coming for them."

I sort of figured that's what he'd want me to do. I had one favor to ask of him. "Tomás . . . I mean, Sheriff, do you mind if I take a few moments to track down Mollie and show her I'm alive? You know she's gonna hear about this right about the time I get young Charlie's remains to Bill Wallace's place."

Cimarrón didn't really have a full-time undertaker. Bill owned the mercantile and did whatever undertaking needed to be done on the side. He was a successful businessman and mayor of the village, which made him the head of the village council. You might say he had his finger in several pies. It seemed like an odd assortment of pies to me, but then what do I know about business? Or pies, for that matter. I'm getting off track.

"I prob'ly won't even have time to get him off his horse before she's tearin' around lookin' for me."

Tomás laughed, which was unusual for him. I wasn't so sure I saw the humor in the situation. Reckon it depends on where you're standing.

"Yes, of course, see your wife. You are right, she is liable to be very upset if you do not find her and show her you are alive." He chuckled again. "She may be upset anyway. It seems a good time to get out of town for a while. Perhaps I should ride out and visit with Jared. He needs to know what has happened."

Tomás seemed to be in mighty high spirits as he pondered my thorny state of affairs. I can't say I was especially pleased to be providing him with amusement. I also didn't think it was particularly manly of him to run away from my wife like that. I understood, though. I was tempted to hightail it for the hills myself. Since she was my wife, I figured I probably couldn't get away with it. You learn to take the bitter with the sweet.

"Sheriff, I want to have a little talk with John Burr down at the bank before I head back over to Springer. I want more information about the robbery that happened here." I was suspicious of Mr. Burr. "Flynt's gang is a bloodthirsty lot. It strikes me as a bit odd that no one got shot here. I wonder why not. That's different from Springer, from what you're tellin' me. I think there's somethin' goin' on that ain't right."

"I noticed that as well. You may be on to something." Tomás looked worried. "Be

64

careful what you say, Deputy. We cannot accuse a prominent member of the business community of something illegal without proof."

Apparently, Sheriff Marés was afraid I might go off half-cocked on the bank president. I don't know where he would get such an idea. "I decided to postpone talking with Mollie until after I'd stopped by the bank. It was important enough that I visit with John Burr that I would risk having a scene with my wife."

"Deputy Stallings, if you don't leave my office immediately, I will have my assistant fetch the sheriff."

I reckon some folks are just thin-skinned. Our conversation took a turn for the worse when I asked Mr. Burr why he hadn't seemed more upset after the robbery. I also might have mentioned that a man had to be pretty low to foreclose on the three good families whose notes were due. Those folks had money in his bank that they planned on using to make their payments. Without any warning, their money was gone and Burr was in position to take their land. It seemed like a little more than a coincidence. Burr took offense at this . . . thin-skinned, like I said. From there, our talk went right on down the hill. I do recall mentioning that I thought he was greedy and I may have questioned whether or not he was an illegitimate child. I was pretty hot so I really don't recall every word I said. I have a feeling that Mr. Burr does.

"All right, Mr. Burr," I said. I started to say "Mr. Fancy-pants bank president" but at the last minute, I remembered that Tomás had told me to be careful not to lose my temper. It was probably a little late to think about it but what the heck. "I'll be keepin' my eye on you." I reckoned that would put the fear of the Lord into him.

As it turned out, he didn't seem too concerned about that, although his face was the color of a ripe tomato fresh from the garden. I think I got under his skin. I have a way of doing that. It's just a knack, something I was born with. Even though I was fuming mad myself, I did recall something important from our little talk before it got out of hand. I remembered that unlike when I'd talked with him right after the robbery, this time he seemed more worried and upset. I'm beginning to think he had a hand in the bank robbery. I admit I don't understand all the connections yet, but I suspect he and Jake Flynt had a plan and something went wrong with the plan.

■ ■ ■ ■

"Oh, saints be praised, there you are, Tommy, darlin'." Mollie saw me from across the street as I walked out of the bank. She crossed the street at a dead run and flung herself on me, nearly knocking me down in the process. I recovered my balance and hung on to her. "I was so worried about you!"

It was a challenge to calm myself down after my little dust-up with one of the most powerful men in town and comfort my wife at the same time. I managed it, however.

"It's all right, Mollie, I'm fine," I said with as much composure as I could muster. "I ain't got a scratch on me." I let go of her and held my arms outstretched so she could inspect me.

She stepped back and looked me up and down. "Sure and it's a fact, you don't." She smiled at me although there were still traces of her tears showing on her cheeks. "I've been so vexed since I heard the news."

I knew it couldn't have been more than twenty minutes since she'd heard the news. I went straight from Bill Wallace's place to the bank and that discussion hadn't taken very long. She hadn't had long to worry.

Still, I wasn't about to make light of her concern or her suffering. While that goes against my cowboy nature, I'd found over the course of our marriage that this approach was not especially effective in maintaining marital harmony.

"I'm fine." People were looking at us curiously. I smiled sheepishly at some citizens passing by, then took Mollie's arm and began walking down the street toward Tomás's office.

"I need to check in with the sheriff, darlin'. Why don't we go down to his office where we can have a little more privacy." I didn't really need to see him about anything, I just wanted to get away from the gawkers. Mollie went along quietly. That doesn't happen all that often so I'm grateful for the times when it does.

When we got to the office, it was empty. Looks like Tomás hadn't wasted any time getting out of town.

"Tommy, I'm so afraid they're going to gun you down. I don't want to lose you."

I wish she'd call me Tom. Tommy is such a little boy name. Once again, it didn't seem like this was a good time to bring that up. "Well, Mollie, I dang sure don't want you to lose me, either," I said with a good deal of enthusiasm. "I do my best to be careful.

There's some risk involved in the job and there's not much I can do about that. I am chasin' outlaws, after all."

"I know, Tommy, I just don't know what I'd do without you. You're the best thing about livin' in this uncivilized part of the world."

She burst into tears. As usual, I was bewildered. "Why are you cryin' now?" I asked as gently as I could. "I told you I was all right." Right about the time I thought things were looking up, she'd started with the tears again. I really don't like crying.

"I miss me home," she wailed.

Now I was really confused. We had a nice little place on the edge of town. A little cottage, nothing fancy, but it was comfortable and it was free. The village paid for it, me being a deputy. We even had a stable and a small corral out back for my horse and mule. If she missed the place, she could walk down there in less than five minutes and be home. Before I opened my mouth, I tried to puzzle out what she meant. I don't usually do that.

"Darlin', I'm not sure I know what you're talkin' about. We have us a home here for as long as I'm a deputy. What is it that you miss?"

"I miss the green, Tommy," she said passionately. "Everything is brown here . . . all the time."

I think I mentioned earlier that things had already started to green up. I remained befuddled. "We're about to get us some good rains in the next month, Mollie, darlin'. It'll really get green then."

"You don't know what you're talkin' about, Mr. Stallings." She turned away in disgust. "You've never seen green."

I was getting a little frustrated now. I didn't want to have a fight with my wife just before I rode out to track down a bunch of killers, so I tried to be reasonable.

"That's pert near the silliest thing I ever heard, Mollie O'Brien Stallings," I said reasonably. "Dang near every tree in these parts is green."

"Psshhhh," she hissed. She looked at me like I was an imbecile. "You know nothin' about green." Apparently, she didn't appreciate my reasonable tone.

I liked it better when she was saying she didn't know what she would do without me. "All right, little miss educated schoolteacher, tell me about green."

Lucky for me, she decided to ignore my sarcastic tone. "Tommy, I miss me home in Ireland. They really do have green there like you've never seen. I miss the people, I miss the pubs, I miss the rains."

Then she started crying again. Did I mention I don't like crying? "Oh," I said in as comforting a manner as I could muster, considering how baffled I was. Seems like there ought to be some kind of instruction manual for this stuff. "You miss your *home.*"

"That's what I've been tryin' to tell you," she said with exasperation. "I swear, Mr. Stallings, sometimes you're a bit thick."

That stung. Once again, I tried again to be reasonable. "Well, that ain't very nice, Mollie, you callin' me names." With effort, I restrained myself from replying in kind and tried to sound self-righteous. I held my breath to see if it would work.

She sighed heavily. "You're right, I know it. When I am upset I get angry. Next thing you know, I'm sayin' things I don't mean." Once again, I saw that mischievous grin start to materialize out of nowhere. How she can switch from distraught to playful in a heartbeat is a mystery to me. "Although you really are a bit thick, Tommy Stallings . . . in a lovable way, of course."

I decided to ignore that. "Mollie, I don't want to fight with you. I got a job to do. I don't want to ride out with you mad at me."

Her face took a softer look. She pulled me to her and whispered, "I love you, Tommy

Stallings. Go do your job."

Once again, I decided the time was not right to remind her about my name.

CHAPTER 7

Tomás rode out towards Jared Delaney's place, which was still called Kilpatrick Ranch in memory of the couple by whose side they had stood against outlaws and corrupt politicians in years past. He was thinking about those times as he rode up to the ranch house when his reverie was interrupted by yelling. His initial alarm was replaced with a smile as he realized it was Jared and Eleanor's almost five-year-old son, Ned. Apparently, he was engaged in chasing rustlers and was telling them to put up their hands or he'd shoot. He pointed a small, hand-carved wooden gun in the direction of his father who immediately surrendered and raised his arms. Ned ran squealing to his father who scooped him up in his arms and swung him around in the air. About mid-turn, Jared saw Tomás and began disentangling himself from the wiggling bundle he was holding.

"Howdy, Sheriff Marés," he said with a welcoming grin. "What brings you out our way?"

Tomás dismounted and tied his horse to the rail in front of the house. "Two things really," he said with a sly grin. "The first one is that my deputy had to tell his wife that there had been an attempt on his life. He did not expect that she would react calmly to the news that someone had tried to kill him. I also anticipated that the meeting might become somewhat emotional. Since she is not my wife, I decided it was a good time to make a visit out here."

"That Mollie is a piece of work, is she not?" Jared's grin faded as the rest of what Tomás had said sunk in. "You say someone tried to kill Tommy?"

"Sí, one of Jake Flynt's men, Charlie Atkins, tried to ambush him," Tomás said. "Fortunately, he was not very good at it. Tommy heard him and was able to sneak up on him. When he tried to take him prisoner, the boy went for his gun. Tommy had to shoot him."

"Charlie Atkins, huh?" Jared looked thoughtful. "Isn't he Dave Atkins's little brother?"

"Sí," Tomás replied. "They were both riding for Jake Flynt."

"I can't say that surprises me all that much. Dave went on one drive with me. I never hired him for another. He was mean and a bully to boot. He liked to pick on the younger hands." Jared leaned down to his son who was hanging on his leg and said, "Ned, go tell your mama that Tomás is here." He turned to Tomás and said, "We're about to have a meal, why don't you come in and grab a bite to eat."

Tomás's ambivalence was written all over his face as he struggled with the decision of which was more onerous, impolitely refusing an invitation to dine with the Delaneys or eating Eleanor Delaney's cooking. Jared came to his rescue.

"We're having venison that I smoked and some beans, too. I made 'em." He grinned. "I think you'll survive." As they began walking toward the house, Jared said, "You said there were two things that brought you out here. What was the second?"

Tomás said, "I want to discuss what is going on with this Jake Flynt gang . . . the bank robbery, the decision to move the sheriff's office to Springer, who may be working behind the scenes." He frowned. "All of this seems too familiar."

As they stepped onto the porch, Jared said, "This Flynt character sounds like he's bad business. You figure he's working for some of our old friends?"

Tomás shrugged. "I am not sure, I only have a suspicion. We continue having these dangerous snakes to deal with and when we kill one, another replaces it. We never manage to cut the head off."

Jared started to respond but whatever he was going to say was lost as Eleanor Delaney, holding a beautiful little girl in her arms, came to welcome him.

"Tomás, it's so good to see you. How are your parents?"

Tomás doffed his hat. "They are well, Señora Eleanor, thank you for asking. My mother complains that she is working too hard, yet she will not allow anyone to help her in the kitchen. My father just shrugs and goes about his business." He smiled. "Things are the same."

Eleanor laughed as Tomás described the ongoing ritual between Miguel and Anita Marés. "It's comforting to know that some things don't change." She shifted her daughter, Lizbeth, to her hip and said, "We were about to sit down to eat. Won't you join us?"

Around Colfax County, Eleanor Delaney was infamous for being one of the worst cooks in the history of the county. Somehow, she seemed to be oblivious to her culinary shortcomings and cheerfully continued preparing meals for her family that were practically inedible. It was no wonder that Jared, unlike many husbands, had taken to helping out with the cooking chores. Eleanor was under the impression that he was among the most thoughtful of all husbands in the New Mexico Territory. Tomás knew, however, that Jared's actions were less about maintaining marital bliss and more about survival.

"It would be my pleasure." Tomás steeled himself in the event that Eleanor had somehow managed to slip in a side dish that she had prepared without her husband's knowledge. They walked into the house and Jared pulled up an extra chair for Tomás.

"What brings you out our way?" Eleanor passed around platters of food and they loaded their plates with the venison that Jared had prepared.

With a wink in Jared's direction, Tomás said, "I felt a need for a ride in the country and some air. There were things I wanted to discuss with Jared so it seemed like a good time for a visit. I would be interested in your thoughts on these things as well."

Although her gastronomic skills were lacking, Tomás knew that Eleanor Delaney possessed a sharp intellect and a spirit that was unconquerable. He valued her opinion as much as he did Jared's. "That sounds serious," Eleanor said. "Why don't we eat, then we can sit a spell on the porch. We wouldn't want to spoil our meal with unpleasant talk." Eleanor smiled affectionately at her husband. "Did you know that Jared prepared this venison? I don't know where he finds the time, but I certainly appreciate it."

Tomás studiously avoided looking at Jared. "One of life's mysteries, I suppose. He never showed much skill as a camp cook when we were on trail drives."

Jared cleared his throat and changed the subject. "I'm sorry you missed Estévan. He went up to the north section to check the fence line. We've had some cows bustin' through the fence up there. I don't know what gets into those critters' heads."

Tomás smiled, both at Jared's rapid change of topic as well as the image of his younger brother mending fence. "My brother has never wanted to step down off his horse to engage in work of any kind. I do not know how you have worked this miracle. It appears he has become a good hand."

Jared laughed. "I ain't sayin' he didn't complain about it, I'm just sayin' he's doin' it. Not many cowboys are eager to fix fence."

"Es verdad," Tomás said. "Still, I am glad to see my brother more settled. For a time after the death of Juan Suazo, I feared that he had lost his way."

Eleanor spoke up. "That was a difficult time for all of us. It seemed like no matter what we did, we couldn't stop those murderous thugs from the Santa Fe Ring. Estévan was hurt and angry. He had to blame someone." She shook her head. "Unfortunately, for a time, it was Jared."

Jared said, "It took awhile before he got it through his thick skull that Juan would never have blamed me for what happened and that Maria Suazo didn't either." He laughed. "Your brother is hardheaded, Tomás."

Tomás smiled. "He takes after our mother. I am more like our father." He paused. "When we are done, I want to speak with you about what you mentioned, Eleanor . . . about how we cannot seem to stop the corrupt politicians from Santa Fe."

"Why don't you and Jared relax on the porch, Tomás," Eleanor said. "I'll clean up and join you in a few minutes." She looked at Jared tenderly and said, "It's the least I can do for my obliging husband."

Tomás and Jared settled into the rockers that sat on the portal. "She really believes that you have become domestic by choice, does she not?" Tomás shook his head in amazement.

Jared sighed heavily. "If she only knew how much I hate kitchen chores. It's a gold-plated testimonial to how bad her cookin' is for me to take over most of those duties."

"Why do you not talk to her about her cooking?" Tomás looked sideways at his amigo. "I am sure my mother would be happy to give her some instructions on preparing better meals."

Jared snorted. "You tell her that. There's no way I'm bringin' it up."

Tomás considered the statement. "When you put it that way, I see your point." Further discussion on the topic was stifled by the appearance of Eleanor Delaney, who took a seat alongside the two men.

Eleanor sighed contentedly. "I love the view out here. It makes all of our hard work and trouble worthwhile."

Jared nodded in agreement. "Yep, we get to live out here in this beautiful country and do what we love to make our livin'." He watched his young son frolic around the yard and looked over at the lovely little girl sitting contentedly in her mother's lap. "Got these two fine young'uns to keep things lively, too. Reckon that balances the scales

80

pretty well against the trouble that comes our way from time to time."

"I hate to change the discussion from life's simple pleasures to something disagreeable," Tomás interjected. "However, it is that very trouble I wish to discuss with the two of you."

"You said one of Jake Flynt's bunch tried to bushwhack Tommy," Jared said thoughtfully. "I thought Flynt was a maverick. I didn't think he had any connection with the Santa Fe Ring or anyone else, for that matter. He's plumb loco from what I hear. Ain't too many folks, even crooks, who'd want to ride with him."

"You are right," Tomás said. "This does not seem like the usual business of the Ring." He took off his hat and scratched his head. "Tommy suspects that John Burr is involved. He says the robbery of his bank seemed almost staged. Burr was not in the bank at the time of the robbery although he is usually there. Did they know that ahead of time? How did they just happen to have a man along who could blow the most secure vault in the territory? However, I do not see a connection between Burr and Flynt."

"Could have been a coincidence," Jared said reflectively. "They knew the vault would be tough, maybe had him there just in case."

"Maybe, maybe not," Tomás said skeptically.

Jared chuckled. "It sure wouldn't be the first time a so-called respectable leader of a community was tangled up with an outlaw."

"A true statement if ever there was one," Tomás replied. "I am also puzzled by the odd way Mayor Wallace is handling the notion of moving the sheriff's office to the new county seat in Springer. It does not make sense." He shook his head in consternation. "I do not know if Tommy is right about Señor Burr but I think he is right to be suspicious. Too many things are not making sense."

"I never liked Bill Wallace," Eleanor said firmly. "He doesn't look you in the eye when he talks with you."

"Yeah, I always check my fingers after I shake hands with him." Jared laughed. "That Burr is the real snake, though. I'm grateful Ned and Lizbeth owned this land outright when they brought me on board. I'd hate to be beholden to Mr. Burr's bank."

"I agree with you," Tomás said. "It makes me want to follow up on my deputy's idea that Burr was in league with Jake Flynt on the bank robbery. It would appear, however, that something may have happened which they were not expecting."

Jared and Eleanor looked at Tomás curiously. "What would that be?" Jared asked.

"It would appear that Garrett O'Donnell made off with the money."

CHAPTER 8

Jake Flynt was enraged. Pierce Keaton hated it when Jake was this way. The bad news was that Jake was this way more and more frequently these days. Pierce figured that was the price you paid when you rode with an outlaw like Jake Flynt. Sometimes he wondered if it was worth it. Still, there didn't seem to be a safe way to leave the gang without Jake killing him. Considering that, it was probably better to stay where he was.

"I think this here might be a better hideout than what we had before, Jake." Hoping to lighten his boss's mood, Pierce tried to sound cheerful. Once they'd discovered that Charlie hadn't been successful in his attempt to ambush Deputy Stallings, Jake decided it would be smart to move. He hadn't been happy about it.

"Shut up, Pierce," Jake said in a quiet, very cold tone. He stood on a rock and looked out to the southwest. If the law came for them, he figured they would come from that direction. After a moment, he turned and said to Pierce, "I want somebody up here on lookout every minute of the day. You understand me?"

"Well, yeah, Jake, I do," Pierce said uncertainly. "We are a little short on men right now with Ben and Charlie gettin' shot and that damned Irishman, O'Donnell, runnin' . . ." He stopped, wishing he could take a deep breath and suck the words back into his mouth. It was too late.

"Don't you mention that sorry Mick's name in my presence, Pierce Keaton," Jake bellowed. "I may shoot you if you say it again."

"Sorry, Jake, sorry," Pierce said rapidly. He really was sorry, too. That damned Irishman had grabbed the bag of money from the job in Cimarrón and lit out to the Big Empty. In between dodging that deputy and whipping sodbusters, they'd been looking for him for the past two days. They'd seen signs of his camps but, so far, hadn't been able to track him down. He kept on the move and it was hard to find somebody in the Big Empty if they didn't want to be found.

■ ■ ■ ■

I kept one eye on my surroundings as I rode back over to Springer. Although I didn't expect Jake to try again so soon after Charlie Atkins's failed attempt to ambush me, you never can tell with outlaws, particularly one as unpredictable as Jake Flynt. It wouldn't hurt to be careful. As I rode along, I thought about what I wanted to ask the folks in Springer about the bank robbery. From what I'd heard so far, it seemed different from what had happened in Cimarrón. Springer sounded like a real, sure nuff bank robbery. Cimarrón seemed wrong. Something strange was going on here and I needed to get to the bottom of it.

As I rode into Springer, the citizens eyed me warily. I could see most of them relax once they saw my badge. A few of them still looked at me with suspicion. I figure they were the smart ones. I rode straight to the constable's little office. Fred Huntington didn't do a lot in Springer to enforce the law. Still, he seemed to know what was going on with everything that happened in town. I figured he could fill me in.

As I dismounted, Fred walked out of his office to greet me. "Afternoon, Tommy

Stallings. How in the world are you?"

"Reckon you might call me Tom?" I probably sounded a might short-tempered. I didn't care. I was tired of being treated like a pup.

"Sorry, uh . . . Tom." Fred sounded hesitant. I don't think he really meant any harm when he called me Tommy. I regretted snapping at him.

"I'm sorry, too, Fred," I said and meant it. "I'm just out of sorts. My backside hurts from ridin' over here. Don't think nothin' of it."

He proceeded cautiously. "What brings you over our way? Is it the bank robbery?"

"Yep, I wanted to ask you some questions. Me and Tomás are doin' our dangdest to catch those lily-livered backshooters. They're mighty hard to track down out in this wide open country."

"Well, we sure do appreciate all you're doin', Tommy . . . uh, I mean, Tom."

He nearly tripped over himself changing how he addressed me so I didn't see any point in making a big deal out of it again. After all, he did correct himself. Now, if I could just get the rest of the world to treat me like a grown man, I'd be happy.

"Much obliged, Fred," I said. "About that holdup. Can you tell me about it from beginning to end?"

"Not a whole lot to tell, Deputy Stallings." I guess Fred had decided the formal route was the safest way to address me. "There was five of 'em rode in hell-bent for leather, shootin' and shoutin'. Winged a couple of folks in the melee, which cleared the streets, I guarantee."

"I heard that. Tomás said they . . ." I stopped. I reckon if I want folks to address me with respect, I owed the same to my boss. "I mean, Sheriff Marés told me they killed one of your tellers. Sorry to hear that."

"They did at that," Fred said sadly. "Bob Howell. Nice fella. New to town. They forced Mr. Burleson to open the safe, took all the cash from it. All the cash from the tellers' drawers, too. Ain't no doubt, they meant business."

That's the way it sounded to me, too. It sounded different from the Cimarrón holdup and fanned the flames of my suspicions. As I was about to step into the stirrup, I could see that Huntington had something else on his mind. He had taken off his hat and was kind of standing on one foot and then the other. He was also having difficulty looking me in the eye.

"Somethin' troublin' you, Fred?"

"Well, I . . . uh, I mean, we . . . well, some

of us was wonderin' when they was gonna move the sheriff's office over here." He looked up with a trace of defiance in his eyes. "We are the county seat now."

"I know that, Fred." Seemed like I had enough on my mind having to track down these danged desperados without getting pulled into a bunch of weaselly politicians' games. "I don't get to make that call, Fred. I reckon we'll burn that bridge when we come to it." I grinned. "If you want to accompany me out there on that wide prairie to look for Jake Flynt and his boys, though, I'd sure appreciate the help. Once the sheriff moves over your way, I expect you'll be doin' a lot more of that kind of thing."

Fred got so nervous when I said that, he looked like he was doing some kind of dance at a hoedown. "Oh, no, that ain't what I was aimin' at, Tommy . . . I mean, Tom." Beads of sweat had appeared on his forehead. I figured I could either keep hoorahing Fred or cut him a little slack. I said, "Fred, you've been a big help, I surely appreciate it." I reached out and shook his hand. "Sorry about snappin' at you when I rode up. These danged outlaws got me on edge."

"No offense taken, Tom," he said. I grinned. Looked like I'd made one convert at least. "Let me know if I can be of any more help."

"I sure will, Fred. Thanks again." I mounted old Rusty and pointed him north out of town. I was starting to get a hunch that might help me figure out who all was involved in this dirty scheme. It wasn't going to do me much good out in the Big Empty though. I still had to track those dirty rotten polecats down.

I headed north out of Springer, hoping to pick up some sign of a group of riders traveling hard. The problem with that is, much as I hate to admit it, I'm not really a very good tracker. You got some folks, lots of them Indians, who could track a hawk through the air. I'm not one of them. I spent most of my time before I became a lawman looking at the backside of a herd of steers. They're pretty easy to track. You just follow the dust and the cow pies. Too bad Jake Flynt and his boys weren't as obvious as that.

I knew they had gone north after the Cimarrón robbery. A few citizens had taken temporary leave of their senses and organized a posse to chase them. We followed them for quite a few miles before we realized we weren't going to catch them. They were riding to the north and east when we gave up the chase. Since then, even with my limited tracking skills, I had seen some evidence of their heading north through the Big Empty. My best guess was that they were either up on Buckhorn Mesa or Black Mesa and I was hoping at some point I might see some signs that they were headed that way. Maybe even figure out which one of those big mesas they were hiding out on, if I was lucky. I pointed Rusty's nose in that direction and ambled along for a bit. After my experience with Charlie Atkins the other day, I ambled with considerable caution, though.

I had covered about seven or eight miles when to my surprise and good fortune, I saw what looked to be signs of a number of riders racing hard on the trail. The kind of deep imprints a horse makes when it is being ridden at a gallop. It had rained right after those sheepherdin' trash robbed the Springer bank so I didn't have to be any great shakes to recognize their tracks. Me and old Rusty both kept our noses looking down as we moved along steadily. I was feeling pretty good until the tracks took an abrupt turn to the right. What in blazes?

I shrugged Rusty around and we followed the trail east. We hadn't gone too far; just crested a hill, when we saw the remains of a campfire. I got down off Rusty and went to look things over. Sure enough, I found what looked like a spot where a lone rider had camped fairly recently. I wondered who it might be. I also wondered why Jake Flynt and his ragamuffin outfit were so interested. I couldn't help thinking about Garrett O'Donnell. I'll bet Jake couldn't, either.

Apparently, Jake and the boys had tried to follow the lone rider, whoever he was, so I mounted up and headed out that way, too. Rusty and me hadn't gone too far when the tracks made a left turn and headed back to the north. Looked like Jake and the boys had given up. I reckon they weren't much better at tracking than I was. That was a little bit of comfort.

I made the same left turn and slogged on up the trail. A mile or so later, I came to one of the many nameless little streams that crisscross this country after the spring runoff. The rains had gotten it flowing pretty good but it wasn't very wide or deep, so Rusty and me trudged on across. When I got to the other side, I looked around, expecting to pick up Jake's trail again. Instead, I found no tracks at all. It took me a minute before I figured out that they'd pulled that old Indian trick of riding down the stream a ways before coming out again. Sneaky devils.

I hate tracking. I decided that even if I followed them all day, about all I would discover is that they'd headed up towards either Buckhorn Mesa or Black Mesa, which I already knew. If I got too close to the wrong place, I'd run the risk of being ambushed again. I knew I'd been lucky before. Charlie Atkins was such a clumsy oaf he'd sprinkled a warning shower of rocks down the front of his hiding place. I didn't think a wily bandit like Patricio Baca would make a mistake like that. I figured it was time to go back and talk with Sheriff Marés about getting some help, not that it'd do any good.

Patricio Baca slid backwards down the rock upon which he'd been laying as he watched Tommy Stallings through his spyglass. Dusting himself off, he walked over to where Jake Flynt was squatting and said, "That deputy turned back." He spat on the ground. "Guess he didn't want to track us down that stream."

"You didn't have a shot at him?" Jake Flynt asked the question half-heartedly. He already knew the answer.

"No, boss, he was out of range." Baca was

uneasy as he struggled with the decision of whether to say something more. Finally, he opted to take the chance. "Boss, I been thinking . . . maybe this might be a good time for us to head up into Colorado. That's what you said the plan was. That deputy, he may be goin' in circles but the circles keep getting tighter. I think he has a notion where we are."

"You telling me you're afraid of that no-account deputy?" Flynt had a sneer on his lips. "Some bad outlaw you are. There's five of us and we got the high ground."

"I know, boss, I know," Patricio said in as mollifying a tone as possible. Being appeasing wasn't his nature. He'd thrived for years in the New Mexico Territory as a horse thief and on more than one occasion, a hired assassin. Still, Jake Flynt wasn't your run-of-the-mill outlaw, he was one mean hombré and more than a little bit loco. Patricio didn't want to bite off more of a fight than he could chew.

"I'm just thinking about what would happen if he brought a posse back with him," he said carefully.

"We're not going to Colorado or any damned where else until we find that damned Irishman and the damned money," Jake said heatedly. "You got me?"

"Yeah, boss, I understand." Patricio had a bad feeling about this. Prudently, he decided not to share his apprehension with the foul-tempered leader.

CHAPTER 9

When I walked into Tomás's office to report in, I found him pinned to his chair by the mayor of Cimarrón. Well, he was sitting there listening intently. I swear, though, it sure looked like the mayor had him pinned.

"*Buenos días,* Tommy," Tomás said in an even more formal tone than I was used to hearing from him. That didn't sound good. "Mayor Wallace was telling me how much the village council would like for us to catch the bandits that are running around Colfax County robbing all of our banks."

"Well, maybe Councilman Wallace would like to drag his fat arse up on a horse and come help me chase all over the Big Empty lookin' for those outlaws," I said.

Well, all right, that's what I wanted to say, what I was itching to say. I'm hotheaded, but I'm not stupid. I took a moment and bit my tongue, not hard enough to draw blood but with enough force to take my mind off telling Wallace what a blowhard he was. Deep breath.

"We're sure tryin' our best, Mr. Wallace," I said as respectfully as I could without gagging. It wasn't easy. "It would really help if y'all could see fit to pay for us hirin' another deputy or two to help me out." I tried on my most winning smile. This used to work pretty well for me with the ladies back when I was single. Who knows, maybe Mayor Wallace would succumb to my charms.

Wallace harrumphed. That's never a good sign when a pompous politician harrumphs at you. It usually means he's about to tell you why he can't or won't do what you want. He didn't disappoint me.

"Deputy, as much as I'd like to accommodate you, we don't have the funds in the village coffers at this time." He smiled his own version of a winning smile right back at me. I didn't find it charming. "Besides, I know you've ridden all over northern New Mexico and southern Colorado. If anyone can find those outlaws, it's you."

If he thought flattery would distract me from the fact that he was turning my request down flat, he was mistaken. I only have so much tolerance for folks spreading cow manure and once it gets deep enough, I mostly don't give a damn about what happens. Apparently, Tomás . . . Sheriff Marés that is . . . noticed that I was winding up to deliver my exact thoughts on the councilman's response. As usual, his cooler head prevailed, at least for the time being.

Tomás rose quickly from his chair and reached out to shake Bill Wallace's hand. "We certainly appreciate your coming by the office to inquire about the investigation, Señor Wallace. Please come by anytime."

As he led the big windbag out the door, I stood fuming. As soon as the door shut on the shadow of his immense old backside, I lit into Tomás. " 'We appreciate you comin' by? Please come by anytime?' What in the heck are you doin', Tomás? You should be tellin' that fat jackass what a terrible job he's doin' for the citizens of Cimarrón by not hirin' another deputy. Instead, I thought you were gonna kiss him on the cheek as he carried his fat butt out the door."

Tomás put his hands on his hips and waited patiently for me to run out of steam. I hate when he does that. I can go on for quite awhile when I get a full head of steam, but usually he comes back with some reasonable explanation that makes sense. About that time, I feel like a durned fool for shooting off my mouth. In the years that I've known Tomás Marés, I've learned to trust him so I decided to shorten my speech and find out what he was really thinking. I was mad as a scalded dog though. I'm not kidding about that.

I was pleased to see that Tomás looked a little surprised when I didn't continue. He waited for another moment in case I'd only stopped for a breath. When it became obvious that I wasn't going to carry on, he spoke. "The man is an idiot. He knows no more about catching outlaws than he knows about how the steam engine on a train works. He could not catch his own fat behind if he used both hands." He smiled at me. "Do you feel better now?"

I was a little surprised, and I have to admit I did feel better, if only just a tad. "Well, if you feel that way, Tomás," I said in a conciliatory tone, "why did you suck up to him like a newborn calf lookin' for its mamma?"

Ignoring the fact that I'd referred to him as a newborn calf in search of a teat, he responded patiently. "I care a great deal more about the safety of the citizens of Cimarrón and Colfax County than I do about crossing swords with a self-important local politician. You understand, do you not, that he and his compadrés on the council have a great deal of influence on the county's decision on whether the sheriff's office remains in Cimarrón."

I had hoped that by cutting my tirade short, I would avoid the part where I felt like a moron. My hopes were dashed. I felt like a schoolboy being scolded by his teacher. "Well, sure, any fool could see that." This, of course, gave him the opening to inform me that I wasn't just "any fool." To his credit, he didn't take advantage of the opportunity.

Tomás continued in measured tones. "If they support moving the sheriff's office to Springer, you and I will be out of a job sooner rather than later. If we lose our jobs, we will not catch these outlaws that are endangering the citizens. Do you think Fred Huntington will run down Jake Flynt and his band of *cabrónes*?" He paused for a breath, then cocked his head at me. *"Comprendé?"*

Sure, I knew that. I also knew that Tomás Marés cared in his own way every bit as deeply as I did about catching outlaws and protecting citizens. He just had a different way of showing it. Sometimes his way worked better. This was probably one of those times. There sure are times, though, that I'd like to really tell those overbearing, conceited, full-of-themselves politicians what a blight they were on humanity. Reckon this wasn't an appropriate time to do that. "Appropriate" is another one of the words I've learned from Mollie, although in my case, she usually uses it as part of the word "inappropriate."

"I know, you're right," I said meekly. I don't usually like being meek. He was so right about this that I couldn't help it. "Sorry I almost lit into that fat, pompous windbag of a mayor who gets to decide our fates."

Tomás walked back to his desk and sat down in his chair. I could have sworn I saw the slightest hint of a grin on his lips. "Although he certainly deserved it, that would not have been a wise decision. He is not someone we can afford to offend. We need him on our side if at all possible." Tomás frowned. "I wonder why he is so unwilling to authorize funds to bring on at least one more deputy."

"That is curious, ain't it," I said. "It's almost like he don't want us to catch 'em."

"That would not seem to make sense, unless there is some reason we cannot see," Tomás said pensively. He shook his head as if to clear the cobwebs. "For now, let us work with what we know. Tell me what you have found out."

■ ■ ■ ■

"Do you think he bought it?" John Burr looked like he'd choked on a chile pepper. He and Bill Wallace were sitting in his spacious, well-appointed, and very private office at the bank.

"Calm down," Wallace said. "I don't think they have any idea what's going on here. Even though Marés keeps that young deputy tromping around all over creation looking for Jake, I don't think there's much chance he'll find him. That's mighty vast country out there. It's more likely that Jake and his bunch will shoot him, which would be fine by me." Wallace scowled. "He's an impudent young man. I don't like how he looks at me."

"He shared some of that impudence with me just yesterday," Burr said with a sour look. "I think I'm going to complain to the sheriff about him."

"I think you should," Wallace said indignantly. "I think you should complain vigorously. We can use situations like this to our advantage to facilitate the move of the sheriff's office to Springer." He glanced nervously out the window of the banker's office. "You don't think Marés will figure out our game, do you?"

"I highly doubt it," Burr replied superciliously. He reached over and pulled a cigar out of the humidor on his desk. He made a show of cutting the tip off and lighting it with a flourish before he continued. "These Spanish folks around here are gullible. I don't know why he would be any different. That's not what's got me worried."

Wallace nodded vigorously. "I know, I know." He wiped a drop of sweat off of his forehead and waved his hand to fan the haze of cigar smoke away from his face. "Any sign of O'Donnell?"

"I haven't heard a word from Jake since he told me that Irish scoundrel absconded with the money. I've been to our meeting spot twice. No one has showed and there were no written messages. I have no idea whether they've had any luck tracking him. It's probably difficult to do while they're on the run."

"It was a good plan, John," Wallace said with a hint of a whine in his voice. "We needed an explosives man and O'Donnell fit the bill. Word around town was that he'd done it all over Ireland before he came here. At the time, I didn't see how anything could go wrong."

Once more, Burr looked as if he'd swallowed a flaming chile pepper. "Exactly my point, Bill. You didn't see it, yet it went wrong anyway. Now look at the mess we're in. The money is gone."

Wallace reacted angrily. "Don't blame this all on me, John. You agreed to the plan as well."

Burr grimaced. "I'm almost wishing we hadn't entered into this bargain with Flynt."

"He is your brother, John," Wallace said with an accusing tone in his voice. "You're the one who came up with that part of the plan."

Once more, Burr's temper flared. "He's not my brother, Bill, he's my stepbrother. Big difference. Anyway, that doesn't change the fact that the money is gone." Burr fixed Wallace with a withering gaze. "If you want to come out of this scheme with your debts settled and stay out of jail, you'd better stay focused on figuring out what happened."

Wallace waved his hand in a gesture of appeasement. "I'm sorry, John, I don't mean to blame you. I'm just upset."

"You think I'm not?" Burr snapped. He leaned forward in his chair. "We can't dwell on mistakes, we need to move forward and deal with this situation. The fact is, we didn't see the wild card . . . that damned Irishman."

■ ■ ■

I filled Tomás in on what I'd learned about the variations between the holdup at Springer and the one here in Cimarrón. There was a ferocity, a willingness to kill anyone in the way, to the event in Springer that was missing from the one here. The way some of the good citizens of Cimarrón described the holdup of John Burr's bank, it was almost as if the robbers were just going through the motions. That is, until the man identified by witnesses as Garrett O'Donnell picked up that bag of money and lit a shuck out of town. Jake and his gang had stopped what they were doing, which was emptying out the tellers' drawers, and mounted up like they were about to follow O'Donnell.

"Remember, that's when old Bill Wolverton come a'runnin' down to your office to say some men were organizin' a posse right there on the spot. When I came out the door, it looked to me for a moment like them outlaws were gonna try to break through our boys and go after O'Donnell. It was only after we started takin' potshots at 'em that the bandits turned and headed out of town to the north."

"How do you know that they didn't plan it that way? Maybe they intended to meet up later and split the money." Tomás always looked at different sides of an issue, which was most likely the right way to go about things. It could sure be annoying, though.

"I don't know that for certain," I said a bit huffily. "What I do know is that it looks to me like Flynt and his boys have been searchin' all over the Big Empty for somebody. I've seen signs of a lone rider myself."

Tomás was curious about the lone rider that Jake's gang and I had tracked for a few miles. By the time we finished talking, he was as suspicious as I was about the real story behind this bank robbery. Facts didn't add up. While Tomás is pretty much a stickler for following rules, he's a pretty smart fellow. As the pieces in this puzzle started falling into place one by one, he began to see the same picture emerge that I was seeing.

"I need for you to go back out tomorrow and try again to see if you can locate their hideout, Tommy."

"I'll do it in a heartbeat if you'll just call me Tom," I said.

I didn't really say that, I just thought it. I knew there were things going on that were way more important than my personal struggle to have folks call me by a grown man's name. Anyway, it was a grown man's job he was giving me. What I said was, "I'll get on it at first light. In the meantime, I'm gonna spend some time with my wife."

"As you should," Tomás said. "I will talk to the witnesses again; the ones who saw O'Donnell pick up the bag of money. I wonder if it looked to them like he was running from Flynt and the others. I did not ask them that before."

CHAPTER 10

Mollie and I sat in rocking chairs on our little portal, watching the sun set. The way the colors change from rose to purple as the sun vanishes behind the hills in the west never fails to lift our spirits. That silly dog she had rescued from Tom Figgs when he couldn't get rid of all the pups his dog birthed was bouncing all around us, licking my hand and sticking his head under my armpit so I would pet him. If they gave out blue ribbons for being a nuisance, he'd win one every time. He'd been the runt of the litter and his mama wouldn't have nothing to do with him. I think it's fair to say that he entered this world not quite right. He's some sort of Catahoula/heeler cross and he was born with a funny-looking crooked nose. It goes straight for awhile, then takes a left turn right there at the end. The left side of his mouth won't quite close either, so he leaks whenever he drinks water. He would have died if Mollie hadn't taken him in and wet-nursed him with warm milk and a washcloth. She named him Willie, for reasons understood only by her. He's good for absolutely nothing. I kind of like him anyway, though I couldn't tell you why.

"I wish you didn't have to be goin' back out to that wasteland again tomorrow," Mollie said, a trace of resignation in her voice.

"I know, darlin', it's hard." I reached over and patted her on the knee. That silly dog licked my hand when I did it. That made my Mollie smile. Maybe that's why I kind of like the dog. "It's my job, though."

"I know, I know," she said, frustration replacing the resignation. "Sure and you've told me that a hundred times."

The last thing I wanted was to spark her temper so I changed the topic. "How is that sodbuster's wife and her young'uns doin'?"

The sodbuster had died in spite of all Doc Adams could do. He'd lost too much blood. Without going into gory detail, it hadn't been a pretty sight.

"That poor woman. She has no idea what she'll do to support herself and those wee bairns." Her eyes blazed. "The man that did that is the devil."

She was sure enough right about that.

"That's why I got to go back out to the Big Empty tomorrow, Mollie. There's too many men who think they can do whatever their evil hearts tell 'em and justice be damned." I was working up a pretty good mad here and I finally had someone who would listen. "We got a choice. We can either keep our heads down and hope we don't accidentally stray into their paths or we can stand up to 'em. I ain't willin' to hunker down like a scared rabbit."

She reached over, took my hand away from Willie's lively tongue, and squeezed it hard. "I know, Tommy Stallings," she whispered. "You find those gobshites and kill 'em."

I think "gobshite" is an Irish curse. I'm not sure what it means but I know it's not a compliment. I love my wife.

John Burr pulled the buggy right up next to the little grove of cottonwood trees. The sky was cloudless and if he strained, he could almost see the Spanish Peaks to the north. He sat in the seat, nervously winding his pocket watch as he looked around. He saw no sign of any other human being. After a few moments, he got out of the buggy and walked a few paces to the east, hoping to catch sight of the man for whom he waited.

The wind was blowing at a pretty good clip . . . seems like it always did that out here. He put a hand on top of his hat to keep it from blowing away. All he could hear was the sound of the cottonwood leaves rustling. He stopped and scanned the horizon. He saw nothing.

"Hello, John, nice of you to come."

Burr whirled around, nearly falling over in the process. "My God, Jake," he exclaimed, "you almost scared me to death." He bent over, taking deep breaths as he tried to bring his heart rate back to normal. "Where did you come from?"

"I was standing in the trees watching you." Flynt chuckled. "It was amusing."

Burr's eyes narrowed as he glared at Flynt. "Well, that's wonderful. You've had your laugh. Now maybe we can discuss what you're going to do to clean up this mess you've made."

Flynt glared back. His hand strayed dangerously close to his pistol. "This mess I've made? It was your idea to bring the Irishman in on the deal."

Realizing he might have overstepped his bounds, John Burr held up his hands in a pacifying gesture. "You're right, Jake . . . you're right. I share responsibility for what's happened. I thought we had that dumb

Mick over a barrel."

"Yeah, well, it looks like he wasn't as dumb as you thought," Flynt said in a disgusted tone. "He managed to get away with almost all the money."

"I was trying to look after your interests, Jake," Burr said. "Just like I've been doing since we were boys."

"Sometimes I think you take too much credit for that, John," Flynt said softly. "Like it was your doing that your daddy married my mama after my pa died."

"Well, of course not, Jake, that's not what I meant," Burr said quickly. "You can't deny that I've helped you out of some tight spots in the past."

"It seems like this time, all you've done is put me in a tighter spot," Flynt growled. "That damned Irishman has my money. How the hell am I supposed to clear out of this country when I don't have a stake? You call that looking after my interests?"

There was a mad gleam in Flynt's eyes that scared John Burr. He had always been the manipulator and planner in their relationship while Flynt had been the explosive one. It seemed to Burr that he was getting more explosive by the minute.

"I thought the threat that the bank would foreclose on him if he didn't comply with our demands would keep him in line. If he had stuck with the plan, I would have forgiven his loan. He would have had that lousy piece of land he covets free and clear. I didn't anticipate that he would double-cross us."

"No, you didn't, John," Flynt said nastily. "You missed that one, didn't you?"

Burr changed the subject. "Where in heaven's name is he anyway?" His voice rose in frustration. He looked all around as if Garrett O'Donnell might be hiding in the same grove of trees Flynt had taken cover in earlier. "Why can't you find him?"

Flynt waited until Burr stopped looking around and turned his eyes back to him. "I haven't found him yet for the same reason that the deputy hasn't found me. There's a huge amount of land out there. A lone rider could be anywhere. If you're lucky, you might cross paths with him. If you're not, you might circle around each other for months, even years." He rubbed a hand over his unshaven face. "O'Donnell seems to be able to live off the land. There's some water out there; fish and small game, too. There's no telling where he is."

Burr took a deep breath and tried to calm down. "That's not very encouraging, Jake. I repeat my initial question . . . what are we going to do?"

"He may not need food, water, supplies. There is one thing he does need and I know what it is." Flynt smiled. There was no warmth in it.

"All right, Jake," Burr said impatiently, "what is it that he needs?"

"He needs to see his wife. That's his weakness." Flynt nodded with a shrewd look. "That's how we'll find him. I sent one of my boys out this morning to that miserable little piece of dirt and scrap lumber that O'Donnell calls a ranch. He'll wait there until he shows up . . . which he will."

"You're probably right," Burr said impatiently, "which makes me wonder why you didn't think of doing this before now."

Flynt glared at Burr. "If you haven't noticed, John, that damned deputy has been lurking out here for days trying to spot us. I was concerned that if he did, he'd bring a whole damn posse down on our heads. That's why we took a shot at him, to see if we could get a little breathing room." Flynt spat on the ground. "Don't know how much good that did us."

Burr decided not to push Flynt any harder. "It's starting to make sense to me now why you didn't want me to have the woman thrown off the premises. You were baiting a trap." Burr smiled. "I like it, Jake. I think maybe it will work."

"Damn right it will work," Flynt said harshly. "And when it does, I'll have my man bring that sorry polecat to me. I want him alive. I'm going to whip all the hide off him and leave him out in the sun to die. I'll enjoy seeing whether he dies of thirst or bleeds to death first."

Burr could not suppress a shudder. While he was not above destroying the lives of people by taking their land and livelihood, he never resorted to physical violence. It occurred to him that he might be in deeper than he would like to be with this man. If so, was it too late to turn back?

"What you do and how you do it is your business, Jake. I just want the money back so we can split it up like we planned. Then you can go wherever you want as long as it's away from Colfax County." Burr hesitated, then asked cautiously, "Where are you hiding out these days, Jake?"

"Never you mind where I'm hidin' out," Jake replied heatedly. He cocked a suspicious eyebrow at the banker. "I'll get the money back, don't you worry," Jake said softly. "Then I'll take a measure of revenge. No one double-crosses Jake Flynt." He stared at Burr intently. "No one. You understand that, don't you, John?"

Burr's mouth was suddenly dry as a desert and he had a bit of difficulty swallowing. As sincerely as a banker possibly could, he replied, "Yes, Jake, of course I understand." His nostrils flared and his breath came more rapidly. "I understand it very clearly."

Our little house is on the outskirts of town so we have room for stables out back. That way, my horse, Rusty, is handy when I need to get on the trail in a hurry. I had saddled him up and was about ready to head out. It was midday and I was getting a later start than I wanted. Sometimes it goes that way.

It had taken longer to gather supplies for the trip than I'd anticipated and my pack mule, Gentry, had gotten a bit stubborn. A stubborn mule, imagine that. She was a beauty and that's not a word you often hear paired up with the word *mule.* She was a zebra dun and right smart. She was great to pack with when it was just me, Rusty, and her. If I tried to trail her with a string of mules, she'd have nothing to do with the others. Wouldn't cooperate at all. She doesn't like other mules. I don't think she realizes she is one. I'm sure not going to be the one to tell her.

The other person who was being stubborn

like a mule this morning was my wife, Mollie O'Brien Stallings. She hadn't spoken a word to me since we woke up and she burnt the bacon she'd fried. I'm pretty sure it wasn't an accident. I can be hardheaded myself, though, when the occasion calls for it. I was about to head out on a dangerous undertaking and there were no guarantees that I'd come through it alive. I wasn't willing to leave things this way so I walked back into the house to say a proper goodbye. She turned away and continued to ignore me. When I reached out to touch her on the shoulder, she slapped my hand and glared at me.

"Why do you act this way, Mollie?" I asked as I tried to control my temper. "You know I have to go, it's my job."

Not quite ready to calm down, Mollie shouted, "You eejit, it's because I love you."

My jaw dropped. "You're mad at me because you love me? Is that what you just said?" I let out a snort of frustration. "That don't make any sense at all."

Mollie's features softened. "Well now, if you think about it, sure and it does." She sighed. "I love you, Tommy Stallings, and I know you love me. You love me when I sometimes act like I got fluff for brains. You even love me when I strike at you like a rattlesnake with me venomous words or when I pretend you're not there. You may get mad at me but I know you won't hurt me and you won't leave me, at least not for good. Deep down in me heart, I know you'll come back to me if you have one breath left in your body. I know that. That's one of the best things about love."

The Irish are such romantics. I was temporarily at a loss for words and I didn't know whether to reach out to her again or not. All that trouble getting Gentry loaded up and now this. I swear these obstinate females are going to be the death of me. I made up my mind that I would *not* leave with her mad at me so I gutted up and held out my hand to her.

"Mollie Stallings, you are the love of my life. I know that ain't somethin' I say near often enough. You married a cowboy, though, so it ain't like it was unexpected. I'll do everything in my power to make it back to you. I don't know what else to say 'cept I sure would like a little kiss before I go."

Her eyes welled over and the tears ran down beside the smile that was now on her lips. She took my hand. Turns out I wound up leaving even later than I'd planned.

CHAPTER 11

The afternoon sun was shining soothingly through the cottonwood trees as I rode up on the spot on the trail to Springer where Charlie Atkins had ambushed me. While I had no reason to believe Flynt would try again so soon and in the same place, I was still pretty doggone alert. Sure enough, as I drew near the bend in the trail, I heard a commotion up ahead. It didn't sound like an ambush to me, though; it sounded more like a person having trouble with his horse. Me and my cooperative horse, Rusty, led Gentry on over to a grove of trees where we did our best to blend in.

"You damn nag," John Burr shouted viciously, "I ought to beat you to death." He came around the bend in his buggy whipping his horse. I hope John Burr is a better banker than he is a horseman. The horse, of course, responded to this ill treatment by crow-hopping like he had a burr in his rigging. Come to think of it, he sort of did. He had a "John Burr" in his rigging. I chuckled out loud in spite of my desire to be quiet. Sometimes I amuse myself. Anyway, all this commotion caused the buggy to slew sideways.

I walked Rusty and Gentry out toward the trail. "He'll prob'ly oblige you a little better if you stop beatin' him, Mr. Burr." I dismounted and walked over to his rig. Burr ceased the whipping and I was able to calm the horse.

"Thank you, Deputy," Burr said. He acted nervous. I had a feeling there was more to it than just a balky horse.

"What brings you out this way, Mr. Burr? You do a lot of bankin' business out here in the Big Empty?" I think he may have noticed a touch of sarcasm in my voice and figured out I was giving him a bit of a hard time. Apparently, being given a hard time was not his favorite pastime.

"I'm not sure that's any of your affair, Deputy. What I do and where I go is none of your business." He saw my sarcasm and raised it with haughty. I wondered what other cards he had in his deck. I decided to call him.

"That's true enough as long as what you're doin' is inside the borders of the law,

Mr. Burr." I smiled. "If your business takes you outside those border lines, then it sure nuff is my business." I swear I saw him flinch when I said that. I got a good eye for that sort of thing. He recovered his composure pretty quickly.

"I don't have time for this folderol, Deputy; I've got a bank to run." With a brusque nod, he urged his horse forward, nearly running me and Rusty down in the process. He took his whip to his horse again and, of course, the horse began crow-hopping again. I'd helped him once, I wasn't about to help him again.

"Good luck with runnin' your bank, Mr. Burr," I called after him. "I'll be keepin' an eye on you to see how that goes." He didn't look back.

As Jake Flynt rode along, he contemplated his next moves. Hank Andrews was on his way to watch Garrett O'Donnell's place. *Probably should have sent him sooner,* Jake thought. *Damn that deputy.* While Andrews was no great shakes at a fast draw, he'd been in some pretty good dust-ups in his time and was no coward. If he got the drop on O'Donnell, he could capture him and bring him to their hideout. Flynt's smile was evil. He had something special in mind for that cheeky Irishman beyond the whipping he gave his victims. It involved a fire, a branding iron, and a knife. He spent a few moments relishing the image in his mind. Before he died, he would regret the day he double-crossed Jake Flynt.

As he thought about the subject of double-crosses, he pondered the question of why John Burr was so interested in where his hideout was located. He already didn't trust his stepbrother. Now, he smelled desperation on him. It crossed his mind that if Burr became convinced that the damned Irishman had gotten away with the money, he might try to cut his losses by turning Jake in. He figured if that happened, Burr would do his best to make sure he didn't live to testify in court. He wouldn't be the one to pull the trigger, of course. The banker didn't have the stomach to shed blood himself. No, he would hire the job out to someone else. Family ties or not, it would be a good idea for him to keep an eye on the man.

As he headed northeast toward the hideout, the wind began to whip up. Jake tightened the stampede string on his hat so it wouldn't blow all the way to Denver. He looked back over his shoulder and noticed storm clouds gathering to the southwest. He wasn't much concerned about the weather; he'd lived through everything this part of the country had to throw at him and he'd survived. He was rather pleased that a storm appeared to be brewing. It would make it more difficult for that damned deputy to track them.

Stallings was another one on his list of men he would make pay for their insolence. He was no match for Jake Flynt. Other, better men had tried. They had failed and Stallings would as well.

CHAPTER 12

Tomás Marés soaked up the last of the juice from his frijoles with his tortilla. When he was trying to puzzle out a problem and develop a strategy to deal with it, it helped to partake of some of his mother's cooking. The strong green chile peppers seemed to open up not only his nasal passages but his mind as well.

"What will you do if they decide to move the office to Springer?" Miguel Marés leaned forward in his chair and placed both elbows on the table. His wife, Anita, took Tomás's plate from the table. As she did, she looked at her eldest child with a mixture of concern and curiosity. He appeared not to notice.

Tomás slowly shook his head. "I am not sure, Papa. I want to continue with this job that I started. If Sheriff Averill taught me anything, it was to finish what you start." He smiled at his father. "It seems to me that you also may have mentioned that once or twice."

During the time Tomás Marés worked as deputy under the sheriff, their dealings with the outlaws that served the corrupt politicians of the Santa Fe Ring had provided a trial by fire. Tomás had survived and learned many lessons. He learned how to enforce the law and more importantly, he learned honor, integrity, and courage. He learned that men of honor will only compromise so much before they make a stand. And he learned that when you make that stand against evil men, you have to be prepared to fight to the death.

Unfortunately, his job as sheriff came in two parts . . . law enforcement and politics. He had to keep the village council happy and, in his opinion, that took up far too much of his time. It helped some that he had allies on the council, including his father and Father Antonio Baca. He also knew he was fortunate to have a deputy who was willing and able to ride the vast country that made up Colfax County and search for the numerous lawless men who tried to take advantage of the people who lived there. Although Tommy Stallings tried his patience on a daily basis, Tomás knew he was lucky to have him. "Of course you are right," Miguel said with a grin. "Me and Nathan were some tough hombrés in our day. That does not answer my question of how you plan to keep the sheriff's office in Cimarrón."

Tomás nodded respectfully to his father. "It is my belief that we need to capture Jake Flynt and his gang quickly and bring them to justice. The people of Colfax County must see us as capable of doing our job from our headquarters in Cimarrón. They need to know that we serve all the people of the county equally. That is my plan." He smiled at his father. "Now, if we can only get Jake Flynt to cooperate."

His father laughed. "Jake Flynt may become so tired of your deputy hounding him that he turns himself in. That Stallings boy can be annoying, *qué no*?"

This time, Tomás did not join in his father's teasing. "Tommy Stallings is a good man. If anyone can find Flynt and his gang and bring them in, it is him." He took a deep breath and exhaled slowly. "It is too much of a job for one man. He needs help. As you know, I have tried repeatedly to convince the village council to see this. So far, I have been unsuccessful. They do not just want results, they want miracles."

Miguel's smile faded with his son's words. "You are right, my son. We have lost too many good men and women through the years to these evil men. You would think, would you not, that the people of Cimarrón might have learned from this? It appears that they have not. There are those of us on the council who understand this and support your requests for assistance. Sadly, we do not have the majority to win this battle. I am worried that you will suffer the consequences for this lack of support." Miguel's expression changed from serious to mischievous. "As annoying as he can be, I worry for young Stallings as well."

Anita Marés returned and asked her son, "More frijoles, *mi hito*?"

"No, Mama, gracias," Tomás replied respectfully. He turned and was about to continue his discussion with his father when he noticed that his mother had lingered by the table. "Was there something else, Mama?" His mother cocked her eyebrow at him, which in his experience indicated that she was getting ready either to reprimand him or ask him a difficult and uncomfortable question.

"So," she said in a long and drawn-out tone. This was supposed to indicate that she was only casually interested in the answer to the question with which she was about to blindside him. The truth of the matter was

127

that until he came up with an answer that she deemed satisfactory, she would likely hector him unmercifully. He steeled himself.

"Sí, Mama?"

"If they decide to move your office to Springer, what will you do? Will you move to that silly little town?"

"As I was telling Papa, I do not know the answer to that question yet. I would finish this investigation into the Jake Flynt gang. After that, I do not know."

"You have strong ties to Cimarrón, *mi hito, qué no*?" She squinted one eye and looked at him somewhat in the manner of a hawk eying a field mouse.

"Of course, Mama," he said. "You know my family is the most important thing in the world to me."

Like the hawk circling, Anita Marés moved in closer. "Of course it is, *mi hito*, but that is not what I am talking about."

Tomás turned a bright shade of red. "Then I am sure I do not know what you are talking about, Mama."

Anita pulled back a bit, perhaps deciding to wait until a later time to move in for the kill. "That is all you tell your mama?"

Mustering some dignity, Tomás tried to put his mother off with a formal tone. "Sí, Mama. That is all there *is* to tell."

His mother bestowed on Tomás a look that fairly screamed disappointment. She sighed heavily. She looked meaningfully at her husband who had been sitting with a bewildered expression on his face. "You see how he is? He is just like you. This is your fault." She looked back at Tomás. "We will speak of this again." She walked out of the room.

Miguel looked at his son and started to ask a question. He stopped and frowned. Another question began to form on his lips, only to die. He took a deep breath and shrugged. He knew his wife well. He would eventually find out what was going on. Until whatever time she was ready to include him, Anita Marés would continue to blame him for whatever sin, real or imagined, that their son had committed. He grinned sheepishly at Tomás and threw up his hands.

"*¿Quien sabé?*"

Indeed, Tomás thought, *who knows?*

Saints preserve us, Mollie Stallings thought as she made her way down the street to the schoolhouse. *He's me bleedin' husband and I almost sent him away with no more than a bleedin' look at me back. I acted like a bleedin' banshee, screamin' at him the way I did. Thank the stars he's got the nerve to come back for more.*

The students had not yet arrived when Mollie slipped in the door. Christy Johnson was already there preparing her lessons for the day. Her plain wooden desk next to the woodstove at the front of the classroom was tidily arranged with a spray of wildflowers neatly tucked into a small blue glass vase. She had placed a McGuffey's Reader on each of the scarred wooden desks and checked that the inkwells were filled, the better for the boys to dip little girls' pigtails in. She noticed a fresh set of initials among the other timeworn markings, carved, no doubt, by a young student with his Barlow knife. She thought it amusing that these young scamps never considered that by carving their initials, they might as well be signing a confession of guilt. She heard Mollie come in and, looking up, was about to remark on the childish folly of their young charges. One glance at Mollie changed her mind. She asked in alarm, "What in heaven's name is the matter, Mollie?"

Mollie immediately burst into tears. "Oh, Miss Christy, I may be the worst wife in the history of the world."

Christy got up from her desk and went to her, enveloping her in a comforting hug. It took a moment for Mollie to stem the flow of tears. Once they slowed to a trickle, Christy stepped back and looked her young assistant in the eye.

"Mollie, I highly doubt that you are the worst wife in the history of the world. Cleopatra poisoned her husbands. You haven't poisoned Mr. Stallings, have you?"

"No, Miss Christy, I haven't poisoned him yet though I've come close to chokin' him a time or two." In spite of herself, Mollie smiled. "I did burn his bacon yesterday mornin', but it's not likely he'll die from that."

Christy laughed. "However hard it is for these men to ride out, it may be just as hard for us to stay home and wait helplessly." Her laughter faded. "I always hated it."

"How did you do it, Miss Christy?" Mollie smoothed her dress and wiped the tears from her face so she would be presentable when the students arrived. "Sheriff Averill was always mixed up in some sort of knockin', bangin' ruckus."

Christy shook her head. "I didn't do well, Mollie. I never got used to it. You may be handling it better than I did." A sad, faraway look washed over her face. She looked as if she wanted to say more. Right then, students began their noisy entrance into the schoolhouse. A new day was beginning.

It's cold as the inside of a damp cave this morning as I look out over the Big Empty. It rained bucketfuls during the night. The sun finally peeked over the horizon and I'm still stiff from sleeping on the wet, hard ground. It won't be long before things warm up, once that old sun climbs up in the sky a bit.

From the rise where I stand, I can see Buckhorn Mesa to the north and Black Mesa just southwest of it. Where are those dirty polecats? If I look out of the corner of my eye, the land between here and those mesas looks like an ocean of green grass. I got the beginning of a plan in mind. I'm not real happy about it; still, it's the best I can come up with and it beats not having a plan. At least this way, I'll have something to deviate from as I forge ahead. I'm trying to accomplish two things: find Jake Flynt's hideout and not get shot. My best chance of not getting shot is to make my move at night. Well, strictly speaking, my best chance of not getting shot is to light out for home as fast as I can and take up another profession. I guess you could say moving at night is my second best chance. That makes it a bit more difficult to locate their hideout, though. I will have a full moon tonight, which should help some. I hope I don't ride into an arroyo.

From where I'm at, it'll be easier to start with Buckhorn Mesa tonight. I can work my way east of there and then when it gets dark, I can head due west up the side of the mesa. If they have one of those fancy spyglass contraptions, they may be able to spot me this afternoon. I'll be out of range so I'm not worried about them picking me off. I can get myself down into a draw where they can't see me and wait until the sun goes down. If I ride old Rusty to the base of that mesa, I should be able to climb on up the side in a few hours.

If they're there, they'll be on top, probably hidden behind some rocks. Then I'll have to decide if I can take them or whether it would be smarter to retreat and bring a posse back with me. I already know it'd be smarter to retreat. Odds are good they'll have someone awake standing guard; the deal is, I don't have a lot of backup in me. It's against my nature. Some would say that doing the smart thing is against my nature, too. As I ponder this, I have a feeling I'll prove those folks wrong tonight. If I find their hideout, I believe I'll beat a path back to Cimarrón for help. Nothing wrong with backing up.

If I head east around midday, I should be in position to make my move at nightfall. That means I have the morning to kill here at my camp. When you're riding on the trail of outlaws, your mind is on the alert at all times. Waiting here at camp gives me some time to think. It also gives me some time to brush the burrs out of Rusty's and Gentry's coats and clean up their hooves. We've slogged through a passel of mud to get here and I got the time on my hands. They work pretty hard for me; least I can do is clean them up and make them comfortable.

I have any number of things I can think about . . . some make me sad, some mad, and more recently, some make me glad. When I think about my wife, I generally have a real good feeling, in spite of her high temper and sharp Irish tongue. I tend to be forgiving of all that. She's had some hard times, back when she was growing up in Ireland and when she first came to Cimarrón. One of the things I love about her is that she's been tough enough to rise above all that.

She's had some help, of course. None of us could make it without help. Miss Christy and Eleanor Delaney took her under their wings after all that mess with Gentleman

134

Curt Barwick a few years ago. Miss Christy and Eleanor got Mollie out of the dead-end life as a working girl at the Colfax Tavern and gave her a job at the school. She started out cleaning the place and helping keep the other students in line. Some of those ranch boys can get a little rowdy with their hi-jinks. Between Miss Christy and Mollie, though, they kept them in line pretty good. After what they both went through in their former lives, a few high-spirited boys weren't much more than a small bump in the trail. At the same time, Miss Christy helped Mollie with her reading and writing. She knows a lot of words. Reckon I should know. She uses them on me all the time.

Speaking of help, I probably ought to say right now that if it weren't for Jared Dela-ney, there's no telling what I'd be doing today. I know that it probably wouldn't be good. I was one angry cowboy when I first hired on with Jared on a drive up through Raton Pass and on to Pueblo. Jared Dela-ney had the gumption to call me out and make it clear that he wouldn't put up with any of my nonsense.

I'm not saying it was easy, but with his help along with some other folks, my boss Tomás Marés being one, I learned to look at life differently. If it hadn't have been for them, I don't think Mollie would have given me the time of day.

Pretty deep thoughts for a cowboy who's digging mud from the hooves of his horse and mule. Don't tell Gentry I called her a mule, she's sensitive about that. I brushed them down good, too. They appreciate that. Any cowboy who doesn't take care of his mounts isn't much of a cowboy. The morning slipped away leisurely. I got Rusty and Gentry taken care of and had myself more coffee. I laid back propped up on a nice soft rock and watched the high thin clouds drift by. It's amazing how fast they run out here. I guess the wind blows as hard up there in the sky as it does down here on the ground. I wouldn't mind moving that fast, I just don't think I'd want to be at the mercy of the wind. Reckon I'll keep my feet planted on the ground and lean into that wind.

I gnawed on a little beef jerky and a cold tortilla when the sun was straight up. Not being sure when I'll eat again, I figure I'd better put something in my stomach while I can. I got Rusty saddled and Gentry loaded up, then did my best to clean up where I'd camped so it wasn't obvious that someone had spent time there. To the west, I can see dark clouds building up along with flashes of lightning. Though it's difficult for me to imagine the wind could blow any harder, I do believe it's picked up. Looks like those monsoon rains will be coming back this afternoon, what we call a regular gully-washer. That won't make traveling easy but at least the rain will provide me with some cover and keep Flynt's boys from spotting me. I'd rather be wet and uncomfortable than get shot at. One's bad but the other is worse.

CHAPTER 13

Tomás dreaded attending this meeting of the Cimarrón village council. He disliked this part of his job. Given a choice between dealing with the politicians and having a tooth pulled, he might go with the tooth. He'd had a sick feeling in the pit of his stomach all morning. He figured they would be looking to him to come up with a plan to ensure that the sheriff's office remained in Cimarrón rather than be moved to Springer, which was now the Colfax County seat.

Oddly, when he stepped back from his own personal investment in the issue, it made sense to him that the office of the sheriff be located in the county seat. The county government was run from the county seat and it was logical that the sheriff, who served the county first and foremost, have his offices nearby. This would not be a popular position for him to take, however.

One of the greatest challenges of his office was that it was an elected position. Therefore, he frequently found himself choosing between the popular course of action and the right course of action.

The difficulty from his own point of view was that in order to continue as sheriff, he would have to relocate to Springer. He had no friends and family there; all his ties were in Cimarrón. Not only would he have to move, he would then need to get reelected after his current term expired. He didn't see that happening.

It was also true that his deputy would have to pick up stakes and move to the county seat as well. He chuckled to himself as he imagined Mollie Stallings's reaction to the news that they would have to move to Springer. *As the saying goes, that dog would not hunt,* he thought. *If it comes to that, I will see that I have business elsewhere when Tommy tells her the news.* He laughed again but his amusement stopped in mid-chuckle.

Although he didn't think anyone was aware of it, he also had someone who would not be pleased if he moved to Springer. A warm feeling crept over him momentarily as he thought about this one. It vanished just as quickly as he thought about his uncertain future. The time was approaching when he would need to make some important decisions about that future. He was torn between his sense of duty and his long-suppressed desire for happiness. He truly didn't know right at this moment what he would do when the time to choose arrived. *Will I follow my head or my heart?* he wondered. *I wish I knew.* He waited another moment for an epiphany that didn't come. Then he turned his attention back to the problem at hand.

He knew that almost everyone on the village council had some political or personal agenda related to this issue, but he wasn't sure how to sort through them and develop a strategy. Several councilmen, Tom Figgs being one, were primarily concerned with the safety of the citizens of Cimarrón. These men knew that Tomás and Sheriff Averill before him had been willing to stand up and protect their town. Though they had not always prevailed, the town was safer than it would have been without their courage and grit. In public, Figgs and the others might express concern for the citizens who lived in the rest of Colfax County; in private, they could care less about those folks.

Of the seven-man council, Tomás knew of three councilmen who took this position. In addition to Figgs, Roger Smith, owner of the St. James Hotel, and Antonio Chavez, who ran the livery, were included in this group. They depended on customers traveling through on the mountain branch of the Santa Fe Trail and it was critical to their commercial success that travelers viewed Cimarrón as a safe place. The New Mexico Territory had a reputation for lawlessness that already made their jobs difficult enough. Without officers of the law on hand and ready to deal with outbreaks of violence, they were afraid people would choose alternative routes, which would sound a death knell for their businesses.

Father Antonio and his own father, Miguel Marés, very much wanted the office of the sheriff to remain in the village of Cimarrón. Both of their positions were personal. Miguel, of course, wanted his son to remain close to his family. Father Antonio had seen his best friend, the Methodist Reverend Richardson, murdered by Santa Fe Ring henchmen a few years back. He knew how dangerous the territory was, even with the sheriff in the village. He was terrified of what might happen if the protective mantle of the law were to move twenty-five miles to the east.

Like Roger Smith and Antonio Chavez, the position of Tom Lacey, proprietor of the

Colfax Tavern, was closely tied to the commercial prospects of his business. Unlike those men, however, his success hinged on less oversight by lawmen rather than more. In addition to serving food and spirits, his establishment had a reputation as a place where cowboys could enjoy the company of young ladies for a fee. Traditionally, the sheriff and his men had not scrutinized this practice too closely as long as no one got hurt. Still, Lacey recognized it as a potential bone of contention between himself and whoever the sheriff might be. As far as Lacey was concerned, the greater the distance between the Colfax Tavern and the sheriff, the better. He was strongly in favor of the sheriff's office moving to Springer.

That left the seventh member of the village council, Mayor Bill Wallace. The position of the mayor was most intriguing to Tomás. As leader of the village and an owner of several legitimate businesses, it would seem natural for him to want the sheriff to operate out of Cimarrón for much the same reasons as his fellow merchants Smith and Chavez. Instead, he appeared to be pushing behind the scenes to move the sheriff's office to Springer. Tomás knew that bank president John Burr had the ear of Wallace. Tommy Stallings maintained that

Burr was something less than an innocent victim in the recent robbery of his bank. Could it be that Wallace was conspiring with Burr in this matter? Interesting.

Banging his gavel on the table, Bill Wallace said in a firm and clear voice, "Let this meeting of the Cimarrón Village Council be called to order." He looked around the table with a practiced politician's smile. "Welcome, gentlemen," he said. "In particular, welcome to our brave Sheriff Marés."

The man is a pompous ass, Tomás thought as he nodded to the mayor and the rest of the councilmen. As his gaze passed by his father, Miguel Marés winked at him. Tomás suppressed a smile. The mayor seemed to be waiting for him to make a speech, something Tomás was not inclined to do under any circumstances. Particularly in regard to this meeting, he had decided he would say as little as possible. He smiled serenely at the mayor and waited.

As with most politicians, Bill Wallace couldn't tolerate silence. He quickly stepped up and began speaking. "As you all know, we are here to discuss the question of whether the sheriff's office remains here in Cimarrón or is moved to the new county seat in Springer. Officially, of course, we don't have the final say since the sheriff works for Colfax County, not our village." He arched an eyebrow meaningfully and looked around the table. "However, we all know that the position we take can make that decision either more or less difficult to carry out. Perhaps we should have some discussion on this topic. Your thoughts, gentlemen?"

The question had barely passed over his lips when Roger Smith leaned forward in his chair. "Bill, I'm trying to run a first-class hotel here. Folks have a choice about what route they take coming west on the Santa Fe Trail. You know as well as I do that they won't travel here and stay in my hotel if they think there is a chance of violence in the streets." He looked around at the other men, frustration clearly written on his face. "I know I'm not the only fella that feels this way." Antonio Chavez nodded resolutely in agreement. "What I don't understand is why you're leaning the other way, Bill. Seems to me you have as much to lose with the mercantile as any of the rest of us." He chuckled mirthlessly. "Although I expect maybe your undertaking business might pick up considerably if the sheriff was no longer close by."

Wallace chose to ignore the jab. "Roger, I'd like to think all of us could look beyond our narrow self-interest here and consider what would be best for Colfax County."

There was a snicker from the other end of the table. Tomás was looking at Wallace so he couldn't be sure who the culprit was. He suspected it was Tom Figgs. Unlike the mayor, the blacksmith was no politician. Wallace looked over his glasses at Figgs.

"Did you want to make a comment, Mr. Figgs?" Although his words were polite, Wallace's tone was frosty. Clearly, his tolerance was being tested.

"Sure, Mayor," Figgs said cheerfully. "My comment is that I'd like us to get through all this gabbin' as quick as we can so we can vote on the council's position. In fact," he said with a smile, "I'd be pretty doggone happy if we could go ahead and do that right now."

Bill Wallace's face was flushed with anger. Apparently, he had hoped to make a speech with the intention of swaying votes his way. Once a councilman called for a vote, though, it was in the bylaws that they had to honor that request. *We sure need to fix that rule,* he thought angrily. *First things first, though.*

"A councilman has called for a vote, gentlemen," he said, his exasperation in clear contrast to Figgs's cheerfulness. He

145

gave it one more try. "Are we sure we don't want to hear what our good sheriff has to say?"

"I thought what I said was pretty clear, Mister Mayor," Figgs said, some of the good humor draining from his voice. "I called for a vote. When a council member calls for a vote, the rules say we vote." He looked around the table. "Ain't that right, boys?"

Wallace shook his head in disgust. Although John Burr would not be happy with him, he knew he was stymied . . . temporarily. "You are correct, sir," he said without enthusiasm. "All in favor of recommending that the sheriff's office remains in Cimarrón?" Five hands were raised. "All opposed?" He and Tom Lacey raised their hands. Wallace looked over at Tomás. "Looks like our official position is that we'd like to keep you around for a while longer, Sheriff Marés." *You and that meddling deputy of yours,* he thought sourly. *For now.*

After the meeting, Tomás was walking back to his office when he heard boots on the boardwalk behind him. He looked back over his shoulder and saw Tom Figgs. Clearly, Figgs was trying to catch up with him so Tomás stopped and waited for him.

As Figgs caught up, Tomás said, *"Buenos*

días, Tom. Is there something on your mind?"

"Yes there is, Sheriff Marés. I was hopin' we could talk in private, maybe at your office."

"Certainly," Tomás said, turning and continuing down the boardwalk. "I would be happy to visit with you at my office."

They walked the rest of the way in silence. Figgs seemed deep in thought and Tomás's mind was working at a steady clip as well. He realized that Figgs had taken him off the hook at the meeting by demanding a vote quickly before the council could grill Tomás about his views on the subject of the location of the sheriff's office. He was also very aware that St. James Hotel owner Roger Smith had openly questioned Mayor Wallace's apparent lack of support for keeping the office here in Cimarrón. He thought that might be the topic of their conversation once they reached his office.

Tomás opened the door to his office and invited Tom Figgs inside. "Have a seat, amigo, and tell me what is on your mind." He walked over to the small wood-burning stove in the corner. There was a coffee pot on top. "Would you like a cup of coffee?"

Figgs waved off the offer of coffee and took a deep breath. He seemed to be searching for how to begin. Finally, he spoke. "Tomás . . . Is it all right if I call you that instead of Sheriff Marés?"

"Certainly," Tomás said. He was nowhere near as sensitive about what folks called him as his young deputy was. "We have known each other long and well enough to be on a first-name basis."

"Well, I appreciate that, Tomás," he said. "I wanted to make sure you knew I meant no disrespect."

Tomás was puzzled by Figgs's cautious approach. Generally, he was a man who spoke plainly with no subterfuge. For some reason, he was choosing his words carefully. Apparently, he was worried about something. Tomás waited for him to continue.

"I was curious what you thought about that meetin', Tomás," Figgs said cautiously. "I was interested, in particular, if anything about it struck you as odd."

Tomás had a sense that Figgs was feeling him out, trying to ascertain his position in this situation before revealing his own. It was as if he wasn't sure he could trust Tomás. For a second, he pondered, in turn, whether or not he could trust Figgs. He thought of no reason why he couldn't and decided to lay his cards on the table.

"There were a number of things that

struck me about the meeting, Tom," he said carefully. "One was that you seemed to be in a hurry to vote and end the meeting. *¿Es verdad?*"

Figgs nodded. "You picked up on that, did you? Yep, I didn't want a lot of gabbin' about this movin' the sheriff's office business. I wanted to have the vote while I knew I could count on my side winnin'."

"You do not think we are all on the same side, amigo?"

Figgs looked at Tomás and grinned. "Oh, I know for a fact we're not, Tomás. Some members of the council are on the side of what's best for the village of Cimarrón. There's a couple who are only on the side of their business. Whatever they figure is best for that, that's what they'll support. That all makes sense to me and I don't have a problem with it."

"And, yet, I have a feeling there is something that you do have a problem with, *qué no?*"

Figgs squinted and looked closely at Tomás. "You're a pretty sharp fella, Tomás. I think the citizens of Colfax County made a wise choice when they elected you sheriff."

"Thank you for your confidence," Tomás said with a wry grin. "Do you plan on telling me what it is you do have a problem with?"

"Well, I'm gettin' to it," Figgs said uncomfortably. "I'm more than a little concerned about who I can talk to about this particular problem. I'm not lookin' to cause trouble for myself or anyone else. Still, when I see somethin' that I think looks shady, I figure I ought to say somethin'." Figgs looked away for a moment. "When you and your daddy, along with old Sheriff Averill and Jared Delaney, were standin' up to those dirty bastards . . . excuse the language . . . that were tryin' to take over this town, I stayed off to the side at a safe distance, more concerned about myself than about doin' what was right." He cleared his throat. "I'm ashamed of that. I never want to behave in such a cowardly fashion again."

"Tom, I understand what you are saying. I also remember that when we were taking on Bill Chapman and his hired gunman, Daughtry, you were one of the few to step up and stand beside us." Tomás sat forward in his chair. "I believe that you will stand up for what is right. If you see something wrong right now, I hope you will tell me. Maybe we can work together to change it."

Figgs looked away again briefly, then looked Tomás square in the eye. "That

150

means a lot to me, Tomás. Havin' your respect means a great deal."

"You have it, Tom," Tomás said quietly. "Now, do you want to tell me what is really on your mind?"

Figgs paused for another short moment before continuing. "I guess I do, Tomás. Here it is. I think our good mayor is up to somethin' that ain't right. I got a feelin' he's in cahoots with old John Burr at the bank. The only way it makes sense for Wallace to want the sheriff's office moved to Springer is if he's up to somethin' that he don't want you to see."

Tomás nodded slowly. "I see. Do you have any proof that Mayor Wallace is involved in something illegal?"

Figgs sighed with frustration. "Naw, I don't have anything to go on that you could use in a court of law. It's just a feelin' I got that somethin' ain't right. Like I said, his tryin' to get the sheriff's office moved away don't make any sense from the standpoint of his business. That makes me think he's got some other reason for it."

"Do you have any guesses about why our mayor is taking this position?"

"I do have a notion, Tomás," Figgs said. "I mentioned his business, which seems to be doin' pretty well judgin' from the traffic of customers at the mercantile." Figgs paused and seemed to consider his next words carefully. "The thing is, it don't seem to be goin' so well that he can live the way he does. You know, he orders some mighty fine clothes for that wife and daughter of his, they come all the way from Denver. That ain't cheap. He also owns some damned expensive horses that he keeps at the livery. They're some fine stock. I know 'cause I shoe them for him. Where's he gettin' all the money to pay for those things?"

"For what it is worth, Tom, I agree with you that more is going on than meets the eye."

Tom Figgs clenched his jaw tightly, clearly struggling to contain his anger. "Tomás, I'm sick of all the dirty dealin's by these damned politicians and businessmen. What I want is to make a good life for me and my family. All I'm interested in is a fair shot at makin' a livin'. I walk the straight and narrow, abide by the law. Why should they have a different set of rules?"

Tomás shook his head slowly. "I have no good answer for you, amigo. Only that it has always been this way. Greedy and powerful men seem to think they can make their own rules. Often times, they are right."

"Damn them," Figgs said heatedly. "I ain't

willin' to set back and watch that happen anymore without puttin' up some kind of a fight."

Tomás sighed heavily. The requirements of the law were often a burden, particularly when the unlawful tended to ignore or manipulate them. Still, it was his sworn duty to uphold the law. "As sheriff, however, I must have proof if I am to do something about it. I would very much appreciate if you would watch over this situation closely and let me know if you find any evidence of wrongdoing."

"I'll sure do that, Sheriff," Figgs replied, appearing a bit embarrassed by his outburst. "I understand you can't arrest people just 'cause you're suspicious of 'em."

"Thank you, Tom." Tomás chuckled. "I wish my deputy was as understanding of this as you are."

Figgs looked momentarily confused by Tomás's comment. Then he shrugged and said, "I'll be keepin' a close eye on things, Sheriff."

Figgs exited the office and left Tomás to his thoughts. What he thought about was Tom Figgs and whether or not he could be counted on. The man had been in town now for eight or nine years and had never caused any trouble for anyone. He came down to

Cimarrón from Pueblo, Colorado, where he'd learned the blacksmith trade from his father. His timing was good as the previous blacksmith had left town a year beforehand, headed for California where he expected to make his fortune. Tomás figured that the move had probably not lived up to his expectations. The man had been gone long enough that folks were mighty tired of taking care of their own horses and were ready for a competent blacksmith to step up and fill the void.

Tom Figgs turned out to be a pleasant surprise. Not only did he know his job thoroughly, he was as dependable as well. If he told you he would come out to your place on Tuesday to shoe your horses, he would be there first thing Tuesday morning ready to go. He did a good job and he charged a fair price. Over time, the folks around Colfax County came to respect him as an honest and hardworking member of their community.

A bachelor when he first came to town, Tom courted the eldest daughter of one of the neighboring ranch families. Jed and Mary Lowry owned a spread southeast of Cimarrón. They had five children, three daughters and two sons, and being practical above all else, they were pleased when Tom

Figgs not only took off their hands one of the mouths they had to feed but also agreed to provide free blacksmith services to them since they were now family. When the marriage produced two young children in rapid succession, Tom Figgs's high status in the family was assured.

When Tom made the decision to run for the village council, he won handily and had served in an admirable fashion. Unlike some other members of the council, he seemed to have the best interests of the village of Cimarrón at heart. His only agenda seemed to be to do his best to make it a decent place to make an honest living and raise a family. *Yes,* Tomás thought, *I believe he is a man I can count on.*

CHAPTER 14

"Oh sweet Jaysus and Mary," Garrett O'Donnell cried out in dismay. "You're still here." It was late afternoon as Garrett rode through the gate at his scraggly little ranch house to find his wife feeding the chickens.

"And where else would I be since I had no bleedin' idea where you were, Garrett O'Donnell?" There was fire in Ashleen O'Donnell's reply but a hint of panic as well. She ran over to her husband as he dismounted and threw her arms around him. "I was so worried, I didn't know what to do. I thought you were supposed to meet me here."

"Things changed, darlin'." Garrett took a deep breath. "I saw a chance to grab the loot from the vault and I thought to meself, why am I puttin' everythin' on the line to hold on to this worthless piece of land?"

Ashleen shook her head in confusion. "Wait, what are you sayin', Garrett? You took the money? What were you thinkin'?"

"I was thinkin' that with all that money, we could clear out of here and make a fresh start in Colorado, Ashleen. We could afford a real ranch, not this rundown place. We could buy healthy cows instead of those skinny, sickly creatures we have. That's what I was thinkin'."

Ashleen shook her head, unable to make sense out of what her husband was saying. "You have the money?"

"Indeed I do, my lovely Irish colleen," Garrett said with a grin on his face. "There's more than five thousand dollars stuffed in my saddlebags. If we can make it to Colorado, we'll be sittin' pretty for the rest of our lives. No more landlords throwin' us off our own property. It'll be ours free and clear."

A terrifying realization dawned on Ashleen O'Donnell. "We'll have everyone in the whole bleedin' territory chasin' after us, Garrett," she said, a note of hysteria coloring her words. "Lawmen and outlaws alike. They'll all be after us."

"Sure and they will," Garrett replied in a voice deadly serious. "That's why I been slinkin' around out in the Big Empty these past days. I would have come sooner but I was afraid Flynt and his bunch would follow me here. I had to make sure I'd lost them. I don't even want to think about what they'd have done if they had caught us here."

"Oh, God," Ashleen said with a tremor in her voice. "Do they know where we live? They could show up any time."

"I'm afraid you're right, darlin'. If they don't know already, I'm sure Burr will tell them, which is why we need to be out of here at first light tomorrow. I have a fair idea of where Flynt and his gang are holed up. We'll be goin' the long way around to avoid them, but it'll be safer that way."

Ashleen shook her head in resignation. "I wish we'd talked about this beforehand."

"There was no time," Garrett said. "I had no idea it would happen. The chance just presented itself. It was either take it and run or continue to be under the thumb of one more tyrant who can't wait to evict us. I didn't leave the old country only to wind up in the same position again."

Ashleen slowly nodded. "You're right, Garrett O'Donnell. Sure and you're right."

Garrett embraced his wife for a long moment, then he said, "We've got no time to waste. We must gather provisions and what few belongin's we need into the wagon tonight." Once again, his face was creased with a huge grin. "And of course, all that lovely money. We'll do that, eat a meal, and then get a good night's sleep so we're ready to leave before dawn."

Garrett O'Donnell struggled to clear the fog of sleep from his mind. A noise had awakened him and he was doing his best to identify the source. He sat up slowly, his movements in stark contrast to the wild beating of his heart. He strained to hear. There it was again. It was the whinny of a horse. It must have been loud for him to hear it over the sound of the rain. Next to him, his wife Ashleen awoke with a start. She grabbed his arm.

"What is it, Garrett?" She couldn't keep the tremor of fear out of her voice.

"I don't know, darlin'," Garrett said as calmly as he could. The last thing he needed at this moment was for his wife to panic. "I think I'd better go see. You go to the boy and girl now. If you hear anything amiss, scoot out the back and make for the barn. Hide out there and don't make any noise."

Although he spoke calmly, Ashleen O'Donnell could tell that her husband was afraid. "Don't you be goin' out the front door either, Garrett O'Donnell," she said insistently. "They could be right outside waitin' to bushwhack you."

"I know that, darlin'," he said in as reassuring a voice as he could. "I'll take the back way, sneak around the side of the house. I need to find out how many of 'em there are."

Garrett O'Donnell pulled on his trousers and boots and fastened his gun belt, all of which were right beside the bed where he'd left them when he slipped in earlier under cover of night. He was also glad he'd had the foresight to add a rear entrance to his little shack when he built it. His father had done that back in the old country and it had served him well in evading British soldiers. It was one of a number of family traditions Garrett had brought with him to America.

It was raining hard as he snuck out the back. He was soaked before he got all the way around the side of the shack. He made his way to the corner of the building, his footsteps muffled by the pelting rain. He squinted as he surveyed the area in front of his house, looking for any shapes that didn't belong. Again, he heard the soft nicker of a horse. A flash of lightning vividly illuminated the landscape. There, he could see it. A lone gunman standing with his horse beside the little grove of trees to the left of the house. Fortunately, the man appeared to be looking in the direction of the front door of the shack when the lightning struck. If there were any more men, Garrett hadn't seen them. It had to be one of Flynt's gang, come to ambush him.

He realized they had figured out he would come home. *Maybe I should have kept a safe distance and stayed on the run,* he thought, *but sooner or later, Flynt would have come for my Ashleen and the wee bairns. He had to know I would show up here.* It was his biggest vulnerability. No help for that now, though. He would have to deal with it. He drew his pistol and made a wide circle to come up behind the gunman.

Treading softly, he kept an eye on the trees where the man was hiding. His heart was in his throat as he snuck around to get the drop on him. About halfway there, another bolt of lightning struck. He froze in his tracks. From where he stood, he could barely make out the man's silhouette. It appeared that he was still watching the front of the house and had not seen him. He gave his eyes a moment to adjust to the darkness after the dazzling flash of lightning, then he proceeded cautiously. It felt like it was taking him hours to get around behind the gunman. As he got close enough to see the man more clearly, he saw that he had wrapped his wild rag around the horse's mouth in an attempt to silence it.

When he was within ten paces of the man, he cocked his pistol. "Put your hands above your head slowly."

The gunman whirled. Garrett barely had time to register that it was Jake Flynt's man, Hank Andrews. Although Garrett had the drop on him, Andrews went for his gun nevertheless. Garrett thought, *Sweet Jaysus, I'm goin' to have to kill the man.* He wasted no more time on such thought. He pulled the trigger twice. Hank Andrews fell backwards.

Garrett ran over to the fallen outlaw, prepared to shoot him again if he needed to do so. When he got to his side, it became apparent immediately to Garrett that no more bullets would be needed. Hank Andrews lay dead with two bullet holes right square in the middle of his chest. *Sure and I've never been that fine of a shot,* Garrett thought. *Must have been Providence guidin' me hand.*

Seeing that Andrews was no longer a threat, Garrett's thoughts immediately went to his wife and children. Ashleen was bound to have heard the shots. She had no way of knowing whether her husband lay dead out in front of their shack. Remembering his last instructions to her, he headed toward the barn, shouting out as he went.

"Ashleen, darlin', it's me. I'm safe." He saw no one at the entrance to the barn. It occurred to him that his wife might think this was a ploy. *Clever lass,* he thought. He entered the barn and called out again. "Ashleen, there was only one of the lousy bastards. I shot him."

Ashleen O'Donnell stepped out from one of the stalls and said, "I wish you wouldn't curse in front of the children, Garrett. I've spoken to you about that before."

For a moment, Garrett was speechless. Then, he burst into laughter. He'd just killed a man and she was worried about his coarse language. "You're somethin' to behold, me darlin' Ashleen, somethin' indeed."

"Well," she responded primly, "we can't forget about the children now, can we?"

Garrett went over to his wife and pulled her to him. She was trembling whether from fear, the chill from the rain, or both, he couldn't tell. He held her until she was still. "No, darlin', we can't forget about the children." He held her away from him at arm's length and looked at her with a sober expression. "We've got to change our plan

163

now. What just happened shows that Jake and his boys are closin' in."

"What are you sayin'?" Ashleen O'Donnell asked with trepidation.

"I'm sayin' you and the wee ones must leave without me in the mornin'. Flynt will be comin' hard for us now." *And Flynt's a monster who'll stop at nothin' to get his money, even if it means killin' an innocent woman and her children. I should have thought of that.* Garrett didn't say this out loud.

"What are you sayin'?" she said, struggling for breath. "Why must we leave without you?" She grasped her husband's hand and squeezed so hard that he winced.

"I need to go back into the Big Empty and draw Jake away from you," Garrett said. "I am going to let him see me and then lead him on a merry chase. If he's after me, he'll be too busy to look for you."

"Maybe you're right," Ashleen responded anxiously, "but I hate the notion of not bein' together. How will we find each other?"

"In the mornin', you head out of here with the children and go due east. All day long. You'll have to camp out on the trail tomorrow night."

"All right," Ashleen replied hesitantly. "Then what?"

"The morning of the next day, you get up and point that wagon northwest. Keep headin' in that direction and before long, you'll see the mountains. That'll be where Raton Pass cuts through up into Colorado. Just a few miles southeast of the town of Raton, there's a small canyon off to the east of the trail. It's a spot where we held cattle when I went on the drive with Jared Delaney. You and the children will lay up there."

"How will I recognize the spot?" Ashleen's face was pale and her voice trembled.

"At the turnoff into the canyon, there's a huge pine tree that was split by lightning. Turn there and go in about a mile. No one will be able to see you from the trail. Wait for me there."

"When will you get there? How am I to know that something bad hasn't happened to you?" Ashleen trembled with apprehension.

"I will try to keep Flynt off your trail for at least three days," Garrett said. "That should give you time to reach the canyon, even if you are slowed down somewhere along the way. Start lookin' for me on the fourth day." Garrett glanced away from his wife and took a deep breath. Turning back to her, he said, "If I'm not there by the sixth day, you need to head north through Raton

Pass to the town of Trinidad. We'll pack you enough provisions for at least a week." He paused. "Sure and you won't be lackin' for money to rent yourself a room for a few days once you reach Trinidad."

"Oh, Garrett, if you don't meet me in that canyon, I don't know if I can leave there without you."

"Ashleen, you must," Garrett said forcefully. "There's no tellin' how this will play out. After I've led Flynt away from you, I have to make a clean getaway from him so he can't track me. If that takes longer than I think it will, you can't be waitin' around in that canyon." *And if he kills me and doesn't find the money, he'll start trackin' you next,* Garrett thought. Again, he kept this to himself. "Go on to Trinidad. If I don't meet you there in a week, head on up to Denver."

"Saints preserve us, Garrett," Ashleen exclaimed, "how in the world will you find us in Denver?"

Garrett looked deep into his wife's eyes. "I'll find you, darlin'. If I have to go to the end of the world, I'll find you."

Ashleen O'Donnell pulled her husband to her in an unyielding embrace. "Don't you let them catch you." The fierce look on her face unnerved Garrett. "Don't you let them."

166

CHAPTER 15

"Boss, we're runnin' short on supplies." Pierce Keaton was hesitant to tell Jake the news. He was afraid he knew exactly what he would do with the information. He was right.

Jake smiled. It was not a pleasant sight. "Well, boys, looks like we need to find us another sodbuster." He clapped his hands together with enthusiasm. "I saw a place to the south of us when we moved over here from Buckhorn Mesa. Remember, Pierce?"

Keaton sighed. "Yep, Jake, I saw it, too. It ain't but a few miles from here. What do you want to do?" Pierce asked the question even though he already knew the answer.

Flynt turned and looked hard at Keaton. "You're not getting squeamish on me, are you, Pierce?"

"Well, uh . . . I mean, no Jake, a'course not," Pierce Keaton stammered. He looked around at his compadres. They were watching him with interest. "I'm ready when you are. Let's mount up."

Flynt and his gang rode south at a steady lope through the rain. With their dark slickers flapping in the wind, they looked like a band of goblins out of a sinister fairy tale. They came to the top of a hill and looked down at the sod house below them. The rain slowed to a gentle mist and through it, they could see smoke spiraling from a rudimentary chimney at the top of the house.

"It's wet but it ain't cold enough to light a fire for heat," Dave Atkins observed. "Reckon that fella's smokin' some meat down there." He grinned. "Looks like we hit the jackpot, Jake."

"You could be right, Dave." He turned to his band and said, "Pierce, Patricio, I want you to ride around the back. Dave, you stay a ways uphill, keep your rifle ready. I'll ride right up to the front door." He smiled his chilling smile. "I doubt this fella will get spooked by a lone rider." He urged his horse forward. "Let's go."

Baca and Keaton made a circle around to the back of the house. They still had the high ground so they could see Jake Flynt as he rode towards the front of the sod house. They saw him dismount, then lost sight of him as he walked up to the front door. They waited apprehensively, not knowing what he would find. After a moment, they heard a shot and a bloodcurdling scream. They immediately spurred their horses down the hill. Dave Atkins did the same. When they arrived, they found Jake standing over a man writhing on the ground from a bullet wound to the leg.

"Look what I found, boys," Jake said offhandedly. "A sodbuster." He turned to Keaton and said, "Pierce, get inside and see what he's got that we can use." He turned his gaze to Dave Atkins. "Dave, you and Patricio take this boy out by that tree. I got something special planned for him." As they drug him toward the small tree in front of the house, Jake Flynt got his whip. He also got his rope.

As he walked toward the door of the sod house, Pierce Keaton shuddered. He didn't know how much longer he could tolerate riding with Jake Flynt. The man was flat-out loco and it seemed like he was getting worse by the day. Things were falling apart and his solution was to find another sodbuster to murder. No one was willing to mention the fact that Hank Andrews hadn't returned from his mission to the O'Donnell ranch, which meant that he had failed to kill the man and recover the money. Pierce wasn't about to be the one to bring it up.

He hoped fervently that he wouldn't open the door to find a woman and some children. He couldn't bear the thought of hearing them scream as Flynt put the torch to their barn with them locked inside. At the same time, he understood that if he challenged Jake on this or any of the other crazy notions he got, he would be signing his own death warrant. *Helluva mess I got myself into,* he thought with another shudder.

He walked into the cabin and let his eyes adjust to the darkness. With relief, he saw that there were no other human inhabitants. Another horrific scream from out front jumped him like a spooked colt. *Guess Jake found his whip. Reckon I'm gonna take my own sweet time lookin' this place over for supplies.* Methodically, he began searching for things the gang could use. He found a big batch of Arbuckle's coffee, which the fellas would like. Some beef jerky over by the cookstove and some canned goods. *And lookee here,* he thought, a huge grin spreading across his face. *We got us a bottle of rye whiskey.* He reached into his pocket for his empty hip flask and refilled it.

Over by the cot, he saw something lying on the rough straw mattress. He walked over to take a closer look and saw that it was a book. It looked like a ledger book, the kind that folks sometimes use to keep track of money and other important information. Curious, he picked it up and opened it. Keaton was no scholar but he had learned his letters and could read some. It didn't take him long to figure out that it was some sort of diary or journal. He read the last couple of pages and saw that the man had been planning a trip into Springer later in the week for more supplies. There was a short passage about how he hoped to stay over for a dance at the community hall on Saturday night. There was a young lady he had his eye on. The journal entry ended with the statement, "I sure hope to get to know Miss Althea Davis better. She's a fine figure of a woman. I think maybe she kinda likes me." Keaton was not the sensitive sort, yet he could read between the lines that the man was lonely and yearning for companionship. Up until the time they rode up to his place, he'd had hope for tomorrow. Now he had no hope.

More screams penetrated the thick walls of the sod dwelling. These cries hardly sounded human. Pierce suspected that Jake was done whipping the poor man and had strung him up and set him ablaze. For a

171

moment, he thought he was going to be sick. He fought down the nausea and tried to force the grisly image out of his mind as he continued gathering all the supplies he could find. He looked about for something to carry his take in and spotted a half-empty burlap sack in one corner of the cabin. He dumped the contents out on the floor and saw that the sack had contained more journals. Apparently, the man kept a thorough record of his life, perhaps in hopes that one day someone else would be interested in his experiences. He doubted that the man could have predicted it would end in such a gruesome manner as this.

Keaton heard no more screams from outside, so he gathered up the supplies, stuffed them in the bag, and with some trepidation, walked out the door. What he saw in the brief seconds before he turned away in disgust sickened him to the bottom of his tarnished soul. What was left of the charred body of the sodbuster hung from the lone tree out front. Jake stood close by surveying his handiwork. Keaton looked over at Patricio Baca, who briefly met his gaze. Baca shook his head and then averted his eyes.

Over his shoulder, Jake hollered, "Store what you found in the cabin over there by

172

that venison. We'll pick it up on the way back."

Keaton was puzzled. "On the way back from where, Jake?"

"On the way back from Springer," Flynt said.

"We're goin' to Springer?" Keaton experienced a sinking feeling in the pit of his stomach, which was already in distress from the horror of Jake's torture of the sodbuster. "Why're we goin' there?"

"Why, Pierce," Jake Flynt said with a pleasant smile that was bizarrely incongruous with the circumstances, "we're going to rob the bank again."

Keaton felt his jaw drop but could do nothing to stop it. He looked at Baca and Atkins, both of whose eyes had widened in surprise as well. Very carefully, he said, "Well now, Jake, there ain't gonna be much money in that bank since we just robbed it. Why would we do it again so soon, if you don't mind me askin'?"

Flynt's smile faded away. He looked from one member of his gang to the other with a brutal glare. Each of them tried to match his stare. Each of them caught a glimpse of the insanity lurking behind his eyes. All of them looked away. "To show those sons of bitches that we can."

■ ■ ■ ■

We're pretty miserable, me, Rusty, and Gentry. At least I've got my slicker and my hat. I figure it must be late afternoon though it's pretty hard to tell. Because of the storm, it's been dark as night for several hours and it's been tricky to keep headed in the right direction since I can't see more than about five hundred feet. Fortunately, a flash of lightning revealed what I figure must be Buckhorn Mesa a little ways to the northwest. Reckon we'll just keep on plodding in that general direction.

I'm still trying to puzzle this thing out as we mosey miserably along through the rain. I can see what Jake Flynt gets out of this deal . . . money and a chance to vent his spleen on innocent people throughout Colfax County. I even think I have a pretty good handle on what John Burr is getting as well . . . money and power, in the form of yet another variation on the Santa Fe Ring's constant attempt to steal all the land in the New Mexico Territory. Flynt and Burr appear to be in this deal together, though for the life of me I can't see how the two men came together to plan this thing. I'm still not sure how Flynt got Garrett O'Donnell involved.

If I'm in Garrett's boots, I might be willing to go along with a scheme that would hurt John Burr and his bank. I reckon he might see Burr as cut from the same cloth as those thieving, arrogant landowners he fought with back in Ireland. He had to be aware, though, that stealing money from the bank probably wasn't going to result in its closing its doors for good and might increase the likelihood that Burr would foreclose on more properties. Garrett has a family to look out for and he's not dumb. I think he's capable of seeing beyond the immediate pleasure of causing trouble for John Burr and understanding that it would eventually come back to harm him. Why would he go along with it then? I wonder what was in it for him. I don't see the sense in it. It has to be that Burr coerced him into it. Coerced is another one of those fancy words I learned from Mollie. Burr probably threatened to foreclose on his ranch immediately and leave the O'Donnells without a home. If that's true, it means that Burr is in on the deal from the start. More and more, that sounded right to me.

I pondered all this for awhile without getting any closer to figuring it out. I did, however, get close enough to Buckhorn

Mesa that I could vaguely make out its shape through the driving rain. It was time to pick a spot to wait for full darkness before I started the trek up the side of the mesa. Up ahead, I saw a short, sturdy piñon tree that looked like it would do. When I got there, I dismounted and tied Rusty and Gentry to the tree. I loosened their cinches to make them a tiny bit more comfortable in these wretched conditions and settled in to wait.

Although I wouldn't have believed it was possible, I must have dozed off squatting there in the storm. The steady drumming of the rain on my hat must have lulled me to sleep. An incongruent noise had awakened me and I was instantly on the alert and vigilant until I heard the noise again. Gentry was blowing through her lips, that noise she makes when she thinks I'm not paying enough attention to her. I relaxed and shook my head to clear the fog of sleep away. When I did, I noticed that the rain had stopped and the clouds had blown on past. We had us a half moon and the stars were twinkling bright as diamonds.

Near as I could gauge, it was somewhere on to the south of midnight. I figured it was about time for me to get going if I hoped to make it up the mesa and then back down again before daylight. Like I said, the rain had stopped. That didn't mean the grounds had dried up, though. The trail around me was soft and sloppy, and I was concerned that it would only get more treacherous as I headed up the side of the mesa. I had planned on taking Rusty but I reevaluated that plan. This looked like a job for the most sure-footed of mounts, which pretty much meant a mule. Lucky for me, I had one even if she wouldn't acknowledge that fact. I didn't care, as long as she handled the trail like a mule.

This change of plans meant I had to unload Gentry's packsaddle, unsaddle Rusty, and put his saddle on Gentry. One good think about having experience taking steers up the trail is that you get pretty darned good at saddling up in the dark. I got that job done, hobbled Rusty, then me and Gentry headed toward Buckhorn Mesa.

I gave Gentry her head as we slowly made our way up the slope of Buckhorn Mesa. There's times you tell your mount where you want them to go and there's times you let them find their own way. I could feel the incline becoming steeper as we moved along and the footing was every bit as treacherous as I had anticipated. Gentry proved her worth, though, making up for all those times she'd been stubborn as . . . well, dang it, stubborn as a mule. I felt a surge of affection for the zebra dun mule. She sure nuff had some heart.

As we got close to the top, it became harder to move with any stealth because Gentry had to strain to deal with the steep and rocky terrain. Luckily, the wind was really howling up here at the higher elevation. I hoped that would cover any noise we were making. If the wind died down and they happened to have a man on watch, things could get pretty hairy fast. It would be quite a fancy trick to gallop down that steep, muddy incline if we had to make a break for it. I didn't like the odds.

About twenty yards ahead, I could see through the dim light of the half moon where the top of the mesa leveled out to flat ground. I figured Gentry had done her job about as well as she could up to this point; now it was up to me. I dismounted, pulled my rifle from the scabbard, and left her as I began creeping up the final distance. In different circumstances, I probably would've hobbled her. Right here, right now, though, I didn't have the time and I was worried that it might make too much noise. Also, since we might have to run for our lives, it didn't make a lot of sense to do anything that would slow us down if things went to hell. I had to trust her to wait for me. One way or another, I probably wouldn't be gone long. Like I said, she has a mighty fine heart. I figured I'd have to depend on that to keep her there until I returned.

That old half moon I was counting on for light didn't provide a lot of it; mostly shadows of lighter and darker gray. Still, I was able to make out a few details as I carefully poked my head above a rock at the edge of the mesa top. I looked hard and didn't see any sign of Flynt and his gang. I saw a group of large rocks about thirty feet off to my left that looked like the spot I'd pick to put a sentry if it was me making the decision. I took a deep breath, then began slithering on my belly in that direction. I believe I mentioned before that I was pretty adept at sneaking up on folks. I'm not sure that's what I'd want as the epitaph on my gravestone but I figure it's a skill that'll prolong the time before I need one. I listened hard for any sounds that might indicate there was another human being other than me up on top of that mesa. The pounding of my heart made that a bit of a challenge. I heard nothing but the wind and my rapid heartbeats. When I got right to the base of the rocks, I spotted an opening between the two biggest ones. I figured my best chance if someone was waiting on the other side would be to jump out with my rifle aimed in the direction of where the fella would most likely be. If he was there, hopefully I'd have the drop on him and could subdue him without firing any shots to alert the rest of the gang. That's how I saw it playing out in my mind. Of course, when was the last time things played out exactly like you saw them in your mind?

Taking my time, I pushed up from my belly to my knees. I could feel the sting where the rocks had pressed into the heels of my hands. Slowly, I got to my feet. I waited for a full minute to see if I heard anything stirring on the other side of the rocks. Finally, I figured it was now or never. I jumped out into the gap between the rocks, my rifle pointed at where I hoped the midsection of the sentry would be if he was there. Nothing. I looked around, my eyes darting, taking in every detail I could see. Still nothing. Looked like they didn't have a sentry. I blew out a breath of relief.

I searched around the area and was rewarded for my efforts. I saw cigarette butts from some roll-your-owns; the kind of thing you see in places where someone has stood guard. I figured it was time to take a look at the rest of the mesa. Although I continued to move stealthily, my heartbeat had slowed and was no longer pounding in my ears. Out on these plains, you kind of develop a sense for when there's other humans around. My sense was telling me that I was alone on top of Buckhorn Mesa.

A thorough inspection confirmed my feeling that I was the solitary human on the mesa top. It also confirmed that someone, and I can only assume it was Jake Flynt and his gang, had camped for quite awhile on the mesa. There were the remains of a campfire, places where it looked like men had laid their bedrolls and some other nastiness that you find in campgrounds where men aren't especially neat in their personal habits. Judging from the mess they'd made, these fellas were a far cry from neat. It appeared that it was time for me to report back to Sheriff Marés. I couldn't tell him where Jake Flynt and his gang were but I could sure tell him where they weren't. Speaking of knowing where things were, I sure hoped I knew where my mule was.

CHAPTER 16

"He's out of control, John." Bill Wallace shook his head with dismay. "I don't care if he is your family, the man is loco. He can't find O'Donnell to get our money back. In the meantime, he's torturing and killing sodbusters for his own amusement. He's going to bring us all down."

Burr held his hand out towards Wallace in a placating gesture. "Calm down, Bill, we'll figure something out. We're in this thing too deep to let Flynt destroy us."

"We'd better do something fast or that's exactly what he's going to do," Wallace said vehemently. "You're the mastermind that came up with this plan, think of something."

"We need to keep our own heads clear if we want to come up with a plan that will work." Burr spoke in a calm, patient tone, which did not accurately reflect how he felt. He had been having similar fears to those of his partner in crime. "Let's look at this logically. What needs to happen for this wreck to straighten out?"

Wallace took a deep breath to compose himself. "Most important thing is to find that Irish rogue and get our money back. Once we do that, he'll be a loose end we'll be able to tie up."

"I agree," Burr said. "He'll have to vanish without a trace. He knows too much. Once we accomplish that, though, we've still got Jake to worry about. He's not just a loose end, he's a loose cannon. I don't think we can risk letting him go on about his business when this is done."

"I'm afraid you're right," Wallace said reluctantly. "I guess he'll have to vanish like O'Donnell." He made a face like he'd just bitten into something disgusting. "Are you sure you can do that? I realize I said I don't care if he's your family but still, he *is* your family."

Burr turned an icy gaze on Wallace. "That's an accident from the past that I had no control over. As far as I'm concerned, Jake is no different from the Irishman."

"Well excuse me," Wallace sputtered, "but one major difference is that Jake Flynt is a homicidal killer who will not be taken out easily. How do you propose we manage that part of the deal?"

"You're right," Burr said. "It's a tricky proposition. We need someone to kill him. Anybody in their right mind isn't going to want to tangle with him." Burr chewed on his thumbnail for a moment as he pondered the problem. "Do you think we need to wait until the Irishman is taken care of before we deal with Jake?"

Wallace considered the question. "Jake hasn't had much luck in finding him so far. I don't know why we would need to keep him around for that chore. There are others in his gang that could handle looking for the Irishman." He snorted with derision. "They couldn't do any worse than he's done."

"Then we need to figure out how to set Jake up and who we want to pull the trigger." Burr nodded. "The sooner, the better as far as I'm concerned. If we knew where he was hiding out, we might be able to arrange an ambush."

"That'd be tricky," Wallace said. "It could lead to a gun battle with the whole gang. We need the rest of those varmints alive to find O'Donnell and take care of him."

"Jake's pretty cagey. He won't tell me where his hideout is. I don't know if he suspects something or if he's just cautious." Burr drummed his fingers on his desk as he calculated the odds. "Our best bet is to catch him when he comes to our meeting place. The problem is, I'm never sure if he's going to be there like we've planned. It's hard to arrange for someone to ambush him when we're not sure if he's going to show."

"Not to mention figuring out who this brave soul is who's going to take on a wild man like Flynt," Wallace said.

"Brave, hell," Burr retorted with a scornful tone. "More likely foolhardy." Burr contemplated the question. "That gives me an idea about who we could get. Someone who's both brave and foolhardy." He smiled cynically. "Both of those descriptions fit our friend, Deputy Stallings."

"Hmmm?" Wallace squinted as he considered Burr's comment. "You may be on to something. If we're lucky, they'll kill each other and solve a number of problems at once. Of course, we still don't know how to arrange it."

"Not yet," Burr said smugly, "but I might be able to figure something out. If it doesn't look like it will work, I've got some other ideas. Give me a little time; I'll come up with a plan."

Tomás Marés glanced with mild irritation at the bootheels resting on his desk. With a touch of sarcasm in his voice, he asked, "Are you comfortable?"

Estévan Marés looked at his brother with a puzzled expression for a brief moment before breaking into a smile. "Sí, gracias, *mi hermano.* I am very comfortable." Apparently, the sarcasm was lost on him.

Tomás threw up his hands in mock disgust although the smile tugging at the corner of his mouth gave him away. He recognized that while his brother had settled down considerably from the wild ways of his youth, he had not changed completely. He still enjoyed pushing the limits.

"I thought that perhaps working for the Delaneys would help you become more civilized," Tomás said. "What would Eleanor Delaney say if you put your dirty boots up on her furniture?"

"I would never dream of putting my boots on Señora Eleanor's furniture," Estévan said with a serious expression. "That would be rude." Judging from Tomás's outraged face, Estévan could see that his provocation had found its mark. He burst into laughter.

Tomás maintained his outrage for another few seconds, then he joined in laughing with his brother. What else could he do? "Of course, you are right," he said. "What was I thinking?"

"Exactly," Estévan said. It felt good to laugh together. There had been a time only a few years before when they barely spoke. When their laughter subsided, Estévan took his boots off his brother's desk and sat forward in his chair. "I have indeed learned a great deal working for Jared and Eleanor, in spite of what you might think from my casual treatment of your furniture."

"They are good people and good friends," Tomás said. "I am thankful that you were able to resolve your differences."

"I am grateful to Maria Suazo for straightening my thinking out so we could make peace," Estévan replied. "I do not think anyone other than the widow of Juan Suazo could have gotten it through my thick skull that Jared Delaney was not the cause of her husband's death."

"Maria can be quite persuasive," Tomás agreed. "She always had a fiery way about her. I was afraid after the murder of her husband that the flame had died." Estévan noticed that his brother appeared to be blushing as he commented on Maria Suazo. He wondered about this.

"Jared tells me that you visited the other day," Estévan said. With a spark of the devil in his eye, he asked, "How was your meal?"

"Mercifully, Jared prepared the meal that

we ate. I do not know how you can stand Eleanor's cooking." Tomás shuddered. "She is a wonderful lady but her cooking could cause a pig to turn away from the trough."

Estévan laughed uproariously. "I will tell you something you would not believe. Like Jared, I have taken to preparing my own meals. I do not tell our mother for fear that she might say something to upset Eleanor."

Tomás chuckled. "I think it is safe to tell our mother, *mi hermano*. She would not say anything to Eleanor because she would not believe that you would cook for yourself."

Estévan feigned indignation momentarily, then laughed along with his brother. "You are probably right. I would not have believed it myself before I tasted Eleanor's cooking."

"Perhaps this is God's way of reminding Jared that nothing is perfect," Tomás said, continuing to chuckle. "We must always take the bad with the good."

Estévan's smile faded as he contemplated his brother's statement. "That reminds me; Jared said you are no closer to catching that filthy *cabrón,* Jake Flynt, and the rest of his band of murderers."

"True, unfortunately. Tommy has been attempting to track them to their hideout. There is so much land to cover; it seems he is always one step behind them."

"Tommy is maybe not the best tracker in the world, *qué no?*" Estévan said with a sly grin. "Still, there is no one more determined when he makes up his mind to do something. What will you do when he finds where they hole up?"

"I will do what we always do in Cimarrón when there is trouble," Tomás said with an air of resignation. "I will call on the few men who can be counted on when there is danger."

"Me, Jared . . . anyone else?"

"Tom Figgs will help," Tomás said. "Our father, of course."

"Tom Figgs is a good man," Estévan said with a nod. "I trust him to stand with us." He cleared his throat nervously. "Do you not think our father has reached an age that perhaps it would be wise for him not to be included?"

"The thought has occurred to me." Tomás stared at his brother and slowly shook his head. "Do you want to be the one to tell him this news?"

Estévan pondered the question for a moment. Like his brother, he slowly shook his head. "So then, you, Tommy, Tom Figgs, Jared, me, and papa." He frowned. "What about the men who jumped on their horses and went with you after Flynt and his gang the day they robbed the bank?"

"It turned out they came straight out of the Colfax Tavern and mounted up. They were drunk." Tomás smiled. "We gave up the chase about the time they sobered up."

Estévan chuckled. "Courage from a bottle . . . I know a bit about that. Not so much lately, though."

Tomás smiled again. He sat back in his chair for a moment and chewed on his thumbnail. Leaning forward, his expression turned serious. "There is something I want to talk with you about. I want to know what you think."

Noting his brother's change in mood, Estévan leaned forward. "What would that be?"

"Tommy believes that John Burr from the bank is involved somehow in this robbery. He also thinks that Mayor Wallace may have something to do with it as well."

Estévan looked puzzled. "Why would Burr take part in robbing his own bank? It would seem that the loss of the money would hurt him most of all. I also do not understand why the mayor would become involved in something like this."

"Here is what Tommy thinks," Tomás said. "He thinks Burr put Flynt up to robbing the bank. The plan was for them to split the

190

money afterwards. In the meantime, Burr could use the loss of the money as a reason to foreclose on a number of ranches. He would take that land and sell it. He stood to make quite a profit given what those Santa Fe Ring rascals are paying. It is possible that Wallace helped him plan this scheme. If he did, he would expect a cut."

Estévan thought about this for a moment. "I could see that happening. John Burr is certainly enough of a *pendejo* that he might do something like that. Wallace is not much better."

"That is how I see it as well," Tomás said. "They have a problem, though."

"What is that?"

"It appears that Garrett O'Donnell was part of the gang who robbed the bank." Estévan looked skeptically at his brother. "And what is more, it appears that Señor O'Donnell has vanished with the money."

Estévan's look changed from skeptical to incredulous. "This is not making any sense to me, Tomás. I believe Garrett gave up all that violence when he came to this country. He came for a fresh start, why would he risk his family and everything he's worked for?"

"That is a big question, my brother." Tomás nodded gravely. "An even bigger

191

question is where is Garrett O'Donnell and what has he done with the money?"

CHAPTER 17

As Fred Huntington rode north out of Springer, his mind was preoccupied with the grudge he had been nursing for days. *I don't know who that Tom Stallings . . . hell, I'll call him "Tommy" if I feel like it . . . thinks he is. Him a high-fallutin' deputy sheriff and me just a town constable. I'll show him a thing or two. Reckon they'll move that sheriff's office over to Springer straightaway once I bring in Jake Flynt and his gang. See how he likes that.*

Ever since the deputy's visit the other day, Huntington had been stewing. There was no call for him to be treated so disrespectfully. He did his job just like that Stallings boy. As a matter of fact, Stallings hadn't done such a fine job, as it turned out, since Jake Flynt and his gang were still roaming around the Big Empty.

Lost in thought as he was, Fred Huntington was slow to notice the group of riders headed his way as he came over the hill. When he finally looked up and noticed them, he squinted for a better look. The man out front seemed to be waving to him in a friendly manner. *I wonder who these fellas are. Seem friendly enough.* As the riders came closer and he was able to make out their features, a random thought eked its way out of the back of his mind. *Say, that fella out front looks a lot like the man on the wanted poster for Jake Flynt.* It was the last thought he ever had.

Patricio Baca was lost in his own thoughts as the gang rode towards Springer. It was becoming clear to him that if he stayed on with Jake Flynt's outfit much longer, his life expectancy would dwindle down to nothing. Flynt was more and more out of control with his vicious behavior, which no longer made any sense in terms of furthering the gang's financial goals. His savagery only served to temporarily slake his sadistic blood lust. Unfortunately, the respite never lasted very long.

Baca was no stranger to brutal crimes. He had been perpetrating them on the citizens of the New Mexico Territory his entire adult life. For him, though, they had always been a way to make money so that he could maintain his preferred lifestyle of drinking, gambling, and whoring. He was not squeamish and had no remorse about the toll he had extracted in human suffering. It was just a by-product of his chosen profession, however, and not the ultimate goal. He realized that for Jake Flynt, inflicting the pain and anguish *was* the goal. *This hombré is loco,* he thought. *I ain't gonna let him get me killed. I got to find a way out of this mess.*

Preoccupied as he was, Patricio was startled when Jake raised his arm in greeting to a lone rider approaching them from Springer. He seemed to be smiling and welcoming the oncoming stranger. *What's he up to? I think he's lost his mind.* Patricio shook his head. As the rider got closer, Patricio saw that the man had a lawman's badge pinned on the left side of his vest. A little closer and he saw the man's expression change from polite anticipation to confusion and then to alarm. At that moment, Jake Flynt drew his pistol and shot the man.

"What the hell," Patricio barked as his horse reared up at the sound of gunfire. *Damned nag* he thought. He struggled to maintain control as Jake spurred his horse forward toward the fallen stranger. Snapping out of his reverie, Baca urged his horse to where Jake had dismounted next to the latest victim to fall prey to his sadistic nature.

He turned to Patricio and laughed fiendishly. "He's still wiggling a bit." Flynt aimed directly at the constable's star that was pinned on the man's chest right over his heart and pulled the trigger. The bullet pierced the middle of the badge as the body jumped with the impact. The deafening sound of the shot reverberated across the prairie. Jake turned to Patricio again and said, "Reckon he won't be wiggling anymore."

Baca took a deep breath and once again told himself that he needed to find a way out of this insanity as fast as possible. He knew that now was not the time, however.

"You gonna leave him here?"

"Nah, let's move him off the trail," Jake replied. He turned to Keaton and Atkins, "Drag this no-account excuse for a lawman over there behind those bushes. Make sure you can't see him. We don't want some dumb farmer to find him and raise the alarm before we're done in Springer."

Keaton and Atkins dismounted. One took the arms and the other took the legs of the dead constable. They grunted and strained, as the late Fred Huntington was a rather portly man, until they managed to carry him about twenty yards off the trail and drop him off behind a stand of sagebrush.

"What do you want us to do with his horse, Jake?" Pierce Keaton asked ingratiatingly as he hopped from one foot to the other like some old-timey court jester. Patricio Baca turned away in disgust. *What a toady.*

"Take that nag over there in the brush where you tossed that lawman and put it down. We can't have the horse trot into Springer without its rider." Jake walked back to his horse to mount up.

"You want us to shoot him?" Keaton was obviously uncomfortable with the notion of shooting a good horse.

"No, Pierce, I want you to talk it to death. Hell, yes, I want you to shoot it. How else are you gonna kill it?"

"I's just askin', Jake," Keaton said. "I'll do it right this minute."

Jake shook his head as he stepped into the saddle. As Pierce Keaton led the horse away to its execution, he looked at Patricio Baca.

"We're going to ride in hard and fast, Patricio, guns blazing. I want to see the stunned looks on their faces when we come back." He looked out over the horizon, squinting against the late morning sun.

"They won't be expecting us so I don't anticipate much resistance. Still, look for armed men first. You see them, you shoot to kill. After that, anybody that moves is fair game." He smiled his vicious smile. "They'll remember Jake Flynt, I promise you."

Patricio started to respond when he was startled by the sound of a shot. He had forgotten about Keaton's unpleasant deed. Once again, his horse spooked and crow-hopped for a moment before he got him under control. Usually a pretty calm customer, he could tell his nerves were getting frayed. *First chance I get, I'm long gone.*

Dave Atkins was already in the saddle when Keaton came back from his dirty chore. He looked a little green around the gills but he didn't have the nerve to say anything to the outlaw leader. Instead, he mounted up without a word.

"I already told Patricio, boys," Jake said to Atkins and Keaton. "We ride in raising hell. Shoot anyone who appears to be heeled, then shoot anybody else that strikes your fancy. When we get to the bank, I want the two of you in first. Pierce, go left, Dave, go right. You see a guard, you shoot him." He eyed them both carefully, looking for any signs of dissent. When he saw none, he continued. "Me and Patricio will be right behind you. We'll hit the tellers, take whatever they got. You boys cover us in case some poor misguided soul decides to do something heroic."

Both men nodded although with a definite lack of enthusiasm. They were not excited to be the first ones rushing into the bank. Although it was true that they wouldn't be expecting to be robbed again so soon, it was highly likely that they had increased the number of guards at the bank. It made no sense for Jake to take this risk for little or no monetary gain, yet neither had the courage to question the decision.

Jake waited for any sign that the gang members might balk at his instructions. When it was clear to him that they understood their parts in his plan, he spurred his horse forward and hollered, "Let's ride."

They loped along for a ways at a pretty good clip before Jake slowed to a steady trot, not wanting to wear out the horses before they got to their destination. To the north of Springer, there was a hill that looked down on the sleepy New Mexico town. Jake stopped there and surveyed the scene below him. He chuckled to himself but did not share what he found amusing. No one asked.

He pulled his wild rag up over the lower

half of his face and tied it snug at the back of his head. He waited until the others had done the same. He let loose an ear-splitting rebel yell and dug his spurs ferociously into the sides of his white-legged sorrel. In an instant, the splendid horse came to a full gallop. The other three men spurred their mounts as well, although with considerably less enthusiasm than their leader. They thundered into town in a swirl of dust and rode hard down the main street in the direction of the bank. Off to their left in front of the mercantile, a man was loading sacks of grain into a wagon. When he saw the riders racing his way, his jaw dropped in bewilderment. As they rode by, Jake shot him. Other citizens began diving for shelter anywhere they could find it.

Patricio fired a few random shots into the air as they rode toward the bank. At this point, he had no stomach for inflicting further suffering on the citizens of Springer. However, if Jake was the only one shooting, he might question the resolve of his segundo. Baca did not want to draw undue scrutiny to the fact that he was growing increasingly reluctant to follow Jake's lead.

They reined in at the hitching rail in front of the bank and loose-tied their horses. A swift glance back up the street showed that it was deserted. The sounds of screaming and crying, however, could be heard from the terrified citizens who were hiding behind any solid object they could find.

"Dave, Pierce . . . in!" Jake barked his order.

The men threw open the door to the bank. It crashed against the wall as Keaton moved in cautiously, looking to his left. Seeing no one who appeared to be an armed guard, he moved more rapidly into the middle of the room. Dave Atkins, who was carrying a sawed-off American Arms 12-gauge shotgun, had moved a little quicker going in and was farther into the room. When he looked to his right, he saw a man talking with one of the tellers. The man was holding a Winchester carbine. Atkins couldn't tell if he was a guard or not. He knew one thing for sure . . . if the man chose to level the rifle at him, he might soon be dead. Then it wouldn't much matter to him if the man was a guard or a brave and concerned citizen. Not a chance he was willing to take. He unloaded both barrels on the man, slamming him up against the teller's cage.

Both men looked around wildly, searching for signs of further resistance. They saw none. The citizens of Springer had been unaware of the malevolence that would rain down on them until they heard the gunfire moments before the outlaws entered the bank. They cowered around the edges of the room. The tellers had all ducked down on the floor of their cages. Gun smoke clouded the room. Everyone, including the two outlaws, remained frozen in the moment.

Jake Flynt sauntered into the bank. A few people were crying noisily. Jake fired a shot into the ceiling and screamed at the top of his voice, "Silence!" The crying tapered off to whimpering although it didn't disappear entirely. Apparently, it was quiet enough to satisfy Jake.

"Howdy folks," he hollered in a cheerful voice. Pulling his wild rag down from around his face, he said, "Surprise. Jake Flynt at your service." He looked around at the people in the bank and reveled in their horrified astonishment. "Bet you weren't expecting me back so soon, were you?" No one said anything. "Well, I wanted to let you know that any time I feel the urge, I'll come into your town and have my way. And there's nothing any of you can do about it. Now, if you'll all stay quiet, nobody else has to die." He turned to Patricio and said, "Get what you can from the tellers."

As Baca went from cage to cage gathering

the meager amount of cash the bank had on hand, Jake continued to survey the scene. When he had finished his rounds, Patricio hurried back over to where Jake stood in the middle of the room.

"I think that's it," Patricio said. "It ain't much."

"It'll do," Jake said.

Casually, he strolled around the bank, inspecting the terrified people as if they were cattle to be led to the slaughter. They shrank away from him as he drew near, which seemed to please him. After making a full circle, he returned to the middle of the room. His gaze swept the room and lit on a young man dressed in rough cowboy attire who was standing protectively in front of a woman who might be his wife. Jake smiled at the young man. The man flinched but said nothing.

Continuing to stare hard at the young cowboy, Jake addressed the room. "You know how I said if you stayed quiet, nobody else had to die?" His words hung in the air. "Well, I lied." He shot the man. "Let's go, boys."

CHAPTER 18

It took me the better part of the day to make it back to town. I was bone-weary and my horse and mule weren't faring much better, so I wasn't in a rush. No sense in pushing so hard that Rusty or Gentry came up lame, particularly after how well they'd served me the past couple of days. Like I said before, both those critters got a lot of heart, even if Gentry does have some highfalutin notions about her rank in the herd. She is a mighty fine mule, no matter what she thinks.

I was tempted to head straight to my little cottage and sleep for about a week. Mollie would most likely be there as it was late afternoon and school had already let out. I could sure stand a healthy portion of her tender loving care followed by about fifteen hours of sleep. My sense of responsibility overcame my indolent nature. Every minute's delay in pursuing these bad hombrés was more time they'd have to wreak havoc on the citizens of Colfax County. I rode up to the hitching post outside the sheriff's office and secured my animals before walking inside. I didn't have time to unsaddle them and brush them down, which I felt bad about. I did loosen their cinches.

"*Hola,* Sheriff," I said as I walked into the office. "I come a long way just to tell you where Jake Flynt and his gang ain't."

Tomás looked up from his ever-present paperwork and said, "I will go you one better, Deputy. I can tell you where they have been very recently."

I looked at him in confusion. "I was talkin' about the hideout they abandoned in the past few days. What in the Sam Hill are you talkin' about?"

"They once again robbed the bank in Springer. In the process, they killed a guard, a private citizen, and the town constable." The tension in his voice made it abundantly clear how Tomás Marés felt about this most recent development.

My knees felt weak and wobbly. I sank down in the chair across from Tomás and tried to get a handle on the information he was sharing with me. "They killed the constable? Fred Huntington?"

"Sí," Tomás said grimly. "They found his body about three miles north of town when they rode out after Jake and his gang." Tomás shook his head in disgust. "It took them three hours to organize a posse. By that time, Flynt could have been anywhere out there in the Big Empty."

I felt like somebody had punched me in the gut. I couldn't believe the terrible news about Fred. I was confused about what he was doing north of Springer since he was the town constable and had no authority outside the city limits. What was he thinking? Also, it was beginning to dawn on me what Tomás had said about Jake and his boys robbing the Springer bank again. That made no sense to me at all.

"Wait a minute, hold up," I said, my confusion and agitation reflected equally in the tone of my voice. "Why would Jake rob the bank again? He just robbed it last week. There wouldn't have been enough money there to make it worthwhile."

Tomás brought me up to speed. "It makes no sense if he was aiming to make money. That, apparently, was not the reason."

I was frustrated now. "What other damn reason would there be for him to rob a bank? Was he practicin'?"

"He was making a statement to us," Tomás said in a reasonable voice that contrasted with my agitation. "He was telling us he can break any laws he pleases and there is nothing we can do about it." A slight edge returned to his voice as he said, "He said as much to the people in the bank as he was robbing it."

"That no-good, lily-livered, back-shootin', egg-suckin' dog." I strung together as many of my favorite insults as I could think of. It still fell way short of expressing what I was feeling towards Jake Flynt. "You're sayin' he came to town, robbed the bank again, and shot a bunch of folks just to show us he could do it?"

"That is what I am saying."

"That lowdown polecat ain't your run-of-the-mill bad man," I said with conviction. "He's a monster."

"I would have to agree with you, Tommy," Tomás said with a note of sadness in his voice. "He is an evil man. Now, more than ever, we must find a way to stop him."

As I was trying to collect my wits, I remembered what I had originally come to tell the sheriff before he blindsided me with this bad news. "Well, the only way we can do that is to figure out where he's hidin' and hunt him down like the rabid dog he is."

"Oh yes," Tomás said. "You were saying something when you came in about knowing where he was not." He looked at me sideways. "I am not sure how that helps us."

"It does help us and I'll tell you how. It appears they were holed up on Buckhorn Mesa for a pretty good spell. They ain't there anymore. I know this for a fact 'cause I checked. It looks to me like they ain't been gone very long." I felt like the fog was lifting and I could think more clearly. "I reckon they decided to change hideouts when they heard Charlie Atkins had failed in his attempt to bushwhack me. They had no way of knowin' how much he told me about where they were so they cleared out."

"And what good does this information do for us?" Tomás sounded danged near impatient. I like it when he gets stirred up.

"If you recall, Sheriff," I responded a tad testily, "I told you I figured they were either on Buckhorn Mesa or Black Mesa. Well, they ain't on Buckhorn . . ." I paused, "which means they're likely on Black Mesa."

Tomás considered my statement. "I am not sure if you are right about this. Still, it makes some sense and it is the best possibility we have at this time." He squinted as he thought about our next moves. After a moment's deliberation, he slammed his fist down on the desk. This time, my hat wasn't in harm's way. I'd learned my lesson about setting it on his desk.

"It is time to organize a posse and search for these *cabrónes.* I will talk to Mayor Wallace about an emergency council meeting. You ride out to Jared's place. Tell him we need him and Estévan here at first light."

I lit out of town with gusto and probably pushed Rusty a little harder than I should have. He was running short on gusto and so was I. After a couple of miles, I slowed down and gave some serious thought to the matter at hand. It was complicated. First off, I was dog-tired. It was a little past mid-afternoon and I wasn't likely to get home until nearly midnight. Filling Jared and Estévan in on the situation would take some time and then riding back in the light of the half moon. There was one silver lining in the thunderclouds that were gathering all around me. I could beg off staying for dinner by saying I had to get back. Last thing I needed was to be riding back to town in the dark with my stomach on fire from Eleanor Delaney's cooking.

I was a little nervous about how my unpredictable wife would react when I got home. I was in such a rush, I clean forgot to tell her where I was going before I left. I was pretty sure she'd find out about it secondhand. She hates it when she finds out stuff secondhand. That meant that when I finally did make it home tonight, instead of me going straight to bed, we'd probably have to "talk." I really hate to "talk." I'm sure glad I love Mollie so much because she can be a bit of a chore at times. I was figuring this would be one of those times.

There was something else I was a bit fretful about as well. Tomás sounded pretty confident that he could get Wallace and the council to approve funds to pay for our hunting expedition . . . well, all right, for our posse. The thing is, I didn't trust Bill Wallace. Even as I rode out to recruit Jared and Estévan, I had a suspicion that our plan might get knocked off the tracks. I was hoping for the best and planning for the worst.

The sun was sitting right smack-dab on top of the hills out to the west when I rode up to Kilpatrick Ranch and gave a "hello the house" shout. The quiet beauty of the lavender sunset was in stark contrast to the unsettling news I was bringing. Off to my right, I could see Estévan at the stable taking his saddle off his horse. He waved at me and continued his chore. I looked back toward the house and saw Jared walk out on the front portal. When he recognized me, a smile broke out across his face. That made

210

me feel pretty darn good although I knew when I told him what was coming out of the chute, that smile would hide someplace pretty quick.

"Tommy Stallings, what brings you out our way?" He stepped down from the portal and walked over to where I was dismounting. "You must've known we were fixin' to sit down to the evenin' meal. I don't expect you rode out all this way for one of Eleanor's home-cooked meals, though," he said with a hint of the devil in his eye.

"As appealin' as that sounds, that ain't the reason I'm here." I must have grimaced as I said it. Jared chuckled.

"Well, what is it then that brings you out our way? You ready to give up law enforcement and head back up the trail with me?"

I could tell he was glad to see me and I hated to ruin his sociable mood. Still, I had a job to do and I knew he'd understand. "All hell's breakin' loose with Jake Flynt and his band of snivelin' curs. They hit the bank at Springer again, killed a bunch of folks, includin' the town constable."

"The town constable? You don't mean Fred Huntington, do you?"

" 'Fraid so," I said regretfully. "I think old Fred took a crazy notion to chase after Jake and his gang on his own. Me and Tomás

211

been lookin' all over for Jake and ain't been able to find him. Fred sorta stumbled into him."

"That's bad news for sure," Jared said regretfully. "I doubt you came out here to just tell me that, though. You boys need some help with this thing?"

"Yep, that's it exactly," I said. "Tomás wanted me to ask you and Estévan to come in to town at first light tomorrow. He wants you to ride with us to track that no-good back-shooter down."

Jared sighed and looked off to the west toward the setting sun. He looked back at me and said, "Reckon there's no way around it, is there? I'll let you ask Estévan yourself but we both know what he'll say."

Estévan came striding over to where we stood. He had a smile on his face and a bounce in his step. Chances are he was about to find some way to give me the hoorah when he saw the look on our faces. He slowed down a bit and his smile vanished.

"It does not look like you have brought good news to us, Tommy Stallings," he said gravely. "What is it?"

"Your brother sent me to ask if you two would join up with us to track Jake Flynt and his gang. Jake's gone plumb crazy. He's killin' folks like he's some kind of rampagin' wolf. We need to stop him and we sure could use some help."

"Sí," Estévan said immediately. "When do we ride?"

"We plan to head out at first light in the mornin'," I said.

Jared must have detected the uncertainty in my voice. "You said you 'plan' to head out. That makes it sound like you don't know for sure. Is there some reason to think the plan could change?"

"The plan's got to be approved by the village council," I said, the disgust in my voice obvious. "They got to make it official, you know, deputize y'all, approve you gettin' paid and such. You know how it is with politicians; they can always find a way to foul up a good plan. No offense to your pa, Estévan," I said. "He's a member of the council but he ain't no politician."

"I understand," Estévan replied. "I am not offended and I do not think he would be either. He will ride with us, qué no?"

"I reckon so," I said. "That is, of course, if we do get to ride."

"What do you need us to do, then?" Jared had that resolute look about him that I had come to know very well when I rode north with him trailing steers through Raton Pass.

213

"Best I can tell you is to show up at the sheriff's office in the mornin' at first light ready to ride. If things play out the way they ought to, we'll head out. If those damned politicians throw a kink in our loop, we'll have to change the plan."

Jared looked at Estévan, who nodded his assent. He looked back at me. "We'll be there." The devilment returned to his eyes. "You sure I can't interest you in some vittles?"

I quickly stepped over to Rusty and mounted up. "Thanks but no thanks. I really got to get home to Mollie. Give Miss Eleanor my best." I headed back south towards Cimarrón before they had a chance to ask me again.

In the morning, as Jared and Estévan prepared to leave before first light, Eleanor offered to make them a quick breakfast. Both men declined politely.

Eleanor chafed at the fact that her rancher husband was once again being called upon to enforce the law. Uncharacteristically, she kept her opinion to herself as Jared said his goodbyes to her before heading out once more on the trail of yet another vicious outlaw. She knew he would go whether she protested or not.

"You be careful," she said. "Don't take risks if you don't have to." She nodded in the direction of the two small beds in the far corner of the house. "We need you to come back home to us."

"Don't worry, Eleanor, darlin', I'll come back." Jared embraced her for a moment and then turned to leave.

"You be careful too, Estévan," she said. "I've sort of gotten use to having you around here as well." With an innocent look, she said, "If you make it home safe, I'll cook up something special for both of you."

The men glanced at each other uneasily, not sure whether or not she was teasing them. Estévan grinned sheepishly and said, "I will certainly keep that in mind, Señora."

Eleanor stood motionless for quite a while as the sound of hoofbeats faded. Later, as the sun appeared over the mountains, she let the tears flow.

Yesterday had been a very long day followed by a very short night. I made it home a little before midnight and as I had feared . . . well, all right, "feared" is a strong and somewhat harsh word. As I had anticipated, Mollie was waiting up for me. She continues to surprise and amaze me. Apparently, Sheriff Tomás Marés himself called on her yesterday right after I left. He explained that before I'd had the chance to let her know I had returned to town, he'd sent me back out. It seems he convinced her that my last words to him as I rode away from his office were "If I don't make it back alive, tell Mollie I love her." I'm sure I would have thought to say that if I hadn't been so doggone tired. Come to think of it, since I was faced with the possibility of having to eat Eleanor Delaney's cooking, there really *was* a chance I might not make it back alive. Anyway, when I got home, Mollie wasn't in the mood to "talk." She was, however, not ready to sleep. As I said, it was a very short night. I owe Tomás. I'm just not sure what I owe him for.

As a result of all that, I was moving a little slow when first light rolled around. I managed to get myself going after two cups of strong black coffee. I was grateful that Mollie was so tired she couldn't drag herself out of bed. I saddled up old Rusty, who was not all that excited about hitting the trail again so soon. I can't say that I blamed him. I headed over to the sheriff's office, doing my best to stay awake so I didn't fall out of the saddle. That would have been plumb embarrassing.

When I got there, I saw Jared's and Estévan's horses tied outside the sheriff's office. Their cinches were loose and it didn't look as if we were ready to ride out in a cloud of dust the minute I arrived. I walked inside.

"Nice of you to join us," Jared said with a smirk.

Estévan was grinning at me. I'm guessing Tomás had filled them in on how he'd left things with Mollie yesterday. They didn't have to be all that good at arithmetic to add two and two together and figure out why I was late. I mustered my dignity and ignored the joshing. Being a fair hand at arithmetic myself, I'd figured out that the plans for our posse had changed and I had a pretty good idea who had changed them.

"What did that bunch of lamebrains on the village council do, refuse to approve you the right to organize a posse?" I looked at Tomás and Estévan and quickly corrected myself. "That 'lamebrain' comment don't include your daddy, fellas." Estévan waved his hand in dismissal, indicating that he understood.

Tomás looked like he'd been sucking on a lemon all morning. "Worse than that, Tommy. Much worse."

I tried to imagine something worse and came up blank. Well, okay, they could have decided to recommend that we move the sheriff's office to Springer right away. With the second bank robbery, I knew that was coming no matter what any of us said or did. Still, it made no sense for them to do that right in the middle of our manhunt for Jake Flynt. Surely that wasn't it. My head was starting to hurt.

"I ain't as awake as I plan to be later in the day, Sheriff," I said with a hint of annoyance. "Reckon you'd better tell me what they did."

Tomás got up and began to pace. He was clearly agitated. "It was a long and heated meeting with a great deal of discussion, argument, and even name-calling. At the end of the meeting, Mayor Wallace told me that he was suspending our investigation until we moved everything in our office over to Springer."

"Why in tarnation would they do that?" I was starting to wake up now. Truth be told, I was plenty hot. "We got a chance to catch Jake Flynt. This'll knock us right off the rails. What is the matter with those fuzzy-headed dinks? You'd think they were on Jake's side." I was running my mouth when I said that. As soon as the words were out, though, the thought crossed my mind that I might have accidentally blurted out the truth.

"Say, how'd they get a majority to vote for this drivel?" I asked suspiciously. "Last I heard, there weren't enough council members in favor of this recommendation."

Tomás stopped mid-pace and whirled around to face me. "Señor Smith and Señor Chavez changed their votes, that is how."

"Wait just a minute here," I said, shaking my head. The more we talked, the more confused I became. I really could've used about ten more hours of sleep and two more cups of strong coffee. "Old Roger and Antonio were all in favor of keepin' us here last time I heard. What happened?"

"They would not say," Tomás said in clipped tones. "It appears that Wallace and Burr got to them. At least they had the decency to look ashamed of themselves."

Estévan spoke up for the first time. "My father says that he called them gutless *corderitos . . .* cowardly lambs. Señor Smith did not know what that meant." His smile was bleak. "He knew that he had been insulted, though. Antonio Chavez could not look my father in the eye."

"Tomás said Tom Figgs all but challenged both them boys to a fistfight right there in the council meeting room," Jared said with some measure of satisfaction. He sounded like he would have enjoyed witnessing that

219

particular part of the meeting. "Said he'd take 'em on one at a time or both together, didn't matter none to him."

"I'd have paid to see that myself," I said. I pondered that possibility for a moment before moving on. "This brings up a couple of questions, don't it? First thing it makes me wonder is, what did Wallace hold over their heads to make 'em change their minds?"

Tomás calmed down enough to return to his chair. I was relieved. I'd never seen him pace like that before. It was making me jumpy. "I think I may know the answer to that question. Roger Smith and Antonio Chavez both took out loans in order to buy their businesses. Would you like to guess who holds the notes on those loans?"

I shook my head in disgust. "I'd guess it was most likely old John Burr down at the bank. Am I right?"

Tomás looked grim. "You are correct, Deputy Stallings."

"How'd you come by that information? I sure can't imagine that Mr. Burr or Mr. Wallace told you."

Estévan joined the conversation. "Our cousin Lupé works at the bank. Tomás asked her if the bank had some way of pressuring them. It turns out that they did."

Tomás took back over the story. "Burr threatened to foreclose on their notes if they did not vote with him. He had been somewhat lenient in the past when they were late making their payments, telling them it was not a problem. Now, all of a sudden, he told them that because they had been late, he could foreclose any time he wished."

I nodded. "Well, that answers my question. The other question is, why would he do that?" I thought about my recent suspicions that Burr and Wallace were tangled up somehow in Jake Flynt's lawless ways. "You know, I was just jawin' a minute ago when I said it looks like they're on Jake's side. As I ponder it, I'm thinkin' more and more that it's the case."

Jared leaned forward in his chair. "I got no problem seein' Burr behind this. He's a snake, always has been. Wallace, though, I'm not so sure about. He's a bit of a windbag but I never thought of him as a crook."

"Greed does strange things to men," Tomás said pensively. "Bill Wallace has seen Catron and those other *cabrónes* getting rich in Santa Fe. I wonder if he could not resist the idea of acquiring his share of those riches."

How in the world did I get myself into this

221

mess? Bill Wallace had a sharp pain in his gut as he walked toward the bank. Unfortunately, he knew the answer to his question. *I should have known better,* he thought. *I knew Burr was a crook but I kept asking him for help. Now he owns me.* Although he was running late for a meeting with John Burr, he found himself walking at a slower pace. Perhaps if he could delay this latest get-together, the problem would go away. *Fat chance.* He picked up his pace. *Might as well get it over with.*

Jared and Tomás were even closer to the target than they realized with their assessment of Bill Wallace's slide down the slippery slope from windbag businessman to thief and accomplice to murder. When he'd come west from Wichita to New Mexico with a nice nest egg in his pocket, he'd had dreams of starting a successful business. Establishing a mercantile in Cimarrón, smack-dab on the mountain leg of the Santa Fe Trail, had seemed like a good way for him to earn the riches he dreamed of.

As often happens, it turned out that the size of his dreams had outstripped the size of his nest egg. He saw multiple opportunities in Cimarrón and being ambitious, he felt the urge to expand his business interests.

He wound up borrowing money from John Burr, who then introduced him to some influential politicians in Santa Fe. To Wallace, it felt like he was joining an exclusive club whose membership was open only to a select few. Sure, they were willing to help him out. It seemed like a fortuitous opportunity.

To his regret, he had failed to clarify the price tag that was ultimately attached to their assistance. By the time he realized, it was too late for him to escape from their clutches. Along the way, he'd made compromises that, if not exactly illegal, were certainly what folks around here called "shady." Now he'd crossed that line. He was neck-deep in illegal activities that he could never in his wildest dreams have imagined himself getting involved in. There seemed to be no turning back.

Bill Wallace had a wife and a young daughter, both of whom he loved dearly. He couldn't imagine the depths of their disappointment if they learned the truth. He knew that changing the past was not an option. There was no way out. He would have to make the best of it.

"You're late." John Burr looked up when Wallace walked into his private office. "We've got decisions to make and damned little time to make them."

"You don't have to remind me," Wallace said as he sank into the chair across the desk from the bank president. "I bought us some time, though."

"If you mean the council's recommendation that the sheriff move over to Springer right away," Burr said brusquely, "you're right. It bought us a little time. That's all it did. We still have some hard choices in front of us and no room for any more mistakes."

"You're right," Wallace said. His slumped shoulders reflected his dejection. "Do you have any answers?"

"As a matter of fact, I do." Burr sat back with a grin. "Do you remember we talked about arranging an ambush for our friend, Jake Flynt?"

"Of course I do," Wallace said, annoyed. "You thought maybe we could set it up for the deputy to pull the trigger. I don't know how you would work that out."

"Me, neither," said Burr. "A better option has presented itself."

Wallace's irritation vanished and he leaned forward. "What are you talking about?"

"Yesterday while you were twisting arms at the village council meeting, I rode out to the meeting place in hopes that I'd have a chance to talk with Jake and see what he's up to." Burr chuckled. "He didn't show up."

"How does it help anything that you didn't meet with Flynt?" Wallace's exasperation had returned.

"It's not who I *didn't* meet with, it's who I *did* meet with," Burr said mysteriously. He sat back in his chair and began tamping tobacco into his pipe, leaving Wallace hanging.

"I don't want to play guessing games with you, John," Wallace said edgily. "Just tell me what happened?"

Burr spent another moment adjusting his pipe, clearly enjoying his partner's discomfort. Then he blew a ring of smoke and leaned forward. "I had a little talk with Jake's segundo, Patricio Baca. He had some very interesting things to say."

"Wait a minute," Wallace said. "How did you happen to meet with Baca at the meeting place?"

"He's been following Jake when he left camp," Burr said. "Baca wanted to know what he was up to. You might say we share the same concerns regarding Jake Flynt. We even have some common goals."

"And those are?"

"Baca also thinks Jake is out of control. Says he's crazy. He's afraid Jake will either kill him or get him killed with his recklessness." Burr took another pull on his pipe.

"Would you quit fooling with that stupid pipe and tell me what you talked about."

Burr smirked. "Baca says that Jake usually rides out of camp at least once a day and is gone for a couple of hours. He didn't know where he was going and got worried about it. That's how he came to follow Jake to our meeting location in the first place." He shook his head. "He said sometimes Jake rides around out there in the Big Empty like he's looking for something."

"I shudder to think what he's looking for," Wallace said nervously.

"Actually, so does Baca," Burr said. "He thinks a lot of the time, Jake is scouting around for isolated homes on the prairie. He's looking for his next victims."

Wallace shuddered when he heard this. "The man is evil."

"Without question," Burr agreed. "What concerns me even more is that he is mentally unstable and increasingly out of control. The good news is that Baca is willing to follow him when he leaves camp and set up an ambush. I will continue to ride out each day to our rendezvous location. It doesn't matter though whether Jake is coming to meet with me or riding out to scout for innocent people to slaughter. The next time

Jake leaves, he plans to follow and bush-whack him. Problem solved."

CHAPTER 19

"Mollie, darlin', there's nothin' I can do about it. The Cimarrón Village Council has sided with Colfax County. The sheriff's office is changin' locations to Springer. I don't like it any more than you do but that's the way it is."

The morning had not started well. We'd talked well into the night about the change looming just over the horizon but had come to no conclusions. I'd barely got my first cup of coffee down before she started in again. To be fair, I have to say that Mollie O'Brien Stallings wasn't being unreasonable. She was upset. I can't say that I blame her either, I'm not particularly happy about it myself. Those cowards on the council caved in to Bill Wallace and John Burr. Unlike Garrett O'Donnell, who was dirt poor, those men have money and power. What they don't have is any guts. As far as I can tell, there's not a dang thing we can do about it other than start packing up. Well, I've been bucked off horses when I least expected it and I reckon this is kind of like that.

"What am I to do in Springer, Tommy Stallings?" She sounded so despondent, it nearly broke my heart. I wanted to just grab ahold of her and hug her. Right now, though, I had a notion that she had some things she needed to get said, so I restrained myself. "I'm learnin' to be a teacher here in Cimarrón. There's no job like that for me in Springer."

"I don't know what to tell you, Mollie," I said miserably. "This is all new to me, too." I was thinking so hard I was afraid my head might explode. There had to be a solution that would work. "I'm already gone a lot. Maybe you could stay here and I could come back when I ain't out chasin' bad guys."

Mollie huffed in disgust. "Sure and you're right about that. You're already gone a lot. Now you're wantin' to be livin' somewhere else other than with your wife?"

"Naw, now, Mollie, you know that ain't what I meant." Trust her to only see the downside of my suggestion. "I'm talkin' about bein' with you here at our little house whenever I ain't on the trail of outlaws. It wouldn't be that different from the way it is now, don't you see?"

She sobbed for a moment. When she calmed down, she said, "I wish you'd never got into this law business in the first place. You're gone all the time and I'm always frettin' that you're layin' somewheres on the side of a trail with a bullet through your hard head."

It occurred to me that when I was a cowboy, I was gone most of the time and there was always the danger of someone finding me lying dead on the side of a trail. The only difference would be that I'd likely have a broken neck rather than a bullet through my brain. I tried to think of a tactful and sensitive way of introducing this bit of logic into our discussion.

"Hell, Mollie, when I was trailin' steers up to Colorado, I was gone all the time and there was always a damned good chance I'd get myself killed. Did you ever stop to think about that?" Mollie burst into tears once again. Reckon tact is not my strongest asset. "I'm sorry, Mollie," I said. "That was a stupid thing for me to say. I just don't know what to do."

To my amazement, she looked up, sniffed, and smiled through her tears. "You're right, Tommy Stallings, that was a stupid thing to

230

say. Of course I understand things wouldn't be all that different if you went back to bein' a cowboy. At least we could stay in Cimarrón."

I breathed a sigh. Maybe we were making some headway here. "Thanks for bein' understandin', darlin'. And you know, that's what it may come down to before all this is done. I may have to see if I can find steady work as a hand."

Mollie's smile got a little wider. "There now," she said, "I knew we could get this all figured out if we talked about it like sensible folks. How soon do you expect Jared'll hire you?"

This was moving faster than I'd had a mind for it to. "Well, Mollie, I didn't mean I was gonna do it right away," I said defensively. "I got a job to finish. We still got to bring Jake Flynt and his bunch to justice and I need to see if there's anything I can do to help Garrett O'Donnell. I can't take off this badge until that's done."

Mollie burst into tears again. So much for being sensible.

Having done as much damage as I could do to my marriage in a relatively short time, I decided to ride into town to see what I could do for Sheriff Tomás Marés. When I got to his current office, I found him packing boxes to take to his new office.

"Where are they gonna put us up, Sheriff?" In all of our consternation and jawing the day before, I'd failed to ask if the city fathers of Springer actually had a plan for where this new jail would be located. Surely after all the time they've been talking about making the change, they've got a plan in place.

"They informed me in a telegram that there is an abandoned building a block from the bank which we can use as our temporary quarters. It has a dirt floor. Fred Huntington had a tiny office with one small jail cell." Tomás let out a bitter laugh. "And the lock is broke on that cell."

Why was I not surprised? "So if by some chance we was to capture Jake Flynt and his boys while we was in the process of moving everything over there, we wouldn't have anyplace to lock 'em up?" I was disgusted. "This just keeps gettin' better and better."

Tomás nodded. "While I doubt that is likely to happen, you are correct. If we capture any lawbreakers, we have no good place to contain them while they await trial."

I grabbed one of the burlap sacks Tomás was using to pack and began stuffing books into it. "Reckon we'll just have to shoot 'em then. That'll save the county some money on feedin' them. It's more efficient, too." I grinned. "That's one of those words Mollie's been teachin' me."

"Speaking of your wife," Tomás said, "how is she taking the news?"

"Tomás, she's hurt real bad about this. We don't know what we're gonna do. She's got a great job here in Cimarrón, somethin' with a future in it. There's nothin' like that for her in Springer."

"I am afraid you are right, amigo." Tomás shook his head. "What are you going to do?"

"I don't know," I said. "That's what we were talkin' about before I came here. She wants me to give up bein' a deputy and go back to bein' a cowboy."

Tomás looked sharply at me. "What did you tell her?"

"I told her I'd sure give it some thought." Tomás continued to look at me with a troubled expression. Although he wouldn't say it out loud, I knew he was thinking I was going to abandon him right in the middle of the biggest manhunt he'd ever been involved in. "Then I told her I couldn't do it until we got this thing with Jake Flynt settled. That was when the dam burst." I shrugged, dejection written all over my face. "It was also about the time I decided you might need some help here in town."

On Tomás's face, there was a mixture of gratitude and regret. "*Gracias, amigo.* I do not think I could do this without you. I cannot tell you how sorry I am for all the trouble this is causing you and your wife."

I have to say, I was touched by Tomás's concern. That's the kind of man he is. I reckon that's why I'm not willing to walk away yet. "Me and Mollie ain't the first to make sacrifices, Tomás. I know that and she does, too, no matter how much of a ruckus she kicks up when she's upset. When it counts, she's right there with me."

Tomás busied himself clearing his rolltop desk of official-looking papers, an inkwell, and an unusual-looking rock that served him as a paperweight. I continued stuffing books into burlap sacks. After a few minutes, he spoke again. "She is indeed, Tommy. You are a lucky man."

Something about his wistful tone reminded me that Tomás was a bachelor. It had never crossed my mind before to consider how he felt about that state of affairs. Most of his peers were married and settled down with good women who loved them or at least put up with their wicked ways. It occurred to me that he might be lonely. That's not something a cowboy discusses with another cowboy, so I took a different tack.

"You're prob'ly right, though it don't always feel like it when she goes to naggin'. Sometimes I'm a little envious of you. I remember bein' footloose and free before I married Mollie."

Tomás smiled but his eyes were sad. "Footloose and free is not all it is made out to be, Tommy."

Reckon I was right, he's lonely. Since there was nothing I could do about that and I had no idea what to say to comfort him, I made light of it. "I'll try to keep that in mind next time Mollie tears into me." Then I did something I wouldn't usually do. I don't know, I guess I lost my head. "Tomás, you ever think about gettin' hitched?"

His face turned a bright shade of scarlet. He looked shocked. Hell, *I* was shocked that I'd asked him. As you've probably noticed by now, sometimes I shoot off my mouth without thinking through what I'm about to say. I backed up as quickly as I could.

"Never mind, that ain't none of my business." There was something a little odd about the way he got nervous that made me curious. If he'd just told me it was none of my damn business and butt out, I'd have thought nothing of it. Instead, he seemed embarrassed. Wonder what old Tomás is up to?

He turned back to the old desk. Tomás's face was returning to its normal color. It looked like he was going to pretend I hadn't asked. He changed the subject.

"You know," Tomás said, "this was Nathan's desk for all the years he was sheriff here. When he first got elected, he ordered it by catalog from a company in Kansas City."

"Reckon if it could talk, it'd have some tales to tell." Whatever problems we faced in Cimarrón these days, odds were that Nathan Averill had faced tougher ones during his long tenure as sheriff.

Tomás eyed the desk wistfully. "I wish it could talk," he said. "Maybe it could tell us what to do."

Before either the desk or I could respond, the door to the office was flung open. Both Tomás and I nearly jumped out of our skins and reached for our pistols. We recognized Tom Figgs in time and did not shoot him. He barely seemed to notice.

"Sheriff, you might have to lock me up right now," he bellowed. "I think I'm about to commit a crime."

"I do not know what you are talking about, Tom," Tomás said in a calm but puzzled tone. "It would help if you lowered your voice and explained what you mean."

Lowering his voice only slightly, he said, "I mean I'm a hair's breath away from beatin' the hell out of a couple of polecats. I'm just not sure which one to start with."

Surprisingly under the circumstances, Tomás responded with just the slightest hint of a smile. "Tom, wanting is not a crime."

Figgs paced around the room for a moment. He muttered under his breath as he began to calm down and get a grip on himself. "I'm sorry boys, I'm just so mad I don't know what to do."

I'd been observing this and decided to join in the fun. "Here's a thought, Tom. If you wait, all the officers of the law in these parts will have headed east for Springer. Then you can pretty much do what you want and get away with it." I smiled. "Reckon that's what I'd do if I's you."

He looked at me and Tomás and shook his head. He stood there silent for a moment and a small grin appeared on his lips. "All right, fellas, I get it. This hits you even harder than it hits me. If you can stay calm, I reckon I can, too." He took a deep breath. "Have you figured out your next moves?"

"Come sit down, Tom."

Tomás gestured to one of the sturdy

wooden chairs by his desk, which was now empty save for two shot glasses and a ceramic mug. Figgs sauntered over to it and sat down. I watched with interest followed by amazement as Tomás Marés reached in a drawer and pulled out a full bottle of whiskey. That sly rascal, he'd been holding out on me all along and I never had a clue. Sure enough, he poured a healthy measure of whiskey in the two glasses and the mug, turned to me, and said, "Why don't you join us, Deputy."

I bowed formally and said, "Why certainly, Sheriff Marés, my pleasure." I took a seat in the other wooden chair and looked over the two glasses and the mug. It appeared to me that the mug had the most whiskey in it, so I took it. He who hesitates gets the shortest shot of whiskey. This was starting to get interesting.

Tomás waited until we were both seated and had ahold of our whiskey, then raised his glass in a toast. *"Salud."*

Tom and I lifted our glasses, or in my case, mug, and echoed his sentiment. I wasn't sure what we were drinking to but I trusted my sheriff. I figured he'd come up with something that made sense. We tossed down the contents, set down our containers, and looked in anticipation at the sheriff.

Tomás looked back at us for a moment and then smiled. "As tempting as it is to beat the hell out of those puppets on the village council and their puppet masters, I have a better plan."

"I'm all ears, Sheriff," I said. I clinked my mug on the desk. "If you got a plan I ain't heard yet, I might need to be fortified a bit more to take it all in." Tomás filled us up again.

"That seems fair," he said pleasantly. He turned to Tom. "Do you think you could round up a few men to help you load all of this furniture and belongings into a wagon?"

Tom looked at him with a curious stare. "I expect I could."

"Excellent," Tomás said with enthusiasm. "Once you have it loaded, I would greatly appreciate it if you would then haul it over to Springer and unload it into the rat-infested building they are sticking us in."

"Rat-infested?" I sat up straight in my chair, nearly spilling my drink. I hadn't heard anything about rats. "Nobody said anything about rats."

Tomás smiled. "It is just an expression, Tommy. I really do not know if there are rats." His smile expanded. "Besides, four-legged rats are the least of our worries. We

239

have more to fear from the two-legged kind."

He was right; I was probably missing the big picture. Still, the thought of those nasty little critters with their twitchy whiskers and grubby little paws gave me the willies. With one last quiver of revulsion, I waved my hand at him, indicating that I'd figure out a way to deal with the problem.

"So, Sheriff," I said quizzically, "while Tom and his pals are movin' everything, what will you and me be doin'?"

He nodded at me. "Good question, Deputy Stallings." He took a small sip of his whiskey and set it back on his desk. "You and I will ride out to Jared's place, round up him and my younger brother, and head out in search of Jake Flynt and his gang, just like we had originally planned." He took another small sip of whiskey and sat back in his chair, looking very satisfied with himself.

"You sure you can do that, Sheriff?" Tom Figgs looked at Tomás a bit uneasily. "The official word from the council was that you were supposed to drop everything else and make this move." He scowled angrily. "Not that I agree with it, dammit. Still, that was how the vote shook out."

Tomás continued to smile. "Technically, what you say is true. However, I did not hear them say that I was the one who had to move it. As far as I am concerned, if I hand this job off to you, it is now taken care of. That leaves me free to return to the business of enforcing the law."

I felt the beginning of a grin. It just kept spreading until pretty soon I was beaming. This was my kind of law enforcement . . . insubordination in order to get results, playing with the rules. I couldn't believe it. Sheriff "by-the book" Marés was acting unconventional. I picked up my mug, downed the entire contents, and said, "What are we waitin' on? Let's get this party started."

CHAPTER 20

Patricio Baca feigned indifference as Jake Flynt saddled up his fine-looking sorrel horse. The morning sun was shining radiantly across the Big Empty and the morning dew was shimmering like diamonds. Pierce Keaton had cooked up a breakfast of beans along with the venison they'd stolen from the poor sodbuster Jake had tortured and murdered. Patricio could swear that the venison was tainted, as if the evil of the deed Flynt had perpetrated on the man had somehow found its way into the meat. The three cups of strong bitter coffee Patricio chugged down could not rid his mouth of the foul taste. He had to make his getaway. Today might provide his best chance.

"I'll be back in a while," Jake said to the group. "Keep a sharp eye out for those lawmen; I expect they're going to come at us hard after our last little spree."

"Where you off to, Jake? Need any company?" Keaton asked. Patricio Baca shook his head in disgust. Apparently the man had decided to sacrifice his dignity and self-respect to stay in the good graces of his homicidal boss. On reflection, Patricio figured he couldn't really blame him, but it didn't seem to be working.

Flynt stared at Keaton. It occurred to Patricio that he had seen more compassion in the eyes of a mountain lion he had once encountered on a trail. No, Keaton's strategy did not seem to be working.

"Did I say anything about wanting company, Pierce?" Jake continued to stare fixedly at Keaton who seemed to wilt under his intense gaze.

"Well, no," Pierce responded feebly.

"Did I tell you to stay here and keep a sharp eye out, Pierce?"

"Yeah, I reckon you did, Jake." Although there was still a chill in the morning air, Keaton was sweating.

"Then why in the hell would you ask me if I wanted your company?"

Keaton began wringing his hands apprehensively. Clearly, he had no idea how to respond to Jake. The tension was thick in the morning air. Baca took a couple of furtive steps backwards. In case there was shooting, he didn't want to catch a stray bullet. Although it didn't make any sense for Jake to shoot Keaton for such a minor transgression, Patricio had given up on the idea that Jake would do the logical thing. Shifting his weight to the balls of his feet, he waited to see what Pierce would say and how Jake would respond.

In a voice that sounded as if its owner was being strangled, Keaton said, "Just tryin' to be friendly, Jake. I meant no offense. Surely you see that."

Flynt continued staring at him for a few more anxious seconds. Patricio tensed in preparation to jump behind a rock. Jake burst into laughter. "Had you going there, didn't I, Pierce." He laughed out loud again. "I'm just having fun with you. No need to get in a dither."

Keaton staggered and Baca thought he might fall over in a faint. It took him a minute to recover before he could stand up straight again. He was trembling and his legs were wobbling. As he cast about for a response, Patricio thought he looked ready to cry.

Keaton composed himself sufficiently to speak. In a flat voice, he said, "Sure Jake, I knew that."

"That's right, Pierce, just having some fun." Jake smiled at the man for another moment and then his smile faded. It was replaced by that cold predatory look Patricio had likened in his mind to that of a mountain lion. "But next time you question me after I've given you an order, I'll kill you. Got it?"

Keaton was struck dumb by the brutality and malice in Flynt's voice. All he could do was nod.

"I'll see you fellas after awhile," Jake said as he turned his horse and trotted out of camp.

I've got to get out of this, Patricio thought. *This is a thunderstorm and it's about to rain down death and destruction on all our heads. I've got to do something.* He saw no reason to wait any longer. Walking over to where his bedroll lay in the dust, he gathered up his rifle and an ammunition belt, which he slung over his shoulder. As he headed over to begin saddling his horse, he noticed Pierce Keaton sitting on a rock. His breath was coming in shallow gasps and he was trembling like an aspen leaf in the wind. He looked up as Baca walked by.

"My God, Patricio." He croaked. "My God. What are we gonna do? He's either gonna kill us or get us killed, one or the other. Reckon it won't much matter which way, once we're dead."

"He may kill you, *pendejo*," Baca said contemptuously, "but he ain't gonna kill me. I ain't waitin' around for that to happen."

Ignoring the insult, Keaton looked at Baca. "What you plannin' on doin', Patricio?"

"That's none of your business, you damn coward. You let him treat you like a dog, then you come back grovelin' at his feet, ready to lick his boots. You make me sick." Baca continued toward his horse.

Dave Atkins had kept his distance during the interaction between Jake and Pierce Keaton. Now, he stood up and walked over to Patricio as he began saddling up.

"No disrespect, Patricio," he said in a level voice, "but I kinda think it is our business. If you got a plan that could help us get out of this tangle, I want to hear it."

While Baca didn't much like Dave Atkins, he did respect him. At least he was a man who would stand up for himself, which was more than he could say for Pierce Keaton. He figured he didn't have anything to lose by telling Atkins about his plan. Once he was done, he planned to hightail it for Colorado anyway. He doubted, and in fact, sincerely hoped he would never see either of these two hombrés again. What they did once he'd done the deed was not his problem.

"What the hell," he said, "I can tell you. It'll be over soon enough." He glanced over at Keaton with a look of scorn. "I'm gonna do what you're not man enough to do. I'm gonna take Jake Flynt down like the mad dog he is. I'm gonna put a bullet in him." He neglected to mention that if things went according to his plan, the bullet would go into Jake's back.

Keaton slowly rose to his feet. A sly grin appeared on his mouth. "Sure you are, Patricio," he said, his voice containing a hint of mockery. "Why don't you stop back by here on your way north and let us know how it turns out." He turned and walked over to the fire to pour himself another cup of coffee.

Patricio glared after the man. He contemplated putting a bullet in his back, just to warm up for the real event with Jake Flynt. Thinking about how far sound carried off the mesa, he decided against it. No sense alerting Jake that something was amiss. It crossed his mind that it might be gratifying to stop back by the camp and shoot Pierce Keaton on his way up to Colorado. He doubted that Dave Atkins would interfere. He had no love for the little weasel. He would see how he felt after he'd taken care of Flynt.

He finished saddling his horse, stuck his Winchester in the scabbard, and mounted. He nodded to Atkins, who nodded back. As he rode away, he hollered back over his shoulder at Keaton. "You better hope I don't come back this way, *pendejo*. The world would be a better place without your filthy carcass in it."

Dave Atkins went about rolling up his bedroll, studiously ignoring Pierce Keaton. Keaton stared after Baca's receding figure for a few moments, then turned toward where Atkins knelt.

"Reckon we've seen the last of Patricio Baca," he said.

Patricio located the tracks of Jake's horse and urged his horse into a gentle trot. He'd followed Jake Flynt before and had a good idea of the pace the man kept. He was pretty sure that he could proceed with relative stealth and still overtake the man within the hour. That gave him a little time to contemplate his next moves once Jake Flynt had been dispatched. He was mulling over whether or not he wanted to go back and kill Pierce Keaton when the click of the hammer cocking on a pistol snapped him out of his reverie.

"Hello, Patricio." The voice of Jake Flynt came from back over Baca's left shoulder, slightly off the trail. "Kinda funny seeing you here. If I didn't know better, I'd say you're following me."

"Ah, no, boss, I just thought I'd ride out and scout around a bit." Patricio could feel the spit drying up in his mouth. "Can't be too careful with that damn deputy lurkin' about." He started to turn in the saddle to see where the outlaw leader was standing.

"Don't make a move or I'll put a bullet clean through you," Jake barked.

Patricio stopped in mid-turn. "Sure Jake, whatever you say," he said in as calm a voice as he could manage given the pounding of his heart. He was jumpy about the direction this encounter was headed. He knew he had to do something to turn it around. "Hey, it's me, Jake," he said. "Ain't no need for gunplay."

"That's where you're wrong, Patricio." Jake spoke in an agreeable voice, almost as if they were discussing what they'd had for breakfast. Baca was not fooled by his boss's cordial manner. He was in deep trouble.

"Hey, now, Jake, what in blazes are you talkin' about?" He knew he had to talk fast or die. "I'm on your side, you know that.

We've rode together for a long time. Why you want to treat me like this?"

"Why do I want to treat you like this?" Jake sounded as if he was contemplating the choice of a second cup of coffee rather than making the decision of whether a man would live or die. "You know, you could answer your own question, Patricio, if you were honest with me." He paused for a long moment. Baca began to sweat liberally. "Do you want to be honest with me, Patricio?"

This was even worse than he'd thought. It sounded like Flynt knew something about what he'd been up to. Of course, he could just be fishing for information, trying to trick him into tipping his hand.

"Jake, I don't know what you're talkin' about. I've always been straight with you." He was feeling frantic. "Hombré, think about it. I've always done everything you asked me to do."

"Oh, I have thought about it, Patricio," Jake said in a calm, measured tone. "I've thought about it a lot." The calmer he sounded, the more terrified Baca became. "I've thought about it so much that I've been keeping a close eye on you." He chuckled. "Didn't know that, did you."

Feeling like he was losing his grip and not knowing what else to do, Baca tried to bluff and bluster his way through. "I can't believe you don't trust me, Jake," he said indignantly. "After all we've been through together, seems like I've earned some respect."

Jake's pistol boomed and Baca felt a bullet whiz by his ear. His horse began to prance and hop. He thought briefly about making a break for it but he knew what kind of shot Jake Flynt was. Jake had intentionally missed with this shot. He doubted he would miss with the next. He knew his chances of making a clean getaway were almost nil. He got his mount calmed down.

"Why do you keep on lying to me, Patricio? You talk about respect and then you lie to me." Flynt began to laugh. In Baca's experience, this was never a good sign since what typically amused him was the death of another human being.

"I ain't lyin', Jake." He was breathing rapidly now. "That's all I got to say. I ain't lyin'."

"Another lie," Flynt said with a chuckle. "It just goes on and on." Baca looked around in desperation, searching for a way out. He saw none. He knew he was a dead man.

"I've followed you, Patricio, like I said. I saw you meet with Burr. You've made a deal with the devil." His voice lowered and Baca

251

strained to hear him. "Did you think you could outsmart me, Patricio? Didn't you know that I'd always be two moves ahead of you?" Baca heard Flynt chuckle. There was no warmth in it. "Now you get to meet the devil for real."

It's over, Patricio Baca thought. *I should have taken off when I first thought about it.*

Jake Flynt's pistol boomed twice. Patricio's gelding sprinted away in terror. When it had galloped about twenty yards, Patricio Baca's lifeless body fell to the ground. The horse wisely kept running.

Things moved pretty fast after me, Tomás and old Tom Figgs came up with our scheme and sealed the deal with a drink . . . or two. Tom left to recruit a few boys to help him cart everything over to Springer. Tomás planned to talk to his daddy and invite him to join us. Although Miguel was getting on in years, I'd been on enough cattle drives with him to know he was a man you could count on in a tight spot. I figured since we were heading out to track one of the most dangerous men the New Mexico Territory had ever seen, chances are we were likely to find ourselves in a tight spot before too long.

Tomás told me to ride out to tell Jared

and Estévan the game was back on. I immediately headed out, feeling giddy and a bit light-headed from our celebratory drinks. I don't usually drink in the mornings and generally stay away from hard liquor altogether. After about an hour on the trail, the giddiness disappeared. Unfortunately, it was replaced with a dull, throbbing ache just above my right eyebrow. Made me kind of wish we'd just shook hands and clapped each other on the back to celebrate rather than having our drink . . . or two.

I was hoping Jared and Estévan weren't out checking cows in one of the far-flung sections of the ranch. We needed to get moving as soon as we could and I didn't want to have to waste time tracking them down. As I rode up to the ranch house, I saw that good fortune was smiling on me. Jared and Estévan were at the corral shoring it up where one of the horses had apparently been scratching its back and busted through a fence post. I chuckled at the sight of Estévan Marés fixing fence. There was a time where he would have seen such work as beneath his dignity.

"Mornin', boys, have you seen any real cowboys around?"

Jared stood up from his labors and wiped

253

sweat from his forehead. "Mornin' Deputy Stallings, what brings you out our way?"

In spite of the dull pain in my head, I grinned. "I've come to save young Estévan here from engaging in work that's beneath his station in life."

Estévan sent me a sour look. Jared looked at me curiously and asked, "What are you talkin' about, Tommy?"

"Things have taken an unexpected turn, Jared," I said. "Looks like we're goin' after Jake Flynt and his minions after all. We need y'all to ride with us."

Estévan straightened up and smiled. "That *is* good news, Tommy. I thought you were just blowing hot air as usual."

I ignored his jibe. After all, I'd started messing with him first and had it coming. "If you want to run into the house for your guns, I'll explain it to you." I dismounted and prepared to follow them in.

"I am a bit bamboozled," Jared said. "Last time we saw you, everything had gone to hell with the council voting to move the sheriff's office immediately. What changed?"

I laughed as we walked toward the house. "What changed was that Estévan's strait-laced brother decided to hell with the rules, he's gonna do his job in spite of those no-good *cabrónes* on the council that were throwin' obstacles in his way."

As we stepped up on the porch, Eleanor Delaney came out to greet me. "Good morning Tommy, seems like I've seen more of you recently than I have in months. What brings you back so soon?"

"Mornin', Miss Eleanor," I said politely, doffing my hat and bowing slightly. "I was just explainin' to your husband and his fence-mendin' sidekick . . ." I couldn't help it; I had to get one more shot in at Estévan . . . "that it looks like we need their help chasin' down Jake Flynt after all."

"Really," she said. "That's certainly different than the last news I'd heard from Jared. What happened?"

Jared and Estévan were paying close attention as they went about gathering up the assortment of firearms they would need for our task. I have to admit, I was looking forward to telling them about the change in Tomás Marés's approach to law enforcement.

"Tomás may have gotten into a patch of locoweed," I said. "He decided to ignore those poltroons on the village council and do his job. We're goin' after Jake Flynt."

With an inquisitive look, Jared asked, "What's he doin' about movin' his office? It sounded to me like the council was pretty clear that he needed to get that taken care of right away." His look changed from inquisitive to apprehensive. "He could lose his job over this."

"Tom Figgs is taking care of the move," I said with a smirk. "They told him to move his office; they didn't tell him how to do it." I couldn't quit grinning. "I don't know what's gotten into Tomás but I sure am enjoin' it."

"Oh, I believe I know what's gotten into him," Eleanor said with a knowing smile.

We all turned to stare at her. When she didn't show any sign of continuing, Jared asked, "What are you talkin' about, Eleanor, darlin'?" We all looked at her, somewhat baffled by her statement.

She looked around at the befuddled expressions the three of us wore and laughed. "You really don't know, do you? None of you knows." She laughed louder.

"What?" Jared asked with a hint of impatience in his voice. "What is it we don't know?"

It took her a moment to calm herself down sufficiently to respond. After a moment, she said, "Tomás has lately come under the influence of a genuine firebrand." She paused dramatically, savoring our bewilderment. "That would, of course, be

Maria Suazo."

Three jaws dropped. Three cowboys were struck dumb. Estévan was the first to find his voice. With a mixture of perplexity and suspicion, he asked, "What do you mean when you say that Maria is influencing my brother? How is she doing that?"

Now it was Eleanor's turn to smirk. "Why, Tomás and Maria are courting. I thought everyone knew."

Chapter 21

John Burr was as on edge as he could ever remember being in his life. With any luck, a huge weight would be lifted off his shoulders if Patricio Baca delivered on his promise to dispose of Jake Flynt. Of course, there was still the matter of locating that damned Irishman and recovering the money from the robbery. However, that seemed like a relatively minor issue compared to the palpable sense of menace that surrounded Jake Flynt. Garrett O'Donnell had proven to be difficult to find but Burr was certain it was only a matter of time before they ran him down. Jake, on the other hand, was a loaded powder keg. The question wasn't *if* he was going to go off, it was *when* it would happen and *who* would be killed in the explosion.

The early afternoon sun was beating down on Burr's head and he was sweating profusely as he waited for Baca to show up at their rendezvous spot. *Well, more accurately, it was mine and Jake's rendezvous spot,* he thought with a touch of dark humor. *Jake will most likely be having a little rendezvous with his maker. I don't think he'll have any need for this spot any longer.* He'd left his buckboard in the shade of one of the large cottonwood trees and was pacing back and forth restlessly. He knew there was really no way to predict when, or even if, Baca would show up. Still, he had a feeling that all of the twists and turns in this crooked path he was on were about to straighten out.

Burr was hopeful that Baca would be willing to stick around and lead the hunt for O'Donnell. From his conversation with Baca, he had the sense that the man was more than ready to leave this part of the country for a good long while. He figured he would have to sweeten the financial incentive in order to convince him to stay long enough to see the job through to the end. He was counting on Jake's not having been honest with his gang about the deal they had in place. He planned to tell Baca that he'd offered Jake a quarter share of the money instead of the third that he'd promised. He could then "generously" offer Baca a third share of the adjusted amount and be no worse off.

With his mind thus occupied, he jumped at the sound of a branch snapping behind him. He quickly turned, expecting to see Patricio Baca. Instead, he saw Jake Flynt. He blinked several times, trying to alter the image his brain was registering. It didn't work. Jake Flynt still stood about ten paces in front of him, holding a broken cottonwood branch and smiling.

"Surprised to see me, brother John?" Jake carelessly tossed away the two pieces of dead wood. Burr couldn't help but notice that his right hand gravitated to rest just above the pistol on his right hip. Apparently, events had not transpired as Burr had expected they would. He would have to bluff his way through it.

"Jesus, Jake, I've told you how I hate it when you sneak up on me that way."

Flynt stared at the banker for a moment. It's hard to imagine both fire and ice emanating from the same source but Burr could swear he saw both in Jake's eyes. He felt as if someone had punched him in the pit of his stomach and he found it difficult to breathe.

Jake broke the silence. "And I told you that nobody double-crosses Jake Flynt." He smiled at Burr but the fire and ice remained in his eyes. "It seems to me that we had this conversation at this same spot not all that long ago, John."

He knows, Burr thought with dread. *What on God's green earth went wrong with Baca's plan?* Burr felt a small spark of relief at the knowledge he carried a Colt .41 derringer in his right jacket pocket. He would have to invent a believable pretext for taking something out of his pocket. He spoke in as matter-of-fact manner as he was able, given the circumstances.

"Jake, I understood you fine the other day. We're family. I'm not here to take advantage of you, I've got good news." He smiled and hoped it was convincing. "I've a telegram in my pocket that contains information on the whereabouts of Garrett O'Donnell. If you'll let me, I'll show you."

"If you as much as twitch, I'll shoot you down in your tracks," Jake said sharply.

Burr held his hands out to his sides. "Sure Jake, whatever you say. What's happened that's got you so spooked? I swear, I came out here to give you good news. Now you're treating me like I'm the enemy."

A bitter chuckle escaped from Flynt's lips. "That's a good one, John. I appreciate a good laugh."

Trying desperately to remain calm, Burr replied, "Glad I could be a source of amuse-

261

ment for you, Jake." Burr felt as if his cravat was strangling him. He wished he'd thought to loosen it on the way out. "Now, can we dispense with all the theatrics and take care of business?"

"Good idea, John," Jake said agreeably. "Let's take care of business." He pulled his pistol out of the holster. "Truth be told, you were expecting to be doing business with Patricio Baca, weren't you."

Oh God, he knows. Burr frantically tried to come up with a plausible story that might explain his conversation with Baca. His mind raced and came up with nothing. Funny, he was, as a rule, adept at manipulating the truth to his advantage. This time, however, he could think of no way to glibly twist the facts. A small voice in his mind stated the simple fact . . . *you're about to die.* Another part of his mind argued that there was some way out of this. The small voice got louder. *You're about to die!*

"Don't know what to say, do you?" Jake seemed to sense Burr's growing realization of his impending doom. "That's unusual for you, isn't it, John?" He chuckled. "Don't waste any more time playing the 'family card.' We both know what that's worth."

Burr wanted desperately to say something, anything, to alter the inevitable upshot of this dispute. He had used words to destroy others in the past. Now, words failed him. He watched as Jake raised his pistol and aimed at the center of his chest. Burr felt a warm wetness spread across the crotch of his trousers. His last thought was, *that really is unfair!*

The echo of the shot reverberated across the valley. Jake watched as John Burr slumped to the ground. He waited in case a second shot was needed. After a minute, it became obvious to him that it wouldn't be. He walked over to where the banker lay in the dust. "Goodbye *brother,*" he said, his voice a savage growl. "I told you . . . nobody double-crosses Jake Flynt." He emptied his gun into the body.

"You're tellin' me you had no idea about this, that your brother said not one word to you about Maria?" I couldn't believe Estévan hadn't known about his brother's romance. Estévan shrugged as we rode at a steady trot towards Cimarrón.

"He did not say a word to me, Tommy." He shook his head, plainly hurt by his brother's secretiveness. "I knew my brother kept his business to himself but I would never have thought he would have kept a secret like this from me."

Jared chuckled. "Talk about playin' your cards close to your vest."

I was a little miffed that he hadn't taken me into his confidence. After all, I was his deputy. More than that, we were partners. Together, we put our lives on the line for the citizens of Colfax County. It seems like the least he could have done was fill me in on his love life. Right after that thought crossed my mind, I realized how stupid it was. Tomás Marés wasn't the sort of fella to share details about his personal life with other folks. Apparently, Maria Suazo wasn't so picky about who she told. I bet Mollie knows. I bet she's gonna gloat when I bring it up, too. Dang.

"Eleanor said she thought everyone knew about this," I said. "Who else you reckon knows?"

Jared pondered the question for a moment. "Christy is bound to know. I'll bet your Mollie knows, too, Tommy."

"Dang," I repeated, only this time out loud.

"And of course," Jared began with a hint of mischief in his voice, "your mama knows, Estévan."

"There is no way," Estévan said animatedly. "My brother would never share this kind of thing with our mama. I don't think she knows."

I looked at Jared. We grinned at each other. "You want to tell him, Tommy?" Jared nodded at me, giving me the go-ahead. I nodded back politely and turned towards Estévan.

"Your mama *always* knows, Estévan."

He looked flummoxed and started to dispute the statement. He stopped himself, realizing the ludicrousness of his protest. He shrugged. "You are right, Tommy Stallings. I hate to admit it but you are right."

As we rode along in silence for a few moments, I contemplated what seemed to me to be the recent erratic behavior of Tomás Marés. First, he flouts the village council, now this. I said, "Old Tomás is full of surprises these days. I wonder what else he's got up his sleeve."

"I do wonder how he wants to handle this hunt for Jake Flynt," Jared replied seriously. "I've been so confounded about his situation with Maria that I almost forgot about the reason we're ridin' into town."

I agreed, we'd let this whole romance thing throw us plumb off stride. I hadn't really told the boys what we knew, or at least suspected, about where Jake and his gang might be hiding out. This seemed like a good time to fill them in.

"I been trackin' these egg-suckin' skunks all over the Big Empty for weeks. I'd narrowed it down to them either bein' holed up on Buckhorn Mesa or Black Mesa 'cause their tracks generally led in that direction. A couple of nights ago . . ." I stopped, confused about the time frame. "Dang it, we been goin' at it so hard, I can't keep straight exactly when things happened." I shook my head to clear the dust out of it. "Anyway, the other night, I snuck up onto Buckhorn Mesa, thinkin' I might surprise 'em. Place was deserted."

"There was no sign of them at all?" Estévan asked.

"Oh, no, they'd been there all right," I said. "I reckon they moved after Charlie Atkins tried to ambush me. They didn't know if I'd gotten the skinny on where they were hidin' out from him. I guess they didn't want to take any chances. They'd moved their camp. I'm bettin' they just slid on over to Black Mesa."

"I doubt they knew the ambush had gone wrong until Charlie didn't show back up after a couple of days," Jared said. "Reckon they figured somethin' was amiss and lit out. You must've just missed 'em." I could see the wheels turning as Jared calculated the time. "I mean, you must have really just

266

missed 'em," he mused. "Sounds like you were up there within a couple of days from when the ambush happened."

"That's right, I been wonderin' about the same thing." I nodded. "That place didn't have the feel like someone had just taken off in a big old tear. It felt like they'd been gone a while." I paused, pondering the evidence. "That don't make sense, unless . . ." I stopped again.

Jared finished my thought for me. "It don't make sense unless they knew about the ambush goin' wrong pretty quick after it happened. That would mean they have an inside source of information."

"Damn that John Burr!" I exploded. "That lily-livered backstabber has been tippin' them off."

Estévan had been listening up to that point. "Why Burr? Why not Wallace? You say you think he is involved as well."

"I can't say for sure, other than it don't feel right," I replied. "For one thing, I don't see Bill Wallace wantin' to get that close to a killer like Jake Flynt. I don't think he wants to get his hands bloody."

"I think Tommy's right about that," Jared said. "Wallace is an opportunist, a little bit shady, but he don't strike me as havin' the stomach for all the violence Flynt's been perpetratin' on everybody." With a grim look, he said, "Burr, on the other hand, is downright cold-blooded. He's the one."

Estévan tipped his hat back and asked, "So what do we do about this?"

I chuckled. I couldn't help it. "Well, before this last couple of days, I'd have said we need to have more evidence 'cause that's what your big brother would say. Now, I don't have any notion as to what he'll do or say. Hell, like as not he might just light a shuck on down to the bank and arrest John Burr on general principle." We had a good laugh at that one.

"We're gonna have to run this by Tomás," Jared said in a more serious tone. "All kiddin' aside, you know Tomás is gonna want to do this by the book. Right now, we don't really have any way to connect Burr and Wallace to Flynt. Without that, it'd be hard to prove anything. You know Tomás is gonna want to be sure he can make the charges stick if any of this mess ever comes to a trial."

"You're right," I said. "It'll be the second thing we mention to Tomás . . ." I paused dramatically, "*after* we hoorah him about this secret romance of his."

"Because it is none of your damn business,

that is why I did not tell you."

Tomás Marés doesn't use cuss words. The fact that he had just done so in response to Estévan's question kind of tipped me off that maybe we'd taken this secret romance joshing about as far as we should. Either Estévan hadn't figured this out yet or else he didn't care. He kept going.

"If it is none of my business . . . your only brother . . . why is it that everyone else in town seems to know about it?"

"*Everyone* in town does not know about it. This is a personal matter. It is not the concern of anyone but me and . . ." Tomás tripped over his tongue at this point. Apparently, he wasn't even ready to mention Maria Suazo's name out loud in our presence. He made, in my opinion, a rather clumsy recovery. "The concern of me and the lady." I wouldn't have thought he could've turned a brighter shade of red but he did. This only seemed to spur his younger brother on.

"How can you say that everyone does not know? Eleanor Delaney knows. Miss Christy knows. Mollie Stallings knows." Estévan paused and then fired his best shot. "Our own mother knows."

Tomás exploded. "That is a vicious lie! She does *not* know." He stood up and clenched his fists. I thought he was going to jump on his brother and pound him into the floor of his now rather empty office. Apparently, Estévan must have had a similar thought. From previous experience, it seemed he'd learned that there was a point beyond which he dared not push his usually mild-mannered brother. Reckon he figured out he'd reached that point. He put up his hands in a placating gesture. Well, it looked placating to me. Maybe he was getting ready to defend himself.

"As you wish, brother," he said. I guess he couldn't just leave it alone. "Still," he said obstinately, "it seems that you could have told me. I am your brother, after all."

Sparks seemed to fly from Tomás's eyes. He took a step toward Estévan. Thankfully, Jared stepped in to save Estévan's hide. He stood up and extended his hand towards his friend.

"Well, even though you weren't quite ready for us to know about this, now that we do, I'd like to offer my congratulations," Jared said. "You and Maria are two of the finest people I know. You both deserve to be happy. I wish you the best."

Tomás stopped his murderous advance on his brother and turned toward Jared. For a moment, he seemed unsure of what to do. Then, with a look of disgust in mine and

Estévan's direction, he took Jared's hand and shook it firmly.

"*Muchas gracias, amigo.* I am thankful at least one of you is behaving like an adult today."

That stung. I'd only made fun of him a little and then I backed off, unlike his kid brother. It was unfair of him to lump me in with Estévan and his childish behavior. I decided to take the high road. "I'm happy for both of y'all too, Tomás," I said. "Mollie's gonna rib me somethin' fierce, though." I saw some of the fire begin to return to his eyes and decided retreat was the safer course of action. "It don't really matter all that much. I forgive you."

He looked at me in stunned amazement. I was afraid I'd really said the wrong thing and he was going to vent his spleen on me. I prepared to retreat . . . well, to run like hell . . . if he came at me. It turned out it wasn't necessary. He burst out laughing. I breathed a sigh.

Shaking his head, he said, "Then, by all means, I apologize for putting you in an uncomfortable position by not sharing my most personal secret with you. What was I thinking?"

"That's all right," I said magnanimously. "No need to beat yourself up about it."

Jared joined in the laughter at that point. I wasn't sure what was so goldarned funny but I figured it was better than the situation a moment ago when Tomás was ready to rip my lungs out. Tomás took a couple of deep breaths. He said, "If it is all right with you jokers, we should turn our attention to more serious matters."

CHAPTER 22

Once Tomás's feathers smoothed out we set about getting organized. None of us knew how long this was going to take so we figured we needed supplies for a week or thereabouts. That meant I would take Gentry, which was all right. She doesn't mind hard work. Miguel Marés had a mule that we would use to help pack the rest of what we'd need. I knew Gentry would not be happy about this everyday, run-of-the-mill mule going along on the trip. As I've mentioned before, she prefers not to fraternize with other mules, finding them too common for her tastes. That means I'll have to ride up front and lead Gentry, with Miguel and his ordinary mule in the back so she doesn't have to look at him. The things I do for my mule.

We were going to be leaving later in the day than we would have liked but I think all of us just wanted to get started. It being summer, we could count on a couple more hours of daylight. We figured we could make five miles towards Springer before we stopped to set up camp for the night. That would give us a chance to talk strategy and come up with a plan.

When I got to the house, I stopped in to tell Mollie the posse was back on again. She'd just gotten back from the schoolhouse and appeared to be straightening up our little place.

"Mollie," I said so she would know it was me and not some intruder coming in the front door, "I'm here to get some supplies." When I walked in, she stopped her puttering and came straight over to me. She gave me a big hug and to my surprise and delight, her eyes were dry.

"I know, Tommy," she said matter-of-factly, "I heard the news from Anita Marés. She says you're gonna ride after Jake Flynt."

"We're dang sure goin' after that dirty scoundrel. I think his day of reckonin' is here."

Mollie sighed deeply, which made me nervous. I changed the subject.

"You know what I just found out, honey?" I walked over and smoothed out one side of the bed cover. "Tomás Marés is courtin' Maria Suazo. Don't that beat all?"

My lovely Irish wife stood straight up across the bed from me and said, "Jaysus and Mary, Tommy Stallings, are you just now finding out about that? I thought everyone knew that. Where in blazes have you been?"

"Some of us have been out chasin' dangerous outlaws and ain't had time for this sort of nonsense. Some of us know to mind our own business and not poke about in other people's personal lives, too." I tried to look wounded and dignified at the same time. "And by the way, I would appreciate it if at least some of the time you would call me Tom. I ain't a kid, you know."

Mollie stared at me for a moment and then laughed so hard she couldn't speak. When she finally caught her breath, she said, "You know, Tommy . . ." With a giggle, she stopped and started over. "You know, *Tom,*" she said, emphasizing the word "Tom" in a deeper voice and managing to make it sound undignified, which just defeated the whole purpose, "we probably wouldn't tease you as often if you didn't make it so much fun."

I guess I looked baffled because she burst into another round of laughter. Since my wounded and dignified approach hadn't worked, I decided to go with sarcasm.

"Well, I'm just so pleased that I can bring so much joy and fun into the lives of my family and friends."

Again, she got a handle on her laughter. Shaking her head and still chuckling a little, she came over and embraced me again. "Oh, Tommy Stallings, I love you. You go catch some outlaws and then come back to me."

We got away midafternoon and kept up a steady trot. There wasn't much talk among us as we wanted to get as far as we could before we camped for the night. I figure we'd made about eight miles when we came to a little grove of cottonwood trees by a stream. It was dusk and this looked like as good a place to spend the night as we were likely to find. We unsaddled our horses and Jared and Estévan led them over to water while me and Miguel unpacked our mules. I took Gentry a few paces off to the east and pointed her in the opposite direction so she wouldn't have to look at Miguel's run-of-the-mill mule. Once I got her unloaded, I took her down to the stream where she got a long drink. The boys had already hobbled the horses and I took care of Gentry before turning her loose. She immediately moved over by Rusty, ignoring

Miguel's mule. Miguel said his name was Pedro. I don't think Gentry much cared.

Tomás had started a fire and was heating up some coffee. He threw on a pot of beans and when everything was ready, we had sat down to eat beans, drink coffee, and gnaw on some jerky.

"For a man that owns a café, Miguel," I said, looking to get a little conversation going, "you sure prepared a meager meal for us tonight. I'd have expected better."

"I would have thought you would have learned not to complain about my cooking after these years on the trail with me, Tommy." Miguel hadn't eaten much and was rolling a cigarette. You have to wonder about a cook who doesn't eat his cooking. "Maybe I will give you one of my special biscuits in the morning."

Miguel had been known to slip a rock on the plate of a cowboy who complained about his meal. I quickly made amends. "I don't know what I was thinkin', Miguel. These beans are startin' to taste better and better."

"That is what I thought you would say."

Tomás had apparently had enough of our casual conversation and was ready to get down to business. "We need to decide what we will do in the morning. Tommy, how do you think we should proceed?"

Since I was the one who'd done the most legwork in this deal, I appreciated that Tomás asked for my ideas first. "Well, I already told you I'd searched Buckhorn Mesa and they had moved their camp. I'm pretty doggone sure they're camped on top of Black Mesa now." I took off my Stetson and scratched my head. "I figure that's where we'll head tomorrow. My question isn't where we're goin', it's how we're gonna approach it. If we ride right up on 'em, we'll be sittin' ducks."

Jared weighed in. "You snuck up Buckhorn Mesa at night, didn't you, Tommy?"

"I did," I said, "and I reckon we could try that. There was only one of me then and there are five of us. The odds of makin' some noise that alerts them are a lot higher."

"You're right about that," Jared said thoughtfully. "I got the beginnin' of an idea, though. It would take a little longer but I think it makes sense."

Miguel took the coffee pot from the fire and refilled cups all around. When he was done, he said, "Let us hear this idea, Jared."

Jared nodded. "Here's what I'm thinkin'. Tomorrow, we head for Black Mesa to get in the general vicinity. We're careful not to get too close."

"Somewhere outside of rifle range sounds good to me." Estévan chuckled.

"That's right," Jared replied and we noticed he wasn't laughing. This was serious business, no matter how we joshed about it to lighten the mood. "When the sun sets tomorrow, I think three of us should make our way around to the north side of Black Mesa and creep up to just below the rim."

"All right," Tomás said carefully. "What will the other two be doing?"

"When the sun comes up day after tomorrow, the other two will ride in the direction of Black Mesa, makin' sure that if anyone is up on top, they can see 'em." Jared pounded his right fist into the palm of his left hand. "The tricky part is that you want 'em to see you but you don't want 'em to shoot you. The distance has got to be accurate."

Miguel sat forward. "I think I see what you have in mind. While the two down below draw their attention, the other three sneak up to the top and get the drop on them. *¿Es verdad?*"

"That's it," Jared responded with an emphatic nod. "We create a distraction and give the three up top a chance to sneak up on those murderin' varmints."

Everyone looked expectantly at Tomás. He's the sheriff and it's his call in the end.

He sat quietly, obviously pondering the possibilities. Then he nodded in accord. "I think it is a good plan, Jared. We will have to figure out some of the details tomorrow before we arrive, such as who will be the two decoys. Still, I think it could work . . . as long as they are up there."

"There sure ain't no guarantees about that," I shrugged. "If they're out traipsin' about, I reckon we'll have to come up with another plan."

"I agree," Tomás said. "Now, I think we should turn in so we are rested in the morning."

I had some trouble falling asleep. I swear I must have turned over at least a hundred times during the night. I finished off the night facing east and it was the first rays of the sun as it rose up out of the Big Empty that woke me. That and the cawing of crows.

Estévan was still buried deep in his bedroll. I could hear snores emerging from beneath his blankets and I laughed. Everyone else was up. Miguel had started the fire and the coffee was hot. I picked up my cup and walked over to where they were squatting.

"What's with the crows? Looks like somethin' died." I held out my cup and Miguel poured me a shot of joe.

"We were just talkin' about that," Jared said. "We figured we'd finish our coffee, then go see what it is."

"Might be a mountain lion got himself a deer, couldn't finish it off," I said as I sipped the scalding coffee.

"Better a deer than a stray calf," Tomás said. "Ranchers hate it when a big cat gets a taste for their calves."

"Since I'm one of the ranchers," Jared chuckled, "I can tell you for dang sure that I hate it." His smile faded. "We got predators of a different kind to worry about today."

"That we do," I said. "Y'all done any more talkin' about who gets to be the decoys that get shot at and who gets to sneak up on those lowlife curs?"

"I am thinking that all of us will likely have the chance to be shot at before this is done," Tomás said. "It occurs to me, Tommy, that it would be logical for you to be one of the decoys since you are the one who has been tracking them for all this time. They would expect to see you and you will draw their attention."

That thought had occurred to me, too. "It does make sense, I reckon," I said reluctantly. "I sure hate to miss out on bein' there when we arrest those boys . . . or shoot 'em, whichever comes first."

"Well, you never know," Jared said. "Once we come up over the north side of that mesa, some of them boys may take off down the south side. If they do, they could wind up right in your lap."

"Who do you want ridin' with me, Tomás?" I had an idea what he was going to say. I sure didn't want to be the one to bring it up.

Tomás glanced out the corner of his eye at his father, squatting by the fire. "We need someone who is steady. Someone who is a good shot with a rifle."

Miguel poked at the coals with a stick, stirring the fire to warm up the coffee. "What you mean is that you do not need someone who is old and slow climbing up the mesa with you in the middle of the night."

"That is not what I said, Papa," Tomás protested.

"That's what he means, though." Estévan had crawled out of his bedroll and wandered over to the fire. "And he is right, Papa. You are the oldest and you do not move like you once did. This is no time for letting pride get in the way. We have a job to do."

I was a little nervous that Miguel was go-

ing to raise a ruckus even though what Estévan had said was plain old common sense.
Tomás was right, too. Miguel was a fine shot
with a rifle. He might not move as quick as
he used to but he was dang sure steady in a
fight. He wasn't going to get spooked and
take off.

Miguel Marés stared at his two sons for a
moment. He tossed the last bit of coffee
and grounds that remained in his cup on
the fire. When he looked up at them again,
he had a trace of a smile on his lips. "Sometimes I forget that I am getting old and that
my two sons are grown men. One speaks
carefully so as not to offend, the other blurts
out the truth in plain language." He reached
down and refilled his cup. "You are both
right. I will ride with Tommy Stallings and
try to distract these *cabrónes* so that you
can sneak up and get the drop on them."

We glanced around at each other, wondering if Miguel had any more to say on the
subject. Apparently, he was done. He began
heating up some beans and tortillas for our
breakfast. After a minute, Tomás cleared his
throat.

"I think we should have Tommy and Papa
ride ahead so that they arrive in sight of
Black Mesa later in the day. We want it to
seem as if they have been searching and are

preparing to make camp. That should keep the attention of Jake and his men on them, both as the sun goes down and again, when it comes up the next morning."

"Are you thinkin' the rest of us will follow behind so we get there after dark?" Jared asked.

"Sí," said Tomás. "We can rest up here for awhile longer, then slip in under cover of darkness. There will be enough moonlight that we will not miss Black Mesa. If we go around the northwest corner, we should be able to find a path to the top."

"What is the plan for the morning?" Miguel asked. "What do you want Tommy and me to do to attract their attention?"

"I reckon they'll have their eyes on you as soon as there's light enough to see," Jared said. "I think you should get up and act like you normally would, drink some coffee, eat some beans. Once the sun is up over the horizon pretty good, I think you should ride towards the mesa. The sun will be in their eyes." He grinned. "They'll be less likely to shoot you that way." He paused, considering. His grin got wider. "Or less likely to hit you, at least."

"Thanks for thinkin' about our welfare," I said with just a touch of sarcasm.

"No probléma," Tomás said. I couldn't

tell if he was joking or serious. "We will give you time to begin heading in their direction before we make our move." He turned to Jared and Estévan. "Once we raise our heads above the rim of the mesa, we must be prepared to move right away."

"Who do we think will be waiting for us up there?" Estévan spoke casually, almost as if he were planning to go to a church social rather than a showdown with dangerous outlaws.

"They've lost a couple," I said. "We know that. I reckon Pierce Keaton, Hank Andrews, Dave Atkins, and Patricio Baca are still with Jake."

"Any chance Garrett O'Donnell is with them?" Estévan asked as he helped himself to some beans on a tortilla."

"Naw," I said. "Garrett took off the other direction when they robbed the bank in Cimarrón. They been lookin' hard for him and I don't think it's 'cause they want to invite him to rejoin the gang. If they did find him, he's either in a shallow grave or he's food for the crows. Of those other three, the one you got to look out for the most is Baca. He's a pretty bad hombré himself."

"*Es verdad,*" Tomás said. "We will try to take them alive. I have a strong feeling that they will not allow that to happen." He took a deep breath. "We must be prepared to shoot to kill. That is what they will be prepared to do."

I reckon we all knew that. Still, with Tomás saying it right out loud, it sorta put a damper on the conversation. It didn't seem like there was much else to say on the subject. I took a sip of my coffee and glanced over to where the crows were still circling.

"Speakin' of food for crows," I said, "I think I'll mosey over and see what those birds over there are chowin' down on."

Nobody said anything so I set my cup down on a log and walked over in the direction of the little grove of cottonwoods to see what I could find. What I found sure enough changed our plans.

Garrett O'Donnell didn't hear what Tommy Stallings had to say about Jake and the boys looking hard for him. If he had, he would have agreed with his conclusion that they weren't interested in inviting him to rejoin them. He'd had some close calls where he'd seen Pierce Keaton or Dave Atkins out making a wide circle, obviously searching for him. Once, he'd seen Jake Flynt, although he didn't know if his purpose was to look for him. Mercifully, Jake had been a good distance away and Garrett had only recognized him because of his big white-legged sorrel. He'd fired a shot in Flynt's direction before taking off even though he was out of range. He felt like he was walking on a very narrow limb, letting Flynt and his gang catch sight of him from enough of a distance that he had time to lose himself in that Big Empty. If he got too close or wasn't able to cover his tracks, the game would be over.

As worried as he was about the gang on his trail, he was more worried about his wife and children. Jake had already sent one man to his ranch to look for him. That man was now lying in a shallow grave. It was lucky that he'd been there and had managed to get the upper hand. There was no doubt that they would try again. He prayed that whoever Jake sent didn't pick up Ashleen's trail. He suspected that the longer he was able to evade the gang, the madder Jake was getting.

Garrett had good reason to believe that the word "mad" . . . as in loco . . . was the right word. The other day, he'd heard shots. After waiting a couple of hours, he'd snuck over to where he'd heard the shots and found the body of Patricio Baca. At least he thought it was Baca. The man's face had been beaten and torn, most likely with the barrel of a pistol. It looked like raw meat.

If Flynt was torturing and murdering the members of his own gang, Garrett knew he wouldn't hesitate to kill the wife and children of a man whom he thought had betrayed him. *Sure and it's a fact,* Garrett thought. *I did betray him.* The thought of what Flynt would do to Ashleen and the children before he killed them terrified Garrett.

It's past time for us to clear out of this God-forsaken country. I only hope Ashleen and the wee ones are well on up the trail towards Raton.

CHAPTER 23

"What do we do now?" Estévan turned away from the body on which the crows had been feasting for some time. The body of John Burr was barely recognizable.

No one answered immediately. These men were no strangers to swift and merciless death, yet there was something repugnant and evil at work here. Not for the first time, they were comparing Jake Flynt to a rabid wolf in their minds. Courts and trials be damned, there was only one cure for this sickness. Tomás spoke.

"We need to ride back to town and speak with Bill Wallace. I think his life is in danger as well." In a grim tone, he continued. "I also think we might use this to pressure him into telling us what their scheme is."

"Why do we give a donkey's damn about Bill Wallace?" I was having trouble understanding Tomás's point of view on this deal. "If he is in danger, he put himself there.

Seems like that'd be his problem, not ours. Our problem is trackin' down this loco outlaw before he kills any more innocent folks."

"Even if Bill Wallace is involved in this, that does not mean the law will not protect him," Tomás said quietly. "I would remind you that he has a wife and daughter as well."

He had me there. Whatever Wallace may or may not have done, his wife and child didn't deserve to have this wickedness rain down on them.

I nodded grudgingly. "I see your point. Somebody needs to take Burr's body back to town and talk to Wallace. That don't mean all of us have to go. If you and Miguel did that job, Jared, Estévan, and me could stay on Flynt's trail."

After a moment's deliberation, Tomás said, "I think not. I want us all to return to town now. We can leave again together in the morning to track down Flynt. If you are right about where he is hiding out, there will not be a great deal of tracking to do. We will follow the same plan as before."

For a moment, I was puzzled, then it dawned on me. "You're worried that three of us ain't enough to take Jake, aren't you?"

Estévan spoke up. "Brother, there is not a man alive that the three of us cannot take.

You are being an old woman."

I could see Tomás bristle for a brief instant before his calm nature reasserted itself. "I believe you could take Flynt, brother. I also think that with only three of you, the chances that one or more of you would be killed are too great to risk. It will be less risky with the five of us. He will still be out there tomorrow."

Jared, who had been quiet up to this point, joined in. "I kinda have to agree with Estévan on this one, Tomás. We all knew what we were gettin' into when we agreed to ride along. I hate to give that devil an extra day to hide out."

Tomás looked around at his compadres . . . his father and brother, his former trail boss, Jared Delaney, and of course, me. He squared his shoulders. I got this feeling that a subtle and immeasurable shift was occurring. When he spoke, it was in a calm voice full of authority.

"I appreciate your thoughts on this matter. I, however, am the sheriff. It is my call. We all return to Cimarrón now."

Well there you go. Atta boy, Sheriff Marés.

We rigged a travois from the trunks of some young piñons and Miguel's bedroll to carry Burr's body. Being drug up the trail like that made for a pretty bumpy ride and it didn't look any too comfortable. I doubted John Burr would do any complaining. As we made our way back towards Cimarrón, we talked about Burr's murder.

"I wonder why Flynt decided to kill the man," Estévan said. "If they were partners like we thought, it does not make sense."

"It makes sense if Flynt thought that Burr was trying to double-cross him," Tomás replied. "This makes me think that their plan is coming unraveled. I suspect that John Burr was trying to pull something underhanded in order to save himself. Jake must have found out about it."

"That's why I think you're right about talkin' to Bill Wallace," Jared said. "I believe he's in this deal up to his ears. He can tell us everything if he has a notion to do it. I think he might do that if he's scared enough."

Miguel Marés had been quiet up to that point. "I think Señor Wallace has very good reason to be scared. This Jake Flynt, he is a killer. He does not seem to care who he murders. All they have to do is get in his way and he cuts them down." Miguel made the sign of a cross.

My mind was racing as I contemplated what Miguel had said. "Tomás, I'm worried about Garrett O'Donnell's family. If Jake has the nerve to kill John Burr, I see no reason why he would extend any mercy to the family of another man who betrayed him."

Tomás nodded grimly. "I am afraid you may be right, Tommy. She and her little ones may be in grave danger."

I made a snap decision. That's one of the things I'm known for. "We're travelin' pretty slow cause we're haulin' Burr's body. Why don't I swing by O'Donnell's ranch to warn Mrs. O'Donnell? I think me and old Rusty can hotfoot it over there and still get to town about the time y'all make it in."

Tomás made a snap decision of his own. "Go. Do not waste any time."

I didn't need any more encouragement. Leaving Gentry with Tomás and the others, I spurred old Rusty. We peeled off headed southwest towards Garrett O'Donnell's scraggly little patch of land. As we swung into a good lope, I thought about what I should say to Mrs. O'Donnell. I hoped that telling her she and her children were in mortal danger would convince her to come into town with me. I wasn't sure what to do if she refused. It didn't take me long, it being only about five miles away. Nothing was stirring as I pulled up to the ragged little house, which made me doggone nervous. I sure hoped I wasn't too late.

"Mrs. O'Donnell," I called out. "Are you there? You all right?"

There was no answer. I glanced over to the stable and noticed that it appeared to be empty. I thought back to my recent visit a few days ago . . . was it a few days or a week? I'm almost sure there'd been a buggy by the dilapidated old barn. It wasn't there now. I walked up to the front door and knocked loudly.

"Halloo the house."

No response. I waited a couple more seconds, then took a deep breath and threw open the door. It took a moment for my eyes to adjust to the lower light in the house. Once they did, I could see that it was empty. Ashleen O'Donnell and her children were gone.

I took a closer look around and saw no sign of a struggle. I reckon if Jake had come for her, the woman would've fought to protect her little ones. There would have been blood, too, probably a lot of it. Mercifully, there was none of that. I couldn't bear to think of those little children being murdered by a monster like Jake Flynt. It looked like Ashleen O'Donnell had flown. Now,

where in the Big Empty was Garrett O'Donnell?

CHAPTER 24

"I have no idea what you're talking about," Bill Wallace replied indignantly. "Furthermore, you've got a lot of nerve accusing an elected official of this kind of reprehensible behavior."

Tomás had decided to bring Jared along with him when he questioned Wallace. Jared was well-respected and he thought it might smooth things a bit. They looked at each other and Jared rolled his eyes slightly. After all their experience with crooked politicians, the suggestion that they might be above reproach and suspicion was ludicrous. Tomás chose to ignore this.

"Señor Wallace, I mean no disrespect. We do not, however, have the time to engage in this little game. Jake Flynt has murdered your partner, John Burr, and we are afraid that you may be next on his list. The only way to keep yourself and your family safe is to cooperate with us."

When Tomás mentioned the potential danger to his family, Bill Wallace began to sweat. He reached out for the cup of coffee on his desk. His hand was shaking so badly that he spilled half its contents when he picked it up. Warily, he glanced out the window of his office as if he expected to see Jake Flynt ride up at any second. He turned back to Tomás and Jared.

"I want a deal," he said to Tomás.

Tomás stared at him. "A deal?"

"Yes," he said, "a deal. If I tell you everything, I want my part in this kept quiet."

Tomás looked over at Jared. "I think we are done here." He rose and started walking toward the door.

"Wait," Wallace said in a panicky voice. "Just wait." He pulled out a handkerchief and wiped his face. "Okay, maybe not that kind of deal. If I help you, though, you have to take that into consideration if any of this comes to trial." He took another swipe at his face with the handkerchief. "I'm in danger if I tell you details about the arrangement between John Burr and Jake Flynt. If he finds out I talked to you, Jake will kill me."

Jared couldn't contain himself. He laughed. "Bill, you don't seem to have a handle on the situation. Jake already believes you double-crossed him. He's probably already plannin' to kill you, and most likely your family, too. We're your only chance. You got nothin' to deal with."

Wallace glared at the two of them for a long moment. Then he seemed to fold in on himself. He lowered his head and put his hand over his eyes. Jared thought he saw a teardrop fall on the desk although it might have been sweat. His nose appeared to be running as well. "I didn't mean for it to come to this," Wallace said. "I'm not a bad man."

"That may well be," Tomás said firmly. "That is not for me to judge, however. If you survive this, you will have your day in court. If you are not a bad man, as you say, you will help us now so we can stop this monster Flynt before he kills anyone else. That will help towards making you a more sympathetic figure when it is time for you to be judged."

Bill Wallace told them the whole sordid story. Once he started talking, Bill Wallace had quite a tale to tell.

"Can you believe Flynt and Burr were from the same family?" I shook my head in amazement. "What are the odds?"

"It is strange, is it not?" Tomás was sitting

in a chair in his nearly empty office. I was standing because there was only the one chair. Everything else had already been carted over to Springer.

"So Wallace admitted to you that John Burr put the squeeze on Garrett O'Donnell, promisin' to forgive the mortgage on his dusty little ranch if he blew the bank vault? Or else he would foreclose and O'Donnell would lose everything?" I still wasn't certain that Tomás recognized the distinction between Garrett and the rest of that outlaw band.

"Sí," Tomás said, "along with a great deal more information, he did tell me that." He looked sideways at me. "What are you trying to say, Deputy?"

I hate it when Tomás pulls rank on me. Of course, he does outrank me but that's beside the point. "What I'm tryin' to say, Sheriff . . ." I drug out the word so he'd know I was being cheeky. "I'm sayin' that Garrett O'Donnell ain't one of 'em. He ain't an outlaw like the rest of those *banditos.*"

Tomás was tired and he had a lot of hard work ahead of him. He was probably tired of me being cheeky with him, too. Anyway, he took a tone with me. "As I have told you more than once, Deputy, Garrett O'Donnell took part in a bank robbery. That makes him a bank robber. Why he did this thing and whether he should be treated with leniency is not something you or I get to determine. That is left to a judge and jury. *Comprendé?*"

I was tired, too. I sparked back at him pretty hard. "I comprendé all right. I comprendé that it ain't fair. What about doin' what's right? What about givin' people justice?"

Tomás smacked the flat of his hand hard on his leg. It sounded like the crack of a bullwhip. "You are out of line, Deputy. Don't talk to me about what is fair. My family was living on this land for more than a hundred years when you gringos arrived. You call us beaners and pepper bellies and you use your laws to take our land. What do you know about what is fair?"

"I know it damn sure wasn't fair that my parents and sister got wiped out by Indians. You ain't the only one that's had hard things to deal with."

Jared had been standing off to the side listening as our discussion escalated into a heated conflict. Now he stepped up and said, "Maybe both y'all ought to cool down and take a deep breath. We got a dangerous job ahead of us; we can't waste time fightin' with each other."

Tomás stared at me for another moment and then he took Jared's advice. He took a deep breath and I could see the tension drain out of him. "I am sorry, Tommy," he said. "I understand you went through terrible times when you were a child. It was not right of me to suggest that you do not know about the injustice that life sometimes deals us."

I felt like an idiot. Tomás Marés was my amigo and I respected him as much as any man I knew. "Well, I'm sorry, too. There ain't no doubt you and your family have gotten a dirty deal. If it was up to me, I'd hang every one of those no-good politicians that have stolen your land." I took my own deep breath. "I ain't never called you a beaner, neither, and I'd pummel anyone I heard sayin' such nonsense."

Tomás looked at me for another moment, then he shook his head and laughed. "I think you continue to miss my point that you are not allowed to take the law into your own hands. Still, I appreciate that you stand with me." He looked over at Jared. "We need a plan to protect Bill Wallace so we can get back on the trail of that monster, Flynt."

"Your father and Estévan are with Wallace

301

right now," Jared said. "What do you have in mind?"

"I will ask Tom Figgs to find another good man to stand guard on Wallace. I am not sure he deserves our protection," Tomás said and stared at me pointedly, "but that is not for me to decide. Under the law, he will be protected."

All right, I get it. I don't necessarily agree, but I get it. We're not going to take the law into our own hands. I was tired of arguing with Tomás anyway. Once we get this whole situation with Jake Flynt taken care of, maybe I'll try again. Sometimes he's just so durned hardheaded.

I was ready to get back on the trail and whatever I could do to get things moving, I was willing. I'd even play messenger boy and go track down Tom Figgs. "You want me to go find Tom?"

"Sí, that would help."

Jake shaded his eyes from the midmorning sun as he gazed out on the Big Empty from a boulder atop Black Mesa. He pondered his next move. He hadn't even been sure he'd wanted to return to what was left of his gang. The killing fever had been on him something fierce and it was all he could do not to gun down Pierce Keaton. It was lucky for Keaton that he'd had the good sense not to ask about Patricio Baca. *If he'd said a word, I expect I would have shot him down where he stood.* He'd gotten a grip on himself, though, and let the worthless cull live another day. You never know, Keaton might come in handy. Still, he intended to kill the man before he took off for Colorado. The notion caused him to smile.

Colorado was indeed where he planned to end up when he'd tied up the remaining loose ends in this wreck. A man with a pocket full of money could have a mighty fine time in a place like Denver. Thinking about money spoiled the good mood he'd been experiencing as he thought about shooting Pierce Keaton. If he didn't catch up with that damned Irishman and get his money back, this whole thing would have been a waste of his time . . . well, except for all the folks he'd gotten to torture and kill. There was that.

Thinking about torture and killing led to his contemplating what he would do to O'Donnell when he caught up with him. He would die a slow and agonizing death, that's for sure. It occurred to Jake that if he took the time to head over to that little scraggly piece of land the Irishman referred to as a ranch, he could rape and murder his wife. Probably in front of the children. Then he could torture them as well. Of course, doing it the other way around had possibilities as well. He imagined the agonizing screams of the mother as she saw her children tortured and killed. *Yes,* he thought, *that could work.*

He smiled as he thought how Garrett O'Donnell would react to this news. He'd have to be sure to pay close attention to all the particulars so he could describe the scene in detail. He figured that would be even more painful than the physical torture he planned to inflict on the man. Yes, he had a plan.

Jake hopped down from his perch on the boulder and walked over to saddle his big sorrel horse. As he passed by the campfire where Keaton and Atkins squatted, he said, "I'll be back late this afternoon. You boys keep watch here. Tomorrow, we're gonna find us an Irishman."

Dave Atkins just nodded. Pierce Keaton bounced up and followed Jake over to his horse.

"Where you headed now, Jake?" Keaton was careful not to ask him if he wanted any company. Apparently, he had learned that much from his previous experience.

Jake shook his head as he saddled up and

tried to keep a grip on his temper. He needed Keaton if they were going to make an all-out push to find O'Donnell the next day. He comforted himself with the thought of how much he was going to enjoy the look on Pierce's face when he looked down the barrel of Jake's pistol and realized that he was about to meet his maker.

"If I want you to know where I'm going," Jake said with exaggerated patience, "I'll tell you." There was a menacing edge in his voice. "If I don't tell you, Pierce, what do you think that means?"

Keaton obviously recognized the warning signs and started backing away toward the campfire. "Ruh . . . reckon I don't need to know," he sputtered.

"That's right." Jake turned, mounted up, and rode off to the southwest.

O'Donnell's place was a little more than ten miles away. Jake took his time, contemplating what he would do to Mrs. O'Donnell and her children when he caught them. He wanted to get back to camp before dark for a good night's sleep before the hunt for Garrett O'Donnell tomorrow. That meant he couldn't linger too long. As he considered his window of opportunity, he urged his horse into a trot. Better to get there a little sooner so he had more time to enjoy his work. There were some things he didn't like to rush.

It was just after midday when he crested the hill that looked down on the O'Donnell ranch. *Ranch,* he thought scornfully. This dried up patch of ground could barely support a flock of chickens, much less a herd of cattle. *The conceit of some people.* He rode slowly down toward the front gate, taking his time so as not to spook Mrs. O'Donnell. The closer he got, the more obvious it was that the place was deserted. The animals were gone and the place had an empty look about it.

Jake could feel his fury rising up as he realized his murderous urges were not to be satisfied. With difficulty, he tamped the feelings down. He needed to understand what this meant and to do so, he needed a clear head. If she and the children weren't here, where in the hell were they? It's possible that damned deputy had anticipated his move and brought them into town where they would be safe. That would be bad enough. The other possibility was that O'Donnell himself had taken his family and cleared out of the area. If they made a clean getaway, his chances of recovering the money were gone. That was unacceptable. He figured he'd have to track them down.

With John Burr gone, he didn't have a reliable source of information in Cimarrón. He wasn't sure he could count on Bill Wallace to tell him what he needed to know and, anyway, he didn't have a plan in place for contacting the man. He might be better off starting with the assumption that the O'Donnell family had taken off on their own. When he considered the possibility of catching up with all of them at once, he smiled. He might have to postpone the gratification of his sadistic urges until he tracked them down but that would make it all the more pleasurable when he caught them.

Flynt rode back toward the gate, studying the ground. Sure enough, he saw the unmistakable tracks of buckboard wheels leading out to the east. If they'd been heading to town, they would have likely turned to the west. Jake was frustrated by this turn of events. He needed to find the Irishman and his family, get the money, and take his revenge on them before heading north to Colorado. He was puzzled that they appeared to be headed for the northern plains of Texas. Still, he figured he would follow the tracks until he needed to turn off to return to his hideout. *I'll catch that filthy Mick if I have to follow him all the way across Texas.*

He would need Keaton and Atkins with him in order to manage both Garrett O'Donnell and his wife. Knowing their children were in mortal danger could make them difficult to subdue. He figured they could pick up the tracks first thing in the morning. A woman and children traveling in a buckboard would not likely make good time. If luck was with him and they'd only left the day before, he could probably catch up with them tomorrow by late afternoon. For a moment, he sat in the saddle and savored the thought of dealing with the entire O'Donnell family at once.

CHAPTER 25

I tracked down Tom Figgs and he followed me back to what was left of the sheriff's office. I filled him in on the way about Tomás's plan to take Bill Wallace into protective custody. Although he was disappointed that he wasn't invited to our little party with Jake Flynt and his boys, he took consolation in the fact that he would have the chance to see Mayor Wallace disgraced and humiliated.

"I knew he was up to somethin'," Tom said enthusiastically. "It just didn't make any sense what he was doin' otherwise." He laughed out loud.

"You're sure enjoyin' yourself, Tom," I observed. "If I didn't know any better, I might suspect that the mayor was not one of your favorite folks in our little village."

"If you thought that," he said, "you'd be right. He always acted uppity, like he was better than the rest of us. Turns out he was just a crook all along, no better than them damned no-good Santa Fe Ring devils we been buttin' heads with. I'm glad to see him get his comeuppance."

I was having difficulty enjoying the downfall of Mayor Wallace as much as Tom was. I'm not sure I would have said it out loud but I tended to agree with Wallace's own assessment of himself. I didn't see him as a bad man; he just wasn't overloaded with character. Once a person decides that what they want is more important than the needs of other folks, they can slide down that slippery slope that leads to poor choices.

I was starting to feel pretty self-righteous until it occurred to me that this little bit of wisdom probably applied to me as well as it did to Bill Wallace. I sure don't seem to have much trouble losing sight of what's important to the people in my life that matter to me when I get my mind set on something. I ain't much of one for reading the Bible but I do remember old Reverend Richardson, rest his soul, telling me once that there's a passage in there about letting the person who ain't never done nothing wrong throw the first stone. Reckon I'll hold off chunking rocks at Bill Wallace.

"He got greedy, Tom," I said. "I think it blinded him to what's really important. He's got a nice wife and a daughter who looks like she might grow up into a fine young lady one day." I shook my head, feeling kind of sad for Wallace. "After it's too late, seems like he's thinkin' about how all this is gonna change their lives."

Figgs frowned. "I guess I wasn't thinkin' about his family. You're right, too. His wife is a nice lady. Reckon she sees things in her husband the rest of us don't see."

I laughed out loud. "You could probably say the same thing about your wife and mine, too. They know us for who we really are and they love us in spite of it, bless their hearts."

"Ain't that the God's truth," Figgs replied. He grinned. "All right, I won't be too hard on old Mr. Bill Wallace. Reckon he ain't the devil himself after all."

A goose must have walked over my grave because a chill went down my spine when Tom Figgs said that. "No he ain't, Tom, but I'll tell you who might be. That Jake Flynt might just be the devil himself." I shuddered. "You ain't had the pleasure of seeing his handiwork. I got a pretty strong stomach but he's done things that sicken me. And he might be comin' after that nice wife and sweet daughter of Bill Wallace. That's what you got to keep right up in the front of your mind."

Tom nodded. "It don't sound like a job for just one man. I think maybe I'll ask my father-in-law and my two brothers-in-law to help me out with this deal."

"I think that's a real fine idea, Tom," I said grimly.

We walked into what was left of the sheriff's office and found Tomás and Jared waiting for us. They were leaning against a wall and deep in conversation.

"*Hola,* Tom," Tomás said. "Thank you for helping out. Did Deputy Stallings tell you what I need?"

"He did," Tom said. "He made it pretty clear this ain't no ordinary outlaw we're dealin' with here. I'm gonna get my family to help me with lookin' after Wallace and his ladies."

"That is a wise decision," Tomás replied. "This Flynt is a monster. I think he is half loco as well. There is no telling what he will do. The only thing you can count on is that he will try to kill you if he comes. Do not ask questions. Shoot to kill."

"So that's the way it is then." Figgs took a deep breath. "Might be a good idea for you to deputize me and my in-laws. If we're gonna do any killin', it'd be best if it was

312

official."

"You are right. Can you round them up quickly? We need to be on the trail as soon as we can."

"I'll get 'em right now," Figgs said. He paused and looked around at the men in the sheriff's office. "You know what I appreciate? When I tell 'em what I need 'em to do, they'll start complainin'. Thing is, while they're complainin', they'll be grabbin' their rifles. That's two things I can count on 'em for. They'll always complain and they'll always be there when I need 'em." He grinned. "Reckon the second part makes it easier to live with the first part." He walked out of the office.

Tomás turned to me and said, "Perhaps you might want to speak with your wife briefly before we leave. I am sure she would appreciate it."

I thought about my realization earlier that I didn't pay nearly enough attention to the wants and needs of the people in my life. Since there was no one in my life who was more important to me than my dear, sweet Mollie, I figured I might follow Tomás's advice. "That's a good idea, Sheriff. Reckon I'll do that right now."

As I turned to walk out, Jared asked Tomás, "Anybody you want to have a little talk with, Tomás?" I looked back, curious as to how he would respond.

A ghost of a smile appeared on his lips. "Perhaps I will go say goodbye to . . . someone."

He followed me out the door. We stood there awkwardly in front of his shell of an office. I sure didn't feel like teasing him any more about being sweet on Maria Suazo. None of us knew if we'd make it through this deal with Jake Flynt alive. I didn't begrudge Tomás his chance to be happy with a pretty special lady. Still, I didn't know quite what to say. I figured I ought to give it a shot though. Like I said, we didn't know if we would survive the next twenty-four hours. Reckon I'd rather say something stupid than regret not saying anything at all.

"Tomás, I'm sorry I hoorahed you about Maria. No matter how many times Mollie blisters my hide when she's upset, I thank the stars that she's in my life." It occurred to me that mentioning the hide blistering might not have been the best thing I could have done. It's a part of marriage but it's sure not my favorite part. "I guess what I'm sayin' is that she makes me want to be a better man." Now I was really getting embarrassed. "Not that you asked my opinion, of course."

"Tommy, I have learned that whether I ask for your opinion or not, you will most likely give it to me. In this case, your opinion is most appreciated. I agree that having Mollie in your life has made you a better man." He grinned. "I even think that the hide blistering helps with that." He turned and headed towards his parents' café. "I will see you back here shortly."

I was still thinking about his last comment about the hide blistering helping make me a better man so I didn't really have much else to say to him as he walked away. He was probably right. That didn't mean I had to like it, though. I took a deep breath, turned, and headed toward the schoolhouse. I was hoping I would get a loving reception from my wife rather than a hide blistering.

I knocked on the door and entered the school. During the summer, the ranch kids worked with their families so there weren't as many students present. Christy was working with a small group of young readers while Mollie appeared to be helping a girl with her penmanship. They both looked up when I came in.

"Do you mind if I have a word with my wife, Miss Christy?" I belatedly took off my hat. Sometimes I forget my manners.

Christy nodded assent and went back to teaching her young charges. Mollie spoke softly to the girl with whom she was working and then followed me as I walked outside.

"What's wrong?" she asked anxiously. "Did you capture Flynt?"

"A lot's happened," I said quietly. I didn't know how to squeeze all that had occurred during the past day into a short explanation without starting a long conversation. "I don't have time to tell you about all of it. We had to come back to town to take care of some unexpected business. The thing is, we still got to go after Jake Flynt." I shook my head in consternation. I had so much I wanted to say but I didn't really have the words to say it. Dang, sometimes being a cowboy ain't easy. "I just wanted to tell you . . . well, the thing is, I wanted to say . . . well heck, Mollie, I just wanted to tell you I love you. That's all."

She teared up and grabbed me in a fierce embrace. As she nestled against my chest, she said, "That'll do, Tommy Stallings."

When I got back to the empty sheriff's office, Jared was waiting there, sitting patiently in the one chair. He raised his eyebrows and asked, "You get her done, cowboy?"

316

I had to laugh at myself. "Reckon I did," I said. "I'm learnin' that sometimes the less you say, the better."

Jared laughed as well. "That's probably one of the most important lessons a fella can learn if he wants to have a happy marriage. That and never criticize his wife's cookin'."

"Seems like you got that second part down, Mr. Delaney," I said with a grin. "Lucky it ain't as big a challenge for me as it is for you." Enough had been said about the awful cooking of Eleanor Delaney. No need for us to dwell on it any more.

Jared just shook his head. "No doubt about it." He stood up and stretched. "I expect Tom Figgs back here pretty quick. Once he arrives, we can take him and his boys over to Wallace's office to relieve Miguel and Estévan, then hit the trail."

"Probably ought to wait until Tomás is done sayin' his goodbyes, don't you figure?" I don't know what had come over me, I was feeling downright protective about Tomás. Maybe I was getting a bit carried away with this "concern for your fellow man" thing.

"Sure," Jared replied. "I don't reckon it'll take him that long, though. He knows we got a tough job ahead. We can't be done with it until we make a start on it. I expect he'll be here pretty quick."

While we waited, a thought occurred to me. As usual, I blurted it out.

"Jared, don't you get kinda tired of bein' the one we all count on to stand up when there's bad trouble?" This man had a wife and two kids. He'd faced down the worst kind of men on three previous occasions. For his troubles, he'd been shot on one occasion and lost a number of his closest friends to the evil poltroons who made up the Santa Fe Ring. "When does somebody else take the lead so you can just enjoy the life you're tryin' to make for yourself, Eleanor, and the kids?"

Jared frowned as he pondered the question. After a moment, he responded. "Do you know how many times Nathan Averill faced down bad hombrés during all the years he was sheriff?"

I thought about the question. "Well, no, I guess I got no idea."

Jared chuckled. "Neither does anyone else. We all lost count years ago because he did it so many times and with so little fuss. Do you know why he did it?"

"Reckon it was 'cause he was the sheriff?" I thought the answer seemed pretty obvious.

"You must not have known too many

318

sheriffs here in the New Mexico Territory, Tommy," Jared said with a wry grin. "Not only do most of 'em not stand up to the bad guys, most of 'em are in cahoots with them. Nathan was different."

"He was, at that," I said. "You know, he always kinda scared me. Not like he was gonna hurt me or somethin', just that I was afraid I wouldn't measure up in his eyes."

"I understand what you mean," Jared replied. "He's the kind of man you want to respect you. If you had his respect, it was worth more than gold."

"That's a fact. You didn't say why he stood up against the bad ones all those years, though."

"You're right, I didn't." He studied his hands as if the answer to the question could be found in them. "You know why he did it, Tommy? It's really simple. He did it because it was the right thing to do. Nothin' fancy, just that. He knew the difference between right and wrong. He was on the side of what was right and he despised what was wrong."

Thinking about the many discussions I'd had with Sheriff Tomás Marés about the difference between what was legal and what was justice, I was about to ask Jared's thoughts on that topic when Tomás walked through the door. He looked somber. That's another one of those words Mollie's taught me. I decided not to ask any questions or make any smart remarks. Jared, being an old hand at this business, took the same course.

"Any word from Tom Figgs?" Tomás asked.

"Naw," I said, "but we were just sayin' that he'd prob'ly be along directly."

It was clear that Tomás was anxious to get going. "As soon as he gets here, I want to go right over to Bill Wallace's office. We can explain to Bill what Tom will be doing, gather my father and brother, and be on the trail with no more delay."

I got the sense that Tomás was doing a slow burn. He didn't get mad all that often, although we'd had the chance to witness his anger a couple of times already today. There was something different about him now, though. It was almost like he had a fire in his eyes. I'd never seen him quite like this before.

"You sound like you're ready to get this business with Jake Flynt over with," I said carefully. "We want to be cautious, though. Not rush into somethin' without plannin' ahead."

Tomás arched an eyebrow at me. "Am I to assume you are telling me not to go off half-cocked?" He chuckled. "This advice comes from the master of going off half-cocked."

Well heck, I was a little bit offended. Here I was sharing some hard-earned wisdom with him and he makes fun of me.

"Laugh if you want," I said stiffly. "It's still good advice. Jake Flynt may be the most dangerous man we've ever faced. I heard your stories about what a bad hombré Morgan O'Bannon was. I got to meet Curt Barwick up close and personal . . . he shot me, in case you forgot. And that Daughtry fella that worked for old Tom Chapman was pretty bad himself. I'd rather face all three of 'em together than Jake Flynt."

Tomás looked at me and slowly nodded. "I am afraid you may be right, Tommy. This man, Flynt, seems to enjoy his killing even more than those other *cabrónes* you mentioned."

It looked to me like storm clouds were gathering over Tomás's head as we spoke. When he spoke again, there was an edge to his voice that I'd never heard from him before.

"When I see this man, I will shoot him down like the rabid dog he is."

His words hung in the air, filling it with

tension. It occurred to me that this would be the ultimate in taking the law into your own hands. Hadn't Sheriff Marés lectured me on any number of occasions about how wrong this was? I considered bringing this up. Upon reflection, and looking into his eyes that were burning like white-hot coals, I decided I'd just let it slide. Besides, I agreed with him . . . for once.

The door opened. We jumped. I guess we were ready for trouble. Luckily, it was just Tom Figgs along with his father-in-law, Jed Lowry, and his two sons, Randall and Rufus. I don't know why you would name your child Rufus. Sounds more like a name you'd give a dog. Rufus was a big boy, though, so I kept my thoughts to myself. Maybe I was getting the hang of this not going off half-cocked business.

Tomás walked over and extended his hand. "Thank you for coming, Señor Lowry. We really appreciate your help."

Lowry shook Tomás's hand and glanced over at his son-in-law. "Well," he drawled, "Tom's a pretty good boy. With all the free shoein' he's done for us, I reckon I owe him."

All four of the men carried Winchesters. Neither of the Lowry boys said anything but they looked like they were ready for any trouble that might come their way. With any luck, all the trouble would take place out in the Big Empty and Cimarrón would be spared any gunplay.

"Did Tom explain the situation to you?" Tomás asked.

"That he did," Jed Lowry replied. "Said we might just be sittin' around doin' nothin' for a few days or we might get to have us a little dust-up with an outlaw. Either way, we're supposed to be lookin' out for that weasel, Bill Wallace." A concerned look crossed Lowry's face. "Say, Sheriff, I was wonderin'. If that Flynt fella does manage to shoot Wallace in spite of us guardin' him, who's gonna take care of the undertakin'?"

I had to laugh, I couldn't help myself. Jed Lowry was known for being the most practical man in Colfax County. Leave it to him to wonder who would do the undertaking for the undertaker. I notice that Jared was chuckling, too.

Tomás replied in a serious voice. "Of all our concerns, Señor Lowry, that is far down the list. I am sure something can be arranged if it comes to that." He looked around at the men assembled in his empty office. He walked over to his desk and took a Bible out of the top drawer. "If you will all put your hands on the Bible, I will swear you in so you are official. I have no badges to give you."

"I kind of wanted a badge," Rufus said as they all reached in to put their hands on the Bible. "Oh, well."

The swearing in took less than a minute. Tomás put the Bible back in the desk and said, "I will take you to relieve my father and brother now. We need to move fast."

CHAPTER 26

When Jake returned to his camp late that afternoon, he found Dave Atkins cleaning his rifle and Pierce Keaton taking a siesta in the sparse shade of a scraggly piñon tree. Keaton didn't stir as Jake rode in, which made Jake suspect that he'd been drinking. He knew the man kept a flask in his saddlebags although he didn't know how he found a way to refill it. Making no effort at stealth, Jake dismounted and unsaddled his horse. Seeing that Keaton hadn't moved, he went over to the fire and picked up the coffee pot. He considered pouring the remains on Keaton but the pot was cold to the touch. He would relish pouring scalding coffee on the man. Cold coffee seemed dull, however. Instead, he grabbed Keaton's six-shooter out of the holster, which lay in the dirt a few feet away from the sleeping man. Walking to where Keaton lay, Jake bent over next to his ear and began banging on the coffee pot with the pistol.

Keaton almost came off the ground as he scrambled away from the horrible din. He uttered a terrible whining noise and looked around wildly, clearly disoriented.

"What the hell?" He managed to choke out the words in the midst of his whining and gurgling. It took him a moment to clear his head sufficiently to realize what Jake had done.

Jake laughed uproariously. "You should have seen yourself, Pierce. You was dancing around like a tarantula in a skillet."

Either because he wasn't yet fully awake or because his judgment was impaired, Keaton fired back at Flynt. "That ain't funny, Jake. That's a downright mean thing to do to a man."

Jake's laughter ended abruptly. He stared at Keaton for a moment. The man seemed to whither under his gaze. "Naw, Pierce, that wasn't mean. That was me having fun with you. If you want to see mean, say one more word to me."

Keaton turned pale. He clearly wanted to apologize for his outburst but apparently wasn't sure if that would qualify as the "one more word" that would bring down a hail of meanness. He stammered several unintelligible syllables before he was capable of speaking. "Sorry, Jake. Sorry. You startled me is all. I didn't mean nothin' by it, I swear."

Jake's mood, which had gone almost instantly from hilarity to homicidal, switched again to pleasant. Keaton and Atkins found this extremely disturbing. He walked back towards the fire pit with the coffee pot and said over his shoulder, "Oh, that's all right, Pierce. Forget about it."

Keaton reached down by his bedroll and retrieved his flask. He tipped it back and emptied it in one long swallow. When he'd sucked the last drop out of it, he gazed mournfully at it. He had no more whiskey and he had a strong feeling that he would desperately need some very soon. He reached down and replaced the flask in his saddlebags.

"Let me catch you boys up here," Jake said as he set the coffee pot back down by the fire pit. "We've had some interesting developments in regard to Garrett O'Donnell."

Dave Atkins set his rifle down and walked over to where Jake stood. Pierce Keaton also walked warily in Jake's direction. The man was unpredictable. There was no way of knowing when he might lash out and Keaton did not want to be on the receiving end when that happened.

"What's goin' on, Jake?" Atkins reached into his pocket and found a chew of tobacco. He placed some in his mouth and looked at Flynt expectantly.

"It seems like our Irish pigeons have flown the coop," he said cheerily. "I paid a little visit to their dung heap of a ranch earlier today. Guess what I found."

Keaton hesitated. He wasn't sure if it would annoy Jake more if he didn't say anything or if he did. He was momentarily in a quandary yet he seemed incapable of keeping his mouth shut. He said, "What?"

"Nothing," Jake said brightly, as if this was good news. "Absolutely nothing. It appears that the O'Donnell family has decided to move on to friendlier parts. They appear to have headed east."

Pierce couldn't help himself. "What are we gonna do, Jake?"

Flynt sighed deeply and shook his head. With exaggerated patience, he asked, "What do you suppose we're gonna do, Pierce?"

"Why, I reckon we're gonna follow 'em, Jake. They got the money after all."

"Very good, Pierce, very good," Jake said enthusiastically. Keaton was pleased to hear the accepting tone in Jake's voice. If he'd looked closer at his eyes, he might have noticed the glint of malice reflected there and would not have been so pleased.

Dave Atkins was more pragmatic in his approach. "We leavin' this afternoon, Jake?"

"I don't think so, Dave," Jake responded. "I doubt they'll be moving very fast. We have a nice camp set up here and I'd rather not have to make a new camp this evening if we don't find them right away. I think we'll have plenty of time to catch them if we leave in the morning."

"All right," Atkins said. He waited for a moment, then asked, "Anything else?"

"I think that's just about it for now, Dave," Jake said in his friendliest tone. "What I'd like you to do, though, is to get yourself up on that lookout rock and keep an eye peeled for any sign of that damn deputy. I'd hate to get sidetracked right now when we're so close to catching the Irishman."

Atkins said, "All right Jake, whatever you say." He went back to pick up his rifle and headed over to the boulder that overlooked the vast expanse of the Big Empty.

"You want me to do anything now, Jake?" Pierce Keaton danced around like a little kid hoping to please an angry parent. "Just let me know."

Jake stared at Keaton intently. "Not right now, Pierce. Don't worry, though; I've got big plans for you."

■ ■ ■ ■

"Yes, Mayor Wallace, we do have a plan for you," Tomás Marés said as respectfully as he could, given his distaste for the man. I don't believe I would have been half as polite if I'd been the one talking to him. Of course, Tomás tends to be more polite than me anyway, as a general rule. "Tom's father and one of his sons will guard you here at your office while Tom and his brother-in-law will be at your house to ensure the safety of your wife and daughter."

"Why can't I go home?" Wallace had a whiney tone to his voice that annoyed the heck out of me. "I want to be with my family."

I couldn't keep my mouth shut. I'm sure that's a surprise. "Mayor, you don't seem to get the drift here. You're under arrest. You don't get to choose where you go."

Tomás shot me a look. "Thank you, Deputy Stallings, I'll handle this." Turning back to Wallace, he said, "The deputy is essentially correct though, Mayor. You are in custody under suspicion of conspiring to commit a number of serious crimes. Even though our jail here is no longer official, I could still put you in one of the cells." He

330

paused to let the weight of that statement sink in. "Instead, I choose to keep you in protective custody here at your office. I hope you appreciate that I am treating you with leniency that you may not deserve. Let me be clear. You are not free to come and go as you please."

For a second, Wallace looked like he was going to raise a ruckus. I was kind of hoping he would. I remembered his pompous attitude last week when I asked him about hiring more deputies to help with my search for Jake and his gang. Reckon I understand now why he wasn't all that eager to go along with it.

Wallace opened his mouth as if he was about to give one of his politician's speeches. He closed it and seemed to consider his options. He opened it again but instead of words coming out, he let loose a big sigh. As the air poured out of him, he appeared to deflate. His shoulders drooped and his arms hung helplessly by his side.

"All right, Sheriff, I understand. Would it be too much to ask if Tom could take a message to my wife?"

Tomás looked at Tom Figgs. He shrugged. "Why not," Figgs said.

"Please tell her I'm sorry." Wallace looked so crestfallen and remorseful that I almost felt sorry for him. I felt sorry for his wife and daughter, sure enough.

"I'll tell 'em, Bill." Tom Figgs stepped up and looked Wallace in the eye. "And we'll keep 'em safe, too, don't you worry about it. Whatever trouble you wind up havin', you brought it on yourself. That ain't the case with them. They're innocent in all this business."

It took a moment before Wallace could meet Figgs's gaze. He was sweating and taking shallow breaths. With an effort he looked in the other man's eyes. "You're right, Tom, they are innocent. They deserve better than I've given them. I appreciate you looking after them."

I wish Bill Wallace would quit showing these signs of decency. I'd really just like to hate him. Reckon it's not that simple some times. Probably a lot of the time. Lord knows I've done some stupid things in my life that I regretted, but folks like Jared Delaney, Tomás Marés, and of course, my lovely Irish bride have forgiven me and offered me a chance for redemption. I suppose I could keep an open mind where Mr. Bill Wallace is concerned. I'd still like to kick him in his big fat behind, though, for all the trouble he's caused. Course, nobody ever said a swift kick in the butt couldn't be part of the pathway to redemption.

Tomás was ready to be on the trail. Turning to his father and brother, he said, "It is time for us to ride. Are you ready?"

"Perhaps I should say goodbye to your mother. Who knows how this will all turn out?" Miguel Marés looked pensive. Then he shrugged. "I do not suppose we can spare the time. Besides," he said, "she does not listen anyway." A tiny smile twitched at the edge of his mouth and a hint of mist appeared in his eye. "She does not listen . . . but she knows."

CHAPTER 27

We pushed our horses hard. We had a lot of ground to cover if we wanted to be in position while there was still daylight. We left Gentry and Miguel's mule behind, figuring for better or worse, this deal would be over pretty fast and we wouldn't need much in the way of supplies. There was no conversation for the first five miles or so. Reckon we were all deep in our own thoughts about what the next dawn would bring. I sure was. I can't say I've never been scared before. Heck, I've been plenty scared more times than I can count. This seemed different. I've had showdowns with evil men and mostly through sheer luck, I've survived. I knew they would show me no mercy. When the time came, I showed them none. Still, I always just thought of them as men like me. Maybe they had skill with a gun, maybe they were as mean as a snake, but they were just men. Jake Flynt seemed different.

I've heard that when wolves are on the hunt for calves or sheep, they sometimes get into a killing frenzy. I think that's how Jake is. He's got what some call bloodlust. He's like a vicious, wild predator that gets to killing and doesn't want to stop. He's not killing to save himself and he's not killing for a purpose such as robbing someone, he's killing for the pleasure he derives from it. I have a strong hunch that when the morning comes and we square off, he'll stand his ground and fight to the death, even if it would make more sense for him to run for it.

I understand I'm supposed to be the decoy in this little plan of ours, me and Miguel down below to distract Jake and his boys. I believe I may have to throw a kink in that loop when the time comes. I want to be close to Black Mesa when the shooting starts. My best friends in this world will be facing off with an evil predator. I'm not about to wait around down below to see how it all turns out.

I reckon Tomás must have been thinking about tomorrow morning as well. He'd been riding out front setting the pace. Now he slowed down enough for me to pull up alongside of him. He glanced over at me and seemed to be studying me. He knows me pretty well. He's probably figured out that I'm gonna have a mighty hard time staying out of the fray.

"You do understand that you are the decoy tomorrow, do you not?"

"We got a good plan, Sheriff," I said, avoiding answering his question directly. "You know how these plans go though, don't you? Once the shootin' starts, things spin out of control and all bets are off. You can count on me and Miguel to come a'runnin' if you need us."

He stared at me a little longer, then he shook his head. He knows how stubborn I am. I guess he figured there wasn't much point in saying a whole lot more. I had my instructions. How I followed them would depend on how this whole thing shook out. No matter what he said, I wasn't going to stand by doing nothing while he and the others were getting shot up.

He shook his head one more time and smiled. "I know that I can count on you, Tommy." His grin grew wider. "I can count on you to make me loco. But I can count on you to be there when others would run away." He nodded at me. "That means a great deal to me."

That was a heck of a speech coming from a fella who's usually pretty formal and plays his cards close to his vest. I didn't know quite what to say. It made me even more certain that when the shooting started, I'd be kicking old Rusty up the side of Black Mesa. We'd get through this thing or we'd die but we'd do it together. The time for talking was done. I ignored the part about me driving him loco and nodded back at him.

By late afternoon, we'd covered a lot of ground. Tomás slowed down and pulled up in a little grove of cottonwoods. We circled around him and surveyed the situation. We could see Black Mesa off to the east but I doubt anyone could see us, even if they had one of those spyglasses.

"We will split up here," he said. "Jared and Estévan will head north with me. The two of you continue east so that you come out in the open to the south of Black Mesa. Try to make some noise so that you attract their attention." He arched an eyebrow at me. "Do not ride too close, though. Dead decoys will do us no good."

I chuckled. "Me and Miguel appreciate your concern for our well-being, Sheriff. We'll do our best not to get shot. We sure don't want to booger up your plan."

Tomás ignored me. Even with all the practice he's had, it's good to see that he's

337

able to ignore me in tense situations. Turning to Jared and Estévan, he asked, "Are you ready?"

Both men nodded. Tomás turned back towards his father. I wondered what thoughts were running through his head. I couldn't tell from his expression. Once again, it occurred to me that he would be a mighty fine poker player. What do you say to the man who's taken care of you and watched out for you all your life? How do you tell him that things have changed? How do you tell him it's time for you to watch out for him? I guess you don't. Tomás looked at his father for a moment, then touched the brim of his hat with his hand and turned to ride away.

Miguel Marés and I headed east at a pretty good clip. We needed to get due south of Black Mesa before the sun went down and we needed to raise a ruckus doing it. I figured that would be no problem. I can sure nuff make noise when the situation calls for it.

It was closing on sundown. Jake Flynt was brushing down his big sorrel when he heard the unmistakable report of a rifle shot. It sounded like it came from down on the plains below the mesa. Pierce Keaton was cooking up some bacon and beans. Out of the corner of his eye, Jake saw him jump at the sound of the shot. From over on the boulder looking down, Dave Atkins was holding the spyglass to his eye with one hand and motioning to Jake with the other.

"Come take a look at this, Jake," Atkins said.

He hustled over and climbed up the rock. "What is it?" He reached for the spyglass and Atkins handed it over.

"I'm pretty sure it's that damn deputy," he said. "I can't make out who the other fella is."

Jake peered intently through the device, adjusting it slightly. Atkins could see him start to grin. "Yep, it's Deputy Stallings all right. Best as I can tell, the other fella is some old man." He laughed. "They're scraping the bottom of the barrel if they're sending out old codgers like him with their posse."

"What you reckon he's shootin' at?" Atkins asked.

"Near as I can tell, he must have been shooting at some game," Jake said. "Maybe a rabbit."

"Do you think he knows we're up here?" Atkins had a puzzled look on his face. "Firin' a shot like that would give his location away."

Flynt sneered. "I don't think that deputy has any idea where we are. He's wandering around in a fog most of the time."

Atkins didn't look convinced but he wasn't about to question Jake's judgment, no matter how flawed he thought it was. He turned away from Flynt and grimaced but he kept his mouth shut.

As Jake watched, he could see Tommy and Miguel dismount and begin spooling out their bedrolls. Once that was done, he could see the older man begin collecting material for a fire.

"Looks like they're setting up camp," Jake said. He turned to Atkins. "You think you could hit 'em from here?"

Atkins took a step closer to the edge of the boulder and raised his Winchester to his shoulder. He sighted down the barrel for a moment and then lowered it. He turned to Jake and said, "Maybe but I kinda doubt it. It's a hell of a long shot. I'd have to get real lucky to hit one of 'em and that'd likely spook the other one."

"Yeah, I suppose you're right." Jake pondered the situation for a moment. "Besides, I want to watch Stallings die. I want it to be slow and painful, too. A rifle shot to the head is too good for him." He took a deep breath and exhaled slowly. "All right, we'll let them be for now. Looks like they're planning on staying the night. First thing in the morning, I believe we'll sneak on down and pay them a little visit." As the sun went down, the outlaws settled in to wait.

I thought Miguel did a fine job of noise making as he gathered wood and started the fire. Of course, we didn't know for sure if they were watching us or, for that matter, if they were even up there on top of the mesa. All we can do is hope. If that's where they are, I expect they heard my shot. I'd like to think they figured I was shooting at game, which, as it turned out, I was. I got me a nice rabbit to go along with the beans Miguel was cooking up. He finished his cooking, poured us some coffee, and we sat down on a couple of logs to eat our meal. I didn't feel particularly hungry but I knew I'd need some nourishment to keep me going. I didn't expect we'd get much sleep tonight.

Miguel took a sip of his coffee and then asked me, "Do you think he knows?"

"Do I think who knows what, Miguel?" I wasn't sure I knew what he was talking about although I had an idea.

"Do you think my son, the sheriff, knows

that you and I will not stay down here while they face those men in the morning?"

Since I'd already pondered the question, I didn't have to think too long before I answered. "He knows us pretty well, Miguel. I reckon he knows what to expect."

"I hope you are not thinking about telling me to wait down here while you ride up there," Miguel said softly.

I'd been thinking that very thing and wondering how I could go about pulling it off. "Well, Miguel, somebody's gotta stay down here as the decoy. You understand that, don't you?"

He shook his head. "We will stuff our bedrolls with grass."

"I don't know," I said skeptically. "Don't you think we'd be more convincing if at least one of us was down here where they could see us moving around?"

Miguel stared at me for a moment. In an even softer voice, he said, "My sons will both be up there facing *los diablos.* I will be with them. If you try to stop me, I will shoot you."

"Oh," I said, rather lamely. "Well, when you put it that way . . ." I sort of trailed off. I didn't know what to say. He was my friend and he was speaking calmly, yet I had the feeling he meant what he had said. I wasn't quite sure what the appropriate response was when your friend threatens to shoot you. I recovered enough to ask, "What time do we leave?"

"An hour before dawn," he replied, as if he hadn't just threatened to shoot me. We settled in to wait.

Tomás, Jared, and Estévan had made their way north and west of Black Mesa and were now circling around behind it. The shadows were growing longer and they were careful not to get too close before they had the cover of darkness. Then they heard a rifle shot.

"What do you figure?" Jared rose up in his saddle and listened intently.

They held their breath. No shots followed. After a moment, they all exhaled.

"I think Deputy Stallings is trying to attract their attention," Tomás said. "At least that is what I hope is happening. If Jake was going to shoot them, I think we would have heard more shots."

"That is true," Estévan said, "unless, of course, they got too close to the foot of the mesa."

"If that was the case," Jared said quickly, "I expect there still would have been more than one shot. It wouldn't make sense for them to shoot only one of them."

"There is no way we can know for sure," Tomás said. "We will assume they are following the plan and that everything is as it should be."

They rode a little further and Estévan started chuckling. "What is so funny, brother?" Tomás sounded a bit irritated.

"I presume you know what they will do in the morning," Estévan said.

Jared joined in the laughter. "I sure know what they'll do. They'll be up before dawn riding up the south side of Black Mesa. There's no way they'll stay down below when we're up there drawin' down on these lowlife curs."

Tomás exhaled with frustration. "I do not know why we bother to make a plan if they have no intention of following it."

Estévan stopped laughing and looked at his brother. "If you were in their place, what would you do, brother?"

Tomás returned his brother's stare. "I see your point." They rode on in silence.

When the sun was down, they very quietly moved into position at the base of the mesa. They hobbled their horses and began the long, slow climb. They planned to reach a point more than halfway up so that they did not have far to go in the morning. Sometime after midnight when the moon was well up, they arrived at where they needed to be. They planned to begin the last leg of their climb an hour before sunup. They settled in to wait.

CHAPTER 28

Jared's eyes snapped open. Although it was still dark, his years moving steers up the trail had attuned his mind and body to the rhythm and cadence of night blending into morning. He sensed that dawn was only a little more than an hour away. He glanced to his right and saw that Tomás was also moving around. Softly, he walked over to where Estévan lay on the ground.

"I am awake," Estévan croaked in a morning voice.

Jared smiled. Since Estévan had come to work for him, he had discovered that the young man was never particularly eager to greet the morning. "I know you need your beauty sleep," he whispered, "but it's time to move. We got work to do."

With a soft groan, Estévan pulled himself upright and brushed the dried grass off his clothes. He and Jared walked over to where Tomás stood waiting.

"We go fast and quiet the rest of the way up," Tomás said. "Stop just below the rim and wait for my signal. I will announce that they are under arrest but do not hesitate to shoot. I believe they will fight rather than surrender."

There was a steely edge to Tomás's voice that Jared had never heard before. If he'd had any doubts as to the man's fitness for the job, they were gone. He took a deep breath to steady his nerves. "I suspect you're right about the fight. Jake is a killer, that's all he knows to do. Dave Atkins ain't real bright but he's plenty mean. I reckon he'll do whatever he sees Jake doin'. I don't know about Hank Andrews but I know Patricio Baca is a tough hombré." He paused and considered his next words. "From what I hear, Pierce Keaton ain't really known as a fighter. We need to make sure we take care of the others before we pay attention to him. He may not put up much of a struggle if we get Jake, Andrews, Baca, and Atkins down pretty quick."

Jared imagined for a second that he saw Tomás's eyes flash in the dark. "He has ridden with the devil, now he must pay."

"I got no problem with the man facin' up to his actions, Tomás," Jared said carefully. "What I do have a problem with is shootin' a man if he throws down his gun and surrenders. In my book, that's murder."

For a long moment, Tomás stood with his fists clenched, sayin' nothing. "You are right. I must not let my anger control me. We must do this the right way; otherwise we are no better than these *pendejos*. Still, these men are killers. If there is any doubt, use your guns."

Estévan had been listening to the interchange. "Both of you think too much. When this starts, it will happen quickly. If I make a mistake, I do not want it to be that I failed to shoot a man, thinking he was surrendering when he was preparing to kill me. I will not think twice about shooting Pierce Keaton."

Tomás looked at his brother and shrugged. "Perhaps you are right. When the time comes, we will do the best we can do." He reached down and patted the pistol on his hip. "And I believe the time has come. Spread out as we head up. I want for there to be at least twenty feet between each of us." Tomás looked from Estévan to Jared. "Any questions?"

Jared looked at the Marés brothers. He had known them since before they shaved. Their temperaments were so different and yet at their core, they were the same. They were brave and honorable and above all, loyal. If he had to do this dangerous thing he was about to do, he could hardly find better compadres. These were the thoughts that went through his mind. He didn't say them out loud. There was no need.

"Nope," he said instead. "No questions."

"Then we go," Tomás said quietly.

I sat up with a start. I was reaching for my gun when I realized it was only Miguel waking me up for our trek up the side of the mesa. I shook my head to clear the cobwebs.

"I would appreciate it if you did not shoot me this early in the morning, Tommy," Miguel said with a chuckle. "We have work to do."

Of course, Miguel *did* threaten to shoot me last night. Seems like I would be within my rights to threaten to shoot him this morning. As the fog of sleep slipped away and my thoughts became more coherent, I realized that none of this had any bearing on the job we were faced with at the dawn of this day. More than likely, we'd both have several hombrés looking to shoot both of us in less than an hour. No point in us shooting each other.

"All right, Miguel, I won't shoot you."

I could see that he had already stuffed his

bedroll with dried grass. He'd even thought-fully placed a pile of grass next to my bedroll. All I had to do was stuff it in and our decoys were set. As I was completing that chore, Miguel went to fetch the horses from where they'd been grazing much of the night. He took their hobbles off and led them over to where I stood. I reached out to give old Rusty a good morning pat and he nuzzled me. I sure hope I live through this dust-up. Old Rusty would likely miss me if I got killed. Come to think of it, Mollie probably would, too. Good reasons to stay alive.

"Are you ready, Tommy Stallings?" My heart was pounding and I had that funny taste you get in your mouth when you're excited or scared. I was both. Miguel was calm, like he was ready for a morning stroll.

"Reckon I'm about as ready as I'm gonna get," I said. "Let's get on with it."

We planned to ride part way up before dismounting and slip the rest of the way on foot. Yesterday evening while there was still a little light, we had identified a big rock as a landmark for where we'd leave the horses. If there was anything else to discuss, I sure didn't know what it was. Apparently Miguel didn't either. He walked over to his little pinto and mounted up.

Jake Flynt opened his eyes and saw the sun just starting to come up on the horizon. He had wanted to get an earlier start as he anticipated inflicting a great deal of pain on that meddling deputy. He cursed violently as he stood up. Walking over to where Pierce Keaton lay snoring next to the fire, he kicked the man awake.

"Damn you, Pierce, why didn't you wake me up earlier?"

Keaton rolled away from the kick and scrambled to his feet. Disoriented, he could only think to back away as Jake followed him, screaming.

"All you had to do was drag your sorry carcass out of bed and start the fire. How hard is that?" Jake lunged at Keaton and slapped him upside the head. "Why do I keep you around, Pierce? Answer me that. What good are you?"

Still struggling to make sense out of this senseless attack, Keaton tried to speak. Words failed him and all he could manage was a whimper. This infuriated Jake further. He slapped him again.

Dave Atkins had sat up in his bedroll and was watching this exchange with interest.

351

Although he enjoyed seeing Jake torment Keaton, he also realized that the man was as unpredictable as a rabid animal. It wouldn't take much for him to turn his ire on Atkins. Very carefully, he pulled his boots on and stood up slowly.

"Jake," Keaton whined, "I didn't know . . . you didn't tell me . . . I mean, you didn't say you wanted me to wake you up this mornin'." He ducked his chin down against his chest as Jake swatted him once more for good measure. With blurry eyes, he said, "If you'd told me, I'd have done it, I swear."

Jake stopped, breathing heavily from his exertions. He stared at Pierce Keaton, a wild look in his eyes. After a moment, he appeared to calm down. He turned back to his bedroll for his boots. Over his shoulder, he said, "Start a fire. I want some coffee before I head out after that damn deputy."

Pierce Keaton's blood ran cold as he contemplated the unpredictable violence the leader of their dwindling outlaw band was capable of inflicting. He was so horrified he almost lost control of his bowels. *That would've just about done it,* he thought as a shiver ran down his spine. *If I'd of shat myself, Jake would no doubt kill me for sure.* Shaking his head, he forced himself into action. He moved to start a fire, hoping that by complying, he would be spared another bout of abuse. His thoughts were racing as he went about heating up last night's coffee. He couldn't take any more of this; he had to get away today. If he didn't, he was convinced that he would not live to see tomorrow.

Flynt rolled up his bedroll and tossed it carelessly under a tree. Turning to Dave Atkins, he said, "Here's the plan, Dave. We'll have some coffee, then we'll head on down the mesa and sneak up on Deputy Stallings, damn his eyes." He stretched and put on his hat. "When we get down there, I want you to shoot that old man. It may take me some time to deal with the deputy and I don't want that old codger in the way. Once I'm done, we'll come back up here and pack up our stuff. Then we'll head out after that Irishman and his pathetic little family."

Pierce walked over and tentatively held out a mug for Jake. "Here's some coffee, Jake, hot off the fire."

"Why thank you, Pierce," he replied politely as if nothing untoward had happened.

"Uh, you're welcome," Keaton stammered. *This man's crazy as an old hoot owl. I got to leave today.*

"Pierce, while me and Dave go down and

take care of the deputy, I want you to clean up this campsite. I don't want any trace of us to be seen when we leave here. You think you can do that?"

"Sure nuff, Jake, I can do that," Keaton replied. As he said it, he was thinking, *as soon as you get down the hill, I'm skedaddlin' out of here. I think I'll head for the Arizona Territory.*

"All right then, we got us a plan," Jake said. "Dave, get you some coffee and walk with me over here to the rim. I want to make sure those sidewinders are still camped out down below. Bring the spyglass."

They made their way up to the top of the lookout boulder and Jake surveyed the landscape. A thin mist hung over the plains below left over from the cool night air.

"I can't see too clearly," Jake said, squinting. "I think I can make out their bedrolls down by where they were camping. I don't see anyone stirring." He handed the spyglass to Atkins. "You take a look."

Atkins took a long look, moving the glass slightly as he scanned the area surrounding the campsite. "I can't make out much either. I do believe I can make out their bedrolls. Ain't nobody movin' around, that's for sure." He reached up and scratched his head. "It's funny. I don't see their horses anywhere nearby. Course, they might have wandered off a ways to graze."

Jake took the spyglass back and swept over the area again. "I don't see them either." He frowned. "I don't like it, Dave. Something's not right." He handed the spyglass back to Atkins and began to climb down the boulder. "Come on, let's get our guns. We'd better get down there pronto. I think that damn deputy may be up to something."

We were probably three quarters of the way up the mesa when the sun showed the top of its head over the horizon. We were too close to danger for any talking so I signaled Miguel and made a motion that we needed to hurry up. He nodded and picked up his pace. In the dim light, it looked to me like he was struggling. We'd climbed a pretty fair distance. I figured he might be getting tired and a bit winded but there was no time to slow down.

Our plan was to stop about twenty feet from the rim. We would crouch there and wait for Tomás and the boys to make their move. As soon as we heard any noise, be it talking or shooting, we would head up over the top and catch Jake and his curs by surprise. I figured if there was shooting going on, the biggest challenge would be to not get shot by our boys. I'd hate to get shot but I'd especially hate to get shot by one of my friends. Course, when you're dead, it don't much matter. Still, seems to me there's some sort of principle involved.

It took us about fifteen more minutes to move into position. When I thought we were close enough, I looked over at Miguel. When I caught his attention, I squatted down and pointed at the ground, indicating we would stop here. Miguel waved in acknowledgment and then doubled over at the waist, clearly struggling to catch his breath. That worried me. I hoped they'd wait to start the festivities until Miguel had a chance to recover. No such luck.

I heard voices from directly above me and almost immediately, I saw Jake Flynt take a step down the incline in my direction. He saw me right away. That wasn't good. I'd needed both hands for climbing up the mesa and I hadn't yet drawn my pistol. The sun was a little higher now and the light was better. It was bright enough that I could see the twisted, evil grin that spread across his face as he drew his pistol and started to point it at me. I fumbled for my own weapon, knowing I was going to be too late. As I grabbed my gun, I thought to myself that I wasn't really ready to die yet. Of course, I didn't figure that would cut me any slack with a devil like Jake Flynt.

From off to my right, Miguel began blazing away at Jake with his pistol. Reckon he must've caught his breath. Did I say I was glad Miguel was on my side? He didn't hit anything but his hail of bullets drove Jake back over the rim to seek cover. He snapped off a couple of shots over his shoulder as he went. Reckon Miguel saved my life, for the time being at least. We were still in a mighty prickly situation though. The way we were sitting here exposed, they could sneak up to the edge of the rim and pick us off with their rifles. I sure hope Tomás, Jared, and Estévan hadn't slept in.

I shot a look back over to where Miguel had been. He wasn't there. A feeling of dread swept over me. Frantically, I looked downhill. About fifteen feet down the side of the mesa, I saw Miguel sprawled out and motionless. From where I crouched, I could see a bloom of red on the front of his shirt. There was no way to tell if he was breathing or not and I couldn't risk edging over to check on him. Apparently one of Jake's random shots had connected. I would have to hope that he hadn't delivered a killing shot.

From up above, a voice rang out. "Deputy Stallings, how nice to finally meet up with you face to face." There was a taunting tone to Jake's voice. Clearly, he knew he had the upper hand. He probably thought he had some time to play cat and mouse with me. The more time he spent mocking me, the greater the chance that Tomás and the others would get there in time to make him pay. "Well, hey, Jake, I was hopin' we could do some talkin' this mornin'." I tried to sound nervous and scared. It wasn't hard. "Maybe we could work us out some kind of a deal."

I heard him laugh. "I do have a deal for you, Deputy," he said in an almost friendly tone. "I'm going to deal you out more pain than you ever imagined. Before you die, you'll suffer more than you have in your entire young life."

Not exactly the kind of deal I was hoping for. "Come on, Jake, be reasonable." I didn't have to pretend to be frightened now. This was one scary hombré. It seemed to me that this would be a pretty good time for the boys to make an appearance on the north side of the mesa. The silence from that vicinity was deafening.

Jake laughed louder. "Deputy, you been tracking me across this Big Empty for quite a while. Have I done anything to make you think that I'm inclined to be reasonable?"

Well, he had a point there. Torturing and burning sodbusters. Killing innocent people. Robbing a bank a second time when there was no money in it, just to show that he could do it.

"It's never too late to turn over a new leaf, Jake," I replied. A feeble response, I admit.

"Have you heard what the Comanche do to captives when they want them to suffer?" Seeing as how my entire family had been wiped out by the Comanche, I thought it was a particularly low blow of him to bring that up. "They flay them. They cut off their skin . . . while they're still alive. How does that sound, Deputy?"

It didn't sound good at all. Mr. Sheriff Tomás Marés, where in the hell are you?

As if to answer my unspoken prayer, a voice called out, "Hands up, Flynt. We have you covered."

I heard a flurry of shots fired. It was confusing, like it always is in a gun battle. If I had to guess, I'd figure Jake turned and pulled off a shot at Tomás and the others. After that, all hell broke loose. Looked like the party had started. Not wanting to miss the fun, I clambered up the rest of the way to the rim as fast as I could scoot. Poking just enough of my head over the top to get a look at what was happening, I saw Jake pinned down behind the big boulder he'd used as his lookout. Dave Atkins was lying on the ground, blood leaking from a number of bullet wounds in his chest. He looked like he'd be out of the action permanently. There was no sign of Hank Andrews or Patricio Baca. Pierce Keaton was backed up against a little piñon tree with his hands in the air. Clearly, he wasn't interested in risking his life for the likes of Jake Flynt.

Jake was blazing away from behind the boulder, screaming as he fired. "Damn you sons of bitches, I'll kill every one of you. I'll tear your hearts out and eat them."

I could see that Tomás, Jared, and Estévan had come over the north rim, spread out a good twenty feet from each other. As soon as Jake started shooting at them, they'd each found some cover and were keeping a steady stream of gunfire in Jake's direction. They had him pinned down behind his lookout boulder. From my position, I could make out a small portion of Jake's body. I fired a shot in his direction and he moved around the boulder a few feet to get out of my line of fire. I realized that if I slid on over a little ways here at the top of the rim, I would once again have a shot at him. I figured I could force him on around the boulder until he had no choice but to come out in the open. It was as close to having a plan as I've ever had in a fracas like this. I edged over and blazed away. He moved around a bit. I stopped to reload and then began firing again. I emptied my pistol. As I once again began to reload, there was a brief moment of quiet. I heard Tomás's voice.

"Jake, throw down your guns. It's over. Your only chance to live is to surrender."

"You'd like that wouldn't you, Sheriff. Be a real feather in your hat to bring me in for a hanging, wouldn't it?" Jake's voice seemed to be pitched higher. It's funny, though, I didn't hear a trace of fear in it. More like unbridled rage. He didn't sound like somebody who was getting ready to surrender.

"Surrender now or die up here on top of the mesa," Tomás replied firmly. Where I'd heard rage in Jake's voice, I heard steel in Tomás's. "Those are your choices."

Seconds went by, though it seemed an eternity as all of our fates hung in the balance. I risked a glance over the top of the rim.

Jake burst from behind the boulder, screaming an unearthly curse. He had made his choice. I watched in fascinated horror as he furiously fanned his pistols in the direction of Tomás's voice. To my amazement, I watched as Tomás stepped out from behind the rock where he'd been taking cover and walked toward Jake, his pistol extended. Like Elfego by God Baca, he ignored the bloody fusillade of bullets and aimed at the madman. He fired three shots in rapid succession. I could see Jake's body twitch as each one found its mark. The outlaw stood straight up and looked around, a slightly baffled expression on his face. He looked as if he wanted to say something but no words came out of his mouth. With his pistol pointing toward the sky, he pulled the trigger repeatedly. After two more shots, the hammer fell on empty chambers. He continued pulling the trigger for a moment more and then fell facedown on the top of Black Mesa.

I leaped over the rim and ran over to where his fallen body lay. After everything I'd seen with this monster, I wasn't sure he could be killed. I had no compunction about the possibility of pouring some more lead into his body if that's what it took to send him to hell. I stopped about ten feet away, ready to fire. It wasn't necessary. Turned out he could be killed after all. I checked and there was no heartbeat.

I looked around to where Tomás stood

about twenty feet away. Miraculously, he had not one scratch on him. Reckon I'd rather be lucky than good. It looked to me like Tomás Marés was both good *and* lucky. I glanced over and saw that both Jared and Estévan had Pierce Keaton covered. Keaton had both hands high in the air. Over and over, he alternated the phrases, "Don't shoot," and "I surrender." There was still no sign of Andrews or Baca.

Tomás looked around and realized someone else was missing. A worried look crossed his face. "Where is my father?"

I hesitated. I didn't really know what to tell him. I'd seen that Miguel had been shot but I had no way of knowing if he was alive or dead. With a gun battle raging around us, there hadn't been an opportunity for me to check on him. Even with just a quick glance, I had seen that the wound looked serious.

He must have read the truth from looking at my face. "He was shot, wasn't he?"

No way I could sugarcoat it. "He was."

"Is he dead?"

I took a deep breath. "Tomás, I don't know. Jake had us pinned down. I couldn't check on him. It looked serious."

Tomás's face became a mask of controlled rage. He turned and said, "Jared and Estévan. Leave this *cabrón* and check on my father. Now!"

They both looked at him uneasily as he strode over to where Pierce Keaton stood. They could see from his expression that he was prepared to do something rash. Clearly, they were torn between stopping him from making a huge mistake and offering aid to Miguel.

I followed Tomás and said, "The two of you look after Miguel. I'll help the sheriff out here."

Tomás stalked over to where Keaton stood and stared at him with unconcealed hatred. Keaton would not meet his gaze and stood whimpering. Tomás struck out and slapped the man upside the head. Keaton staggered but did not fall.

"Whoa, Tomás," I said in alarm. "No need for that. This man ain't got any fight left in him."

"This man is a murderer," he said, his voice dripping with venom. "He and these other snakes have taken the lives of too many people. They deserve to die."

"I didn't kill nobody, Sheriff," Keaton sobbed. "I rode with old Jake but I didn't kill a soul. I swear it."

"My father is lying down the side of the mesa, you sniveling cur. He may be dead."

Tomás slapped Keaton again. This was not going well. "Tell me why I should let you live."

"Jake shot your pa, Sheriff, not me." Pierce Keaton's words were barely intelligible as he sobbed out his plea for mercy. "Don't kill me for Jake's sins."

Tomás pulled his pistol and put the barrel under the point of Keaton's chin. "Maybe I will just kill you for your sins then . . . eh, *cabrón*?"

I figured I'd better do something fast or the sheriff would travel too far down this road to come back. "Tomás," I said sharply. "Come to your senses, man. This is not how you act. You enforce the law." He didn't look at me. He held his pistol steady under Keaton's chin. I heard him cock the hammer. I was feeling desperate. "Tomás, how many times have you told me that I can't take the law into my own hands? That if I do, I'm no better than these sorry, no-good outlaws we're sworn to hunt down and bring to justice."

Tomás looked over at me, although he didn't take his gun away from Keaton's chin. "And how many times have you told me that we cannot trust the courts, that we must impose our own justice?"

For a moment, he sort of had me stumped.

I had made quite a few speeches along those lines over the last couple of years. "Shooting an unarmed man is not justice, Sheriff Tomás Marés. It's murder. They ain't the same and you know it."

"What I know is that my father is gravely wounded and may be dead. It is all because of the actions of this man and the outlaw gang he rode with. Are you, of all people, saying that I have not the right to avenge my father's death?"

He was asking me hard questions and I didn't have easy answers. If I was in his boots, I'd probably be thinking the same way. That didn't mean it was right. "Tomás, we don't know if your pa is dead, for one thing. Besides, the man who shot him is dead. He's lying right over there on the ground. You shot him yourself. He was trying to kill you, you defended yourself, and he paid the price. I got no problem with that." I took a breath. "This is different."

Tomás smiled grimly. "Maybe I will give this *cabrón* a gun so he is not defenseless. Would that make you feel better, Deputy Stallings?"

I could tell I wasn't getting through to him the way I wanted to. "I understand you're thinkin' about your pa lyin' down the hill gravely wounded. I can only guess what that'd be like. Think about this, though. What would your pa say to you if he saw you right now?" I held my breath.

Tomás flinched as he considered my question. His eyes narrowed. I could see that he was thinking hard. Whichever way this was going to go, I figured it was about to go there fast. In my mind's eye, I measured the distance between me and him, wondering if I could get there and pull his gun away before he could fire it. There was no way.

He took a deep breath and lowered his gun. "Keep an eye on the prisoner, Deputy." He turned and walked down the side of the mesa to see about his father.

Keaton stood motionless until Tomás disappeared over the rim of the mesa. Then he broke into sobs, crying, "Thank you, Deputy, thank you, thank you."

I looked at him with disgust. "Shut up, you worthless rat or I'll shoot you myself." He shut up.

It was almost an hour before Jared came back up to report on Miguel. In the meantime, I'd taken a rope from one of the outlaw's horses and cut it in pieces. I tied Pierce Keaton's hands behind his back and tied his feet together so he was hobbled pretty good. I didn't think he was crazy enough to make a run for it but you just never know. He was not especially gracious towards me when I trussed him up. I don't think he realized I was doing him a favor. If he'd have taken off, I doubt if I could stop Tomás from shooting him.

When I saw Jared appear over the rim of the mesa, I walked quickly in his direction. "What's the story with Miguel?"

Jared looked worried. He shook his head. "I don't know Tommy, he's hurt pretty bad. The shot took him in the chest. It didn't hit his heart but it sure nuff messed up his lungs. It's gonna be touch and go whether he makes it."

"It don't sound like he can ride," I said. "What are they gonna do about gettin' him back to town?"

"They talked about ridin' in and gettin' a wagon back out here to haul him in." Jared frowned. "We decided there wasn't time for that. Estévan went on down the hill a bit to where some young piñons are growin'. They're gonna make a travois with the poles and a bedroll, like we did when we hauled John Burr's body back to town."

That made me nervous. "It's gonna be a mighty bumpy ride, Jared," I said with some trepidation. Burr had been dead. He didn't mind the bumps. "If he's hurt as bad as you say, he might not survive the trip."

Jared nodded solemnly. "That's a fact. The thing is, if he doesn't get to a doctor pronto, he ain't gonna survive anyway. Tomás has a plan to take some of the bumps out of the ride though."

"How's he gonna do that?"

"They're gonna tie one end to Tomás's horse, Paco. Tomás and Estévan are each gonna carry a pole at the other end. They figure they can smooth out the ride a bit that way."

I was skeptical. "I don't know, Jared. That's gonna slow 'em down considerable."

He shrugged. "Reckon it's a trade-off. They're tryin' to come up with the best plan they can under the circumstances."

I didn't know what else to say. Jared was right, they had to do something. This made as much sense as anything I could've come up with. "What does Tomás want me to do?"

"He said to tell you to keep watch on the prisoner until everything is situated. I'm gonna take a bedroll down there now and they're gonna fix up the travois. They'll hand carry him up here. While they do that, I'll bring up Miguel's pinto, then get our horses from the north side of the mesa. Once we got everything together, we'll head on down the west side of the mesa here and make our way back to town."

There didn't seem to be much else for us to discuss. Jared grabbed a bedroll that belonged to one of the outlaws and headed back downhill to where the Marés sons were watching over their father. I went back over to where Pierce Keaton sat in the dirt. I was in a surly mood.

"Where's Andrews and Baca?" After the shooting had stopped, Estevan had done a quick search and there had been no sign of them. It appeared that they had slipped away at some point.

"Hank went to take care of that Irishman and his family a couple of days ago," Keaton said. "He never came back. Kinda looks like he didn't get the job done. And Patricio, well, he set out to back-shoot Jake." He smiled, clearly enjoying the moment. "Guess you could say he didn't get the job done neither."

So Patricio Baca had tried to betray Jake Flynt. Looked like that hadn't gone the way he wanted it to. "You're tellin' me all that was up here was you, Atkins, and Jake?"

"That's right, the three of us was all that was left," Keaton replied.

"You know, if that old man dies, they're gonna hang you for sure."

"Why would they hang me?" Keaton

370

whined. "I didn't shoot him."

"Maybe you didn't," I said harshly. "Still, you're the only one of the gang left alive. Somebody's gonna have to pay. I reckon it'll be you."

Keaton's eyes grew wild, like a cornered animal. "That ain't right," he said indignantly. "Them judges are supposed to be fair. What you're sayin' ain't fair."

"Reckon you should've thought about what was fair before you decided to ride with a murderer like Jake Flynt." I couldn't resist taking a dig at Keaton's cowardice. "You'd have been better off if you'd fought it out like Jake and Dave Atkins. At least you'd have died with a little dignity. Instead, you're just the last man standin'." I looked at him there sprawled in the dirt. "Or in your case, the last man sittin'."

For a moment, the panic shown in his eyes. Then he smiled and I saw a cunning look come over his face. "But I ain't the last man standin', Deputy."

"What are you talkin' about?"

"There's one more still out here in this old Big Empty. That damned Irishman. He's got the money." He smiled at me. "And I know where he's at."

"You know where Garrett O'Donnell is?" I wasn't sure what Keaton's game was.

"Got a pretty good idea," he said with a smug grin.

"Then you'd better start talkin' to me mighty quick," I said sternly.

Keaton shook his head. "I ain't sayin' nothin' until I get some sort of guarantee that I ain't gonna hang for somethin' I didn't do."

I pondered the situation. "I tell you what, Pierce. We'll wait for Sheriff Marés to come back up here with his dyin' father. We'll talk with him about it. You think he's gonna be in a forgivin' mood towards you?" I smiled at him. "Or maybe you could just tell me what you know."

I could tell Keaton was going over his options in his little pea brain. "All right, Deputy, I'll tell you what I know. You got to promise me you'll tell the judge I helped you out, though. You owe me that much."

"I don't owe you nothin', you no-good weasel." I felt like kicking the lowdown varmint. I didn't though. Something about kicking a defenseless man all hog-tied and sitting on the ground didn't seem right to me. I admit it was mighty tempting. I tried to calm myself down.

"You don't deserve any breaks and I ain't all that impressed with your sudden interest in things bein' fair. Fact is, though, if you give me information that leads to the capture of another criminal, I suppose that might help you at your trial."

Keaton squinted one eye as he thought about whether or not he could get a better deal. It looked like thinking that hard was making his head hurt. Apparently he realized he wasn't holding a very good hand.

"I guess that's all I can hope for, ain't it, Deputy." He motioned me closer with a backwards nod of his head. "Jake was all set to go after O'Donnell once he'd got done killin' you. He said the man was ridin' east from here, headin' for Texas. Said there was some tracks we could follow."

I considered this information. Something about it didn't sound right to me. When I'd visited the O'Donnell place to check on Mrs. O'Donnell and found her gone, I figured she'd probably taken the children and headed somewhere. Even though she'd told me before that she might head back east to stay with her brother, that didn't ring true. I had clear memories from our time together driving cattle north of Garrett talking about how beautiful Colorado was. I believe she had other plans.

"All right," I said. "You might've just spared yourself a necktie party if what you're tellin' me is true."

373

"Oh, it's true all right, Deputy," Keaton said earnestly. "I got no reason to lie about this, seein' as how it might make things a bit easier on me and all."

"I didn't make you no promises about things goin' easier," I said irritably. "I just said I'd let the judge know you spoke up."

Keaton looked disappointed. He showed the rare good judgment of not sharing that disappointment with me. He nodded and looked away. I didn't want to be around the no-good skunk so I walked over to where Jake Flynt lay. Dead men never look as scary as live ones do. Still, there was something frightening about Jake, even as he lay growing colder and stiffer. It was almost as if he might suddenly leap up and begin shooting all over again. A shiver danced up my spine.

I realized that if Miguel was alive, it would take all of our efforts to carry him back to town. That meant we were either going to have to bury Jake and Dave Atkins or let the crows have at them. I went over to see if the outlaws had kept a shovel in their camp. I was in luck. They had a medium size spade by the fire pit. Though I would've been happier with a bigger shovel, I figured this would have to do. Since I seemed to be the logical person to dig the graves, everyone else being otherwise occupied, I got to work.

I'd gotten down a few feet on the first one when I heard Tomás and Estévan coming up over the rim of the mesa. I dropped my shovel and walked over to them. They had constructed a stretcher with the two piñon poles threaded through cuts they'd made in the sides of the bedroll. Miguel was unconscious and his skin had a gray pallor. He lay still as death.

"How's he doin'?" I asked. Just looking at Miguel, he appeared more dead than alive. I didn't say that though.

"It is bad, Tommy," Tomás said anxiously. "I do not know if he will make it. Did Jared tell you of our plan?"

"He did," I said. "Sounds like the best we can do under the circumstances." I hesitated, then decided to fill him in on the news shared by Pierce Keaton. "We got a new wrinkle you need to know about."

"What is it?" Tomás sounded distracted.

"Our prisoner tells me that Garrett O'Donnell ain't far from here. They were planning on trackin' him down . . . after they'd disposed of me and your pa, that is." Cautiously, I said, "I might be able to catch up with him if I leave right away. Course, that means Jared would have to handle the prisoner. You and Estévan got your hands full with carryin' your pa."

Tomás sighed deeply as he contemplated the new twist. After a moment's pondering, he made a decision. "We need to finish this if we can. I want you to go after the Irishman."

Jared came over the north rim of the mesa at that point and led the horses over to where we stood. Looking at the two of us, he discerned that something new had transpired.

"What's up? You boys look like you're chewin' on a new problem."

When Tomás explained the situation, Jared immediately said, "I can handle Keaton by myself. I'll put him on a horse in front of me and tie a rope around his waist. If he tries to make a break for it, he'll pop right off the horse. If he does that, I'll make him walk all the way to Cimarrón."

Tomás nodded in agreement. He turned to me. "Go then. Do what needs to be done. We will take care of the prisoner." I could see the pain in his eyes as he contemplated his father's uncertain future. "We will take my father back to town as well. God willing, he will still be alive."

He had it about right. It was in God's hands now. I could only think of one thing to say, so I said it. *Vaya con Díos, amigo.*

I headed down the south side of the mesa

to fetch old Rusty. I didn't know what they would do about burying Jake and Dave Atkins but it was no longer my problem. Here was my problem. Inside my head, I was having a great big old argument. As an officer of the law, it was my duty to catch Garrett O'Donnell and bring him back to face a judge and account for his actions.

Whatever his reasons, it was pretty clear to me that he'd broken the law. On the other hand, I knew quite a bit about his reasons. I'd ridden with Garrett and I knew he was a good man trying his best to look after his family. I can't say I would have done things much differently if I'd been wearing his boots. I was kind of hoping he'd gotten enough of a head start on me that I wouldn't catch up to him. I mounted up and headed down to where Miguel and I had camped the previous night to pick up my bedroll. I didn't know how long this search would take and I figured I might need it. I tied it on behind my saddle. On a hunch, I turned old Rusty and skirted around the mesa headed north.

CHAPTER 29

No sign of Garrett the first day. My thoughts were prancing around my head like a wild mustang on a cold morning. I was worried sick about Miguel. He sure didn't look like a man who was going to live to see the sunrise tomorrow and the trip to town was bound to be hard on him. I was also worried about what Tomás would do to Pierce Keaton if his pa died. Not that I cared two hoots about Keaton, I just didn't want my friend to do something he would regret later.

I was having trouble picking up a trail for Garrett and wondered if maybe I should have headed east like Keaton had suggested. I wasn't having much luck and I had little enthusiasm for the chase anyway. In my heart, I didn't really want to catch up with Garrett O'Donnell. By the end of the day, I'd had no luck. I figured I'd make camp, get some sleep, and give it a try for one more day. I made my bed on the ground. Naturally, it rained that night. The next morning, I got myself going even though I was cold, wet, and had no coffee. Old Rusty wasn't very happy, either. I got him saddled up and we headed north over those rolling plains. Up and down, mile after mile.

As I trotted up the next rise, I could hear the stream gurgling on the other side. I'd discovered it in the past month as I'd trekked all over this country looking for outlaws. In the early spring, it was just a tiny trickle of water winding its way through the sand and gravel of the streambed. Now, with the summer rains and the mountain snow runoff, it was five to six feet wide and maybe a foot deep. No problem to cross and a decent place to water my horse. I crested the hill and looked down. There he was on the other side of the stream. Garrett O'Donnell.

"Hello, Garrett," I said in what I hoped sounded like a friendly voice. I walked my horse down the hill toward him. He had dismounted and was in the process of watering his own horse. "I been lookin' for you."

"Sure and the whole bleedin' world's been out lookin' for me," he replied in his thick Irish brogue.

"Reckon you're right about that," I replied

lightly. "Most of 'em have been lookin' to kill you though. Me, I'm lookin' to help you."

"Is that right, Mr. Deputy Sheriff Tommy Stallings?" Although he said it in a sociable manner, I could hear the suspicion in his voice. He eyed his horse. I could imagine his mind calculating the distance to the rifle in his scabbard. "And how were you plannin' to be doin' that?"

I put my hand on the butt of my pistol where he could see it. I was hopeful that it would discourage him from doing something impulsive, like trying to shoot me. "I know why you were with Jake Flynt and his gang when they robbed the bank in Cimarrón," I said in the same even-keeled voice. "I also know that you're not an outlaw like them other fellas. I think with the help of a good lawyer, we could get you off with only just a little jail time." I cringed inwardly as I said those two words, "good lawyer." They aren't usually spoken together. "I'm acquainted with a fella who's a good man and a good attorney. I believe he'd take your case."

Garrett laughed without any humor. "Sure and a Mick such as meself could expect fair treatment from your territorial courts. They really love the Irish, don't you know, especially them that goes around blowin' up bank safes."

I had to admit he had a point. I tried to convince him anyway. "It beats bein' on the run, though, don't it?" I really hoped that Garrett O'Donnell would see that his best chance was to trust the mercy and judgment of the courts. As that thought passed through my mind, my heart sank. I'd seen the mercy and judgment of the New Mexico territorial courts up close. I was not impressed. I wasn't sure I could sell the notion to Garrett.

"Not if a person has someplace he's runnin' to," Garrett replied. "And a dream about what he might do once he gets there. If I'm to take a risk, I'd sooner take one where I must trust myself rather than some politician judge." His smile was grim. "No offense to your 'good lawyer' friend."

All the pieces to the puzzle fell into place. His wife had left and taken the children, I knew that. What I'd suspected but not known for sure was that they were not heading east. They were headed north, probably to Denver. Garrett had remained on the run in the Big Empty until he was sure his family had gotten away safely. Now he intended to join them. It was my job to stop him. That was the law but it didn't feel like justice to me. I had to make a decision.

"Garrett," I said slowly, "I want you to listen close to every word I'm about to say. Don't move a muscle until I tell you I'm through. Do you understand me?" In the silence that followed, I heard the water murmur tenderly around the rocks that littered the stream.

He eyed me warily, and then he said, "I hear your words, Deputy Stallings. Know this, though. If this is some kind of trick, I'll be grabbin' for me Winchester. Do you understand *me*?" The emphasis that he placed on that last word made his meaning clear. We were a heartbeat away from a shootout.

"I do understand, Garrett," I said with conviction. "This is no trick. Listen carefully. I'm supposed to take you in. We both know that. What that means is about now, I'd have to reach down and draw my pistol so I could get the drop on you." As I said these words, I very cautiously raised my hands until they were up above my shoulders. "As you can see, that'll take me a moment to do. Are you with me so far?"

I could see the confusion in his eyes that was slowly replaced by a glint of understanding. He nodded. "I think so."

"Somethin' else you should know is that I

got me a brand-new holster for my pistol. The wife gave it to me for my birthday. It's pretty fancy, I like it a lot, but the leather's still a might stiff. Makes a quick draw pert near an impossibility."

I could see comprehension dawning on his face. I might've even seen the briefest twitch of his lips. Out of the corner of my eye, I spied a redtail hawk circle in closer to the ground. Some unlucky field mouse, no doubt. I hoped it wasn't an omen. If it was, I hoped I was the hawk.

I continued. "Here's the thing, Garrett. If a fella was gonna make a break for it, now would be the time to do it. He might make it over the next rise before I could get a shot off, what with my gun bein' so hard to get to. The way these old hills roll, I'd have no real way of knowin' which direction he headed out." I shook my head. "He might head east, west . . . hell, I wouldn't have a clue." I smiled. "You know better than about anyone that a man can get lost real easy out here in the Big Empty."

I could see his body lean slightly in the direction of his horse. "I can see the sense in what you're sayin', Deputy Stallings."

"It does make sense, don't it," I said. "Here's the most important thing, though. If a man was to make such a getaway, he'd better ride out of here and never show his face around these parts again. He'd better start a new life somewheres else, leave this old Big Empty country far behind." I paused and stared hard at the Irishman. " 'Cause a fella only gets a chance like this once in a lifetime. You savvy?"

Garrett O'Donnell looked me straight in the eye for a long moment. The hawk rose on a gust of wind and headed north. Then he said, "I savvy, Deputy."

"All right," I said, nodding at him. "I'm through now."

Keeping his eyes tight on me, he took two slow cautious steps to his horse, put his left boot in the stirrup, and mounted up. He nodded back at me and turned his horse, spurring him as he did so. In a second, he'd disappeared over the rise.

EPILOGUE

It was late afternoon that second day when I made it back to town. The first person I needed to see when I got back to Cimarrón was Mollie Stallings, my lovely Irish bride. You might say it was my duty to report in first to my boss, Sheriff Tomás Marés, and if you did, you'd be right. My need was a whole lot stronger than my sense of duty, though. I'd get to Tomás directly, as they say in Texas. Being a deputy was my job. Mollie Stallings was my life.

The shadows were growing longer as I eased old Rusty up to the hitching rail out front of our little house. I could see Mollie sitting in one of the rockers on our tiny front porch. She had that silly crooked-nose dog, Willie, sitting next to her and she was petting him. When she saw me, she bounded out of her chair and raced out to greet me. So did that ridiculous dog.

"Oh, Tommy," she cried. "You're home."

I'd barely dismounted when she flung herself on me and engulfed me in a rib-crushing hug. Willie bounced around our feet, barking and licking at me. I think he wanted to get in on the hug. Not this time, you funny-looking critter.

"Yep," I said, a grin as wide as the Big Empty on my face. "I'm home."

We hugged for quite a spell until I became a bit concerned that Mollie might crush the life out of me. She's small but she's strong. I managed to choke out a plea for mercy. "If you'll please let go of me for just a minute, I can catch my breath. Reckon we can take this little party on into the house."

She only squeezed harder for a second. I could swear I felt a rib pop. Mercifully, she relented and released me. She kept ahold of my hand though. As we walked into the house, she said, "I was so worried when you didn't come home with the others. Tomás told me you'd gone after Garrett." A look of sadness came over her face. "He also told me about his pa."

I felt a stab of pain in my heart as I thought about Miguel Marés. He was as fine a man as I'd ever known and he'd durn sure saved my bacon out there on the side of the mesa. "Did he make it back alive?"

"Tomás said he was just barely hangin'

on," she replied. I could hear the sadness in her voice. "Doc is lookin' after him. Seems he'd lost a lot of blood."

His condition sounded grave. Still, as long as he was breathing, there was hope. I closed my eyes for a moment and said a silent prayer for him. When I opened my eyes, Mollie had that look on her face like she was about to jump on me and give me another bone-crushing hug. Hoping to deflect that for the time being, I said, "Can we sit at the table? I'm worn out from all my ridin'."

Mollie, Willie, and I made our way to the little table and chairs where we took our meals together. Willie quit bouncing around and laid down at Mollie's feet, gazing up at her with an adoring expression on his preposterous-looking crooked face. I don't know what she sees in that dog. He's ugly as an old mud fence.

Mollie sat down and immediately grabbed both my hands. She was looking at me with her own kind of adoring expression. I have to say, it was a whole lot easier to look at than the silly dog.

"So," she said slowly. "Did you find him?"

"Find who?" I asked innocently.

"Garrett O'Donnell, silly, that's who."

"Oh, him," I said, casual as could be.

"Naw, I never even picked up his trail. I think that weasel Keaton was makin' up stories to save his own hide." I sat back in the chair, yawned, and stretched. "I reckon Garrett O'Donnell is long gone from this country."

She gave me a funny look. "You never even saw any tracks?"

"Uh, no," I said. "Never saw any signs at all. Looks like he made a clean getaway."

The look of mischief started in her eyes and slowly spread all over her expressive Irish face. "That's what you're gonna tell the sheriff, is it now?" She began giggling. It took her a moment to compose herself. "You're up to somethin', Tommy Stallings, sure and you are. If that's your story, you'd better be polishin' it up some before you tell it to your boss."

"I don't know what in the world you're talkin' about, Mollie Stallings," I said with righteous indignation. "It's just the plain truth."

She began giggling again. The giggle worked itself down into her belly. Pretty soon she was doubled over with laughter. I sat there with as much patience and dignity as I could maintain while she had her little laugh at my expense. She showed no signs of slowing down.

"I was thinkin'," I said, raising my voice a bit to be heard over her guffaws. "Whenever you get through laughin' at me, maybe we could resume our huggin', only in a cozier location."

She caught her breath and looked at me sideways. "Why, Tommy Stallings, if I didn't know better, I'd be thinkin' you were makin' advances towards me. Don't you have to report in to the sheriff?"

"The sheriff can wait," I said firmly. He did.

"Tell me again," Tomás Marés said, perplexity and perhaps a bit of suspicion in his tone. "You say you found no sign of Garrett O'Donnell?"

I sighed heavily, doing my best to convey the message that all of this was a tremendous waste of time. "Like I told you before, Sheriff, I found some tracks headin' east when I first came down off Black Mesa. Once I got a couple of miles up the trail though, a whole passel of other tracks started crisscrossin' what might have been Garrett's tracks." I shrugged. "You know me, Tomás. I ain't no tracker. I did the best I could do. I reckon that Irishman's long gone out of this country."

"Long gone and carrying more than five

thousand dollars from a bank robbery." Tomás stared at me some more, his eyes narrowed in suspicion.

"It's a shame about the money," I said philosophically. "Course, it ain't your money, Tomás."

Tomás shook his head. "However, Deputy Stallings, it was money belonging to the good citizens of Cimarrón. And you know, the bank needs to have cash in order to stay in business."

Dang. I hadn't thought about that. "What are they gonna do?"

Tomás flashed a smile. "My cousin Lupe tells me that shortly after the robbery, John Burr received two thousand dollars from Santa Fe. It would appear that one of his Santa Fe Ring friends provided him with operating cash to hold him over until he could cash in on his devious scheme to foreclose on those ranches."

"Well ain't that interestin'," I said. "So it looks like the bank can stay in business after all." I leaned over and spoke in a conspiratorial tone. "You know, with John Burr dead and buried, maybe whoever takes over the bank might change his mind about foreclosin' on those homesteaders. That'd make the loss a little easier to swallow, if you ask me."

Tomás gave me a look that said he clearly had *not* asked me. What he said next shocked me near out of my boots, though.

"I had an idea about that. I was thinking we might make a private deal with Bill Wallace. Agree not to make any charges public if he agrees to take over the bank as president. Of course, he would have to agree to do exactly what you just suggested. He would forgive the loans on the ranches that Señor Burr had foreclosed on."

I was speechless. My jaw dropped and my eyes were wide with disbelief. I found my voice. "You thought of that on your own?"

"That and more," Tomás said. "I also believe that as mayor of our village, Señor Wallace may be able to exert some influence to reverse the decision to transfer the office to Springer. I am afraid this could only be a temporary move. Still, it might give us some time to make plans for what we will do about our careers." He stopped briefly, looking uncomfortable. "We also both have personal . . ." He searched for the right word. "Um, personal situations to plan for as well."

"You rascal," I exclaimed. "You go around here actin' straitlaced about everything, then you turn around and plan a deal that old Nathan Averill would be proud of."

Tomás smiled smugly at me. "You act as if you are the only one concerned with justice, Deputy Stallings. You probably think that if I had been on the trail of Garrett O'Donnell and perhaps had caught up with him, I would have taken him into custody without considering the circumstances." His smile vanished and once again he stared at me through narrowed eyes. "Do not believe that you have pulled the wool over my eyes, Tommy. You will not admit it but I am fairly certain that I know what really happened out there in that Big Empty."

"I don't know what you're talkin' about, Sheriff," I said indignantly. "I told you what happened. That's all I got to say about the matter."

He continued to stare at me, then shook his head. His expression conveyed frustration . . . resignation . . . disgust? Perhaps all three. "As long as you and I both know you have not fooled me, I will look the other way. *¿Comprendé?*"

I sure didn't want to admit to the sheriff that I'd broken the law. Still, I was very impressed with how broad-minded he appeared to have become. I wanted him to understand that I approved.

"*Comprendé,* Sheriff." Looked like we had that one settled. I was still curious about how he'd come up with this plan to find some measure of justice for those ranchers and save our jobs, even if it was only for the time being. "Seriously, though, did you come up with this scheme all on your own?"

Tomás looked every bit the rascal as he responded. "I might have had a bit of assistance," he acknowledged. "You mentioned our former sheriff, Señor Averill. As you noticed, the plan does resemble the sort of thing he was known to have implemented on occasion."

Off to the right, a man stood up from the chair in which he'd been leaning up against the wall. Up to this point, he'd remained silent. Now he spoke. "I don't know what you young pups are talkin' about," Nathan Averill said. "I'm just an old retired lawman, can't hardly use my left arm cause of that danged ambush. I'm mostly interested in sittin' on the porch in my rockin' chair, gazin' at the mountains while I wait for my lovely wife to get done with her teachin' for the day." He stretched and ambled toward the door. "If y'all are gonna cast aspersions on my character and imply that I'm a connivin' old son of a gun, I'm gonna take leave of your company."

As he closed the door, Tomás and I began

chuckling. "We're mighty lucky he survived that ambush a few years back," I said once I stopped laughing. "Any time we ain't sure how to handle a problem, it's nice to have him around to discuss it with." A disturbing thought intruded. "How's your pa, Tomás?"

"We still do not know if he will make it," he replied. His eyes were filled with sorrow. "He is awake from time to time but Doc will not allow him to move. He says he needs complete rest if he is to have any chance of living." He took a deep breath. "My mother has not left his side since we brought him home. It has been very difficult, Tommy. If it were not for my sister and Maria, we would have had to close the café." He blushed when he mentioned Maria's name.

The way things seemed to be headed, I figured I needed to help him over his embarrassment about his romance with Maria Suazo. "Tomás, you need to stop turnin' red every time you mention Maria's name. Sure, we hoorahed you a bit but we're all real happy for the two of you. She's a fine woman and you ain't too bad of a fella yourself." He seemed pleased with my little speech. I had an afterthought. "I would appreciate it if you'd try harder to call me

Tom, though. Tommy is a little boy's name. I'm a grown man."

ABOUT THE AUTHOR

Singer/songwriter and author **Jim Jones** is a native Texan, a student of the West, and a lifelong devotee of all things cowboy. He is an award-winning musician, receiving the Western Music Association's 2014 Male Performer of the Year Award and the Western Writers of America's 2013 Spur Award for Western Song of the Year ("Texas is Burnin',"). Jim has produced nine Western Folk albums and three award-winning children's character education music videos.

The first Western novel in his Jared Delaney trilogy, *Rustler's Moon,* came out in 2009 and was a New Mexico Book Awards Finalist in two categories, Best First Book and Best Historical Novel. The second book, *Colorado Moon,* was released in 2011 and received the Western Music Association's 2011 award for Outstanding Western Book. *Waning Moon,* published in 2013, was a New Mexico Book Awards Finalist for

Best Historical Novel.

In addition to his duties as a Western singer, songwriter, and author, Jim has a Master's Degree in Social Work and worked with children, adolescents, and their families for many years before leaving the field to focus exclusively on his singing and writing. He has combined his love of music and stories with his dedication to helping children, resulting in his popular Cowboy Programs for young people. He conducts writing workshops and performs in schools and library programs all over the country, entertaining his youthful audiences while stealthily increasing their knowledge and appreciation for the history of the West at the same time.

Jim's most recent album, *Race with the Wind,* was released on March 1, 2015, and continues to garner rave reviews. He lives in Albuquerque, New Mexico, with his wife and two dogs, Jessie and Colter.

The employees of Thorndike Press hope you have enjoyed this Large Print book. All our Thorndike, Wheeler, and Kennebec Large Print titles are designed for easy reading, and all our books are made to last. Other Thorndike Press Large Print books are available at your library, through selected bookstores, or directly from us.

For information about titles, please call:
(800) 223-1244

or visit our Web site at:
http://gale.cengage.com/thorndike

To share your comments, please write:
Publisher
Thorndike Press
10 Water St., Suite 310
Waterville, ME 04901